Please return/renew this item by the
last date shown to avoid a charge.
Books may also be renewed by phone
and Internet. May not be renewed if
required by another reader.

www.libraries.barnet.gov.uk

BARNET
LONDON BOROUGH

Also by Daniela Sacerdoti

WATCH OVER ME
DREAMS: SARAH MIDNIGHT TRILOGY (BOOK 1)
TIDE: SARAH MIDNIGHT TRILOGY (BOOK 2)
REALLYWEIRDREMOVALS.COM

TAKE ME HOME

Daniela Sacerdoti

BLACK & WHITE PUBLISHING

First published 2014
by Black & White Publishing Ltd
29 Ocean Drive, Edinburgh EH6 6JL

1 3 5 7 9 10 8 6 4 2   13 14 15 16

ISBN: 978 1 84502 746 9

ALBA | CHRUTHACHAIL

A CIP catalogue record for this book is available from the British Library.

Typeset by Iolaire Typesetting, Newtonmore
Printed and bound by Grafica Veneta, S. p. A. Italy

To my mother, Ivana Fornera Sacerdoti, who, as a child, saw.

To Claudio Corduas: the blood is strong, but friendship is stronger.

ACKNOWLEDGEMENTS

Thank you from the bottom of my heart to Ross, who puts up with having a writer for a wife with remarkable good humour, and to my sons, Sorley and Luca, who are, simply, my whole life. Sorry for all the many times my body was there with you and my head was in Glen Avich.

Thanks to both my families, the Sacerdoti and the Walkers, for always rooting for me – especially my mother-in-law, Beth. Thank you, Beth, for a million reasons, and you know them all!

Thank you to Irene, my sister in everything but blood. *Ti voglio bene, amica mia!*

My endless gratitude goes to Sorley McLean because his poems were the seeds of this book. Mary and Robert's story is based on Sorley's poem "The Choice", while Glen Avich itself sparked to life after I read the achingly beautiful "Hallaig". In this book, I quoted Sorley three times: "The dead have been seen alive" and "Every generation gone" in Inary's epilogue are homage to "Hallaig", while Emily's song's final line is inspired by another poem of Sorley's, "Don't Forget My Love". Sorley's poetry breathes inside me and will never cease to inspire my stories.

My heartfelt thanks to Kristen Susienka, the main editor of this book, for making it bloom. You know the story inside out and you felt it nearly as much as me – for this I'm eternally grateful – and for the crazy schedule you and I kept, the phone calls and endless daily emails, thank you! Many thanks also to Janne Moller and Lindsey Fraser for helping me shape the story, and to everyone at Black & White for believing in me.

Many thanks to my agent, Charlotte Robertson. We just started this road together, so here's to a happy future and many triumphs!

A million thank yous to my writerly friends. You feed my mind and warm my heart, you make me laugh and you're there for me when the sun shines and when the rain pours. Roy Gill, Phil Miller and Gillian Philip, every success of mine is yours too. And thank you to the Twitter community for providing writers with a staffroom where we can chat and catch up with each other on days when you've only spoken to the postman and yourself! In particular I'd like to mention Alice Peterson, an inspiration in life and books – and whose lovely book *Monday to Friday Man* made me want to write a nightly skating scene under glittering lights. You know the one, Alice!

Those of you who know me, personally or virtually, know that I'm more than a bit obsessed with music. Here are the artists who soundtracked Inary's story: Máire Brennan, Julie Fowlis, Norrie McIver, Manran, and The Treacherous Orchestra among many. Thank you guys.

Thank you, thank you, thank you to the many thousands of readers who read and reviewed my first Glen Avich story, *Watch Over Me*. It makes me so happy to know that Eilidh is in many hearts now. I wouldn't be here if it wasn't for your trust in me, so thanks for listening to my stories and for making them yours.

And finally, thank you Scotland for making *me* yours. There's nowhere else I'd rather be.

Daniela

Emily's Song

From the depth of winter
Comes new life
Little birds I see from my window
And I wish I could fly

Spring is for the living
I will not let go of this heartbeat
Faltering inside me
Like a fading sun

I'm part of it until my heart stops beating
Mine is the sky and mine are these hills
Until my heart stops beating

I am like a snowdrop
Shivering and still
I raise my head to the sky
This beautiful land

Hold my hand, don't cry
I shall not be afraid
And when I have to go
Don't forget my love

I'm part of it until my heart stops beating
Mine is the sky and mine are these hills
Until my heart stops beating.

PROLOGUE

Across the worlds

Morag Kennedy waved at me from across the worlds, on a clear, sunny day in Glen Avich. She was standing in front of her whitewashed cottage, and the summer sun was shining behind her like a golden halo, making the fields gleam just as golden. I waved back and began walking towards her, hoping she would have some of those lovely sugared jellies she always gave me, but I hesitated. I knew she was ill and I didn't want to trouble her. All of a sudden I realised I was feeling strange – my arms and legs were tingling and there was a low noise in my ears. It was a sensation alien to me, one I'd never felt before.

Just at that moment a cluster of clouds covered the sun, and without its glare I could see Mrs Kennedy properly: she wore the flowery cotton dress she usually put on to work in her garden, her hair in a tidy bob, a cardigan held close by a simple brooch. I did a double take – Mrs Kennedy's face seemed different. She had been ill for so long, her features becoming more and more drawn, her frame getting thinner every day. Even at my young age – I must have been about eight years old – I'd been aware of the pain and fear slowly taking over her mind and spreading over her face, in her eyes, just like the illness was spreading through her body. But that early summer evening she looked herself again. Her smile was

1

serene, her light-blue eyes as bright as they'd been before she got sick.

All of a sudden I heard footsteps behind me, and I turned around to see my brother stepping out of our cottage across the road. I guessed he'd been sent to call me in for dinner, and I wondered why my mum hadn't just called me from the kitchen window like she usually did. Maybe she wanted to make sure I would come in at once; I'd been known to run off into the fields instead, trying to steal an extra hour of play.

"Mum wants you inside, Inary," Logan said in a quiet voice. He was always quite serious, but at that moment he looked nearly solemn. I turned around to say goodbye to Mrs Kennedy, but she was gone.

"Is dinner ready?" I asked my brother.

"I don't think so."

"Then why do I have to come in?"

"Shush, Inary, come inside now!" My mum had appeared on our doorstep; she was slipping her apron off and smoothing her hair. When we reached her, she continued: "I want the two of you to keep an eye on Emily while Granny and I walk across the road. I won't be gone long; time to give my condolences to Karen and Isabel."

I had no idea what she meant. 'Condolences' was too difficult a word for an eight-year-old. "Where are you going?"

She stopped and looked at me tenderly. "Mrs Kennedy has gone to heaven, darling . . . I'm going to tell her children how sorry I am."

"She's not gone to heaven. She's here. I saw her."

Many years have passed, but I still remember the look in my mother's eyes when I spoke those words. Surprise, and at the same time, a sense of recognition.

"Where did you see her, Inary? Did you go into the house?"

"No. She was outside, in the garden. She waved hello to me."

My mum kneeled down and held me very tight. She stroked my face, and her fingers smelled of the raspberries she'd picked earlier in our garden. "You're just like your granny Margaret, aren't you? In every way," she whispered.

I smiled. I loved my granny, and to be told I was just like her felt like the best compliment.

"Let's go, Anne," came Granny's voice from the doorway. "What's wrong?" she added, having seen my mother's face.

"*An da Shealladh*," my mum whispered. They always used Gaelic between them when they didn't want me to understand what they were saying. "She saw Mrs Kennedy, Mum."

My granny's eyes widened. She took my hand and led me to her, gently.

"Oh, Inary . . ."

Suddenly I was confused. I didn't understand if I'd been very good or very bad, and why my mum and my granny were showing such emotion. I had seen Mrs Kennedy just before she died. That was all. I didn't really understand the concept of death, anyway.

Before I could stop myself, my eyes brimmed with tears. "What did I do?"

"Aw, Inary, don't be upset now, pet," my granny said. "You're so little, still. I was much older when it started. All you need to know for now is that you have a gift." She cupped my face and kissed my forehead. Her eyes were shining too. "On you go and keep your sister company, dearie. We won't be long."

They walked across the street to go and see Mrs Kennedy's

daughters, and Logan and I were left in charge of Emily. I went up to her room to sit with her. She was only five at the time, and she'd already gone through two heart operations. She was having a nap; her lips were slightly blue even when she was sleeping.

I usually struggled to sit still for long, but after what had happened I felt strange and somehow disquieted, like all the energy had gone out of me.

It took me a long time to realise that I had seen Mrs Kennedy after she'd died, that her body was lying empty in her house but her soul had gone free. It took me a long time to realise that she wasn't waving hello to me: she was waving goodbye.

1

The night I fell

Inary

"Cassandra kept running, so fast that she felt like her lungs were about to burst. She could sense the change coming. Her muscles were cramping and her bones were aching, about to stretch and extend nearly to the point of breaking. If she didn't find a place to change soon, her secret would be out. What would they do to someone like her? Experiment on her? Lock her in a zoo?"

"Lock her in a zoo?" I read aloud in dismay. I took my glasses off, and for the umpteenth time that afternoon I held my face in my hands. It was the weekend and I was supposed to get on with my writing. Except my head wasn't cooperating. I had worked on Cassandra's story for months, but it just wasn't going anywhere. Several thousand wasted words, several months of wasted work. Cassandra was never going to see the light of day. She was going to join the pile of the Manuscripts That Were Never Sent. And I would spend the rest of my life sorting out other people's books and dreaming of the novel I would never write. I was an editor in a small London publisher, and I enjoyed my job – but recently, it had grown tight on me, like unshed skin.

I sighed and folded my legs against my chest, gazing at the photograph of the hills around Glen Avich on the wall above my desk: the wild, windswept Scottish sky and the black silhouette of the pinewoods, a hint of mist resting on the land and a white, ghostly moon peering from behind a peak. It was such a beautiful picture that I could almost smell the woods and the peat fires, and feel the breeze on my skin. Looking at it usually uplifted me, but this time a sudden, inexplicable sense of dread filled me instead . . .

"I'm home!" My flatmate's voice resounded in the hall.

Trying to shake off the gloomy feeling that had taken hold of me, I ran out into the hall and squeezed her tight. "Lesley!"

"Inary!" She laughed, returning my hug. "What's up with you?"

"Save my life and come out for a drink with Alex and me," I begged. "I've had a hard day."

"Oh honey, I can't. I'm working tonight." Lesley was a music promoter, which often meant working weekends. It also meant a lot of free tickets to gigs, which was a bonus.

"A quick one," I pleaded.

"I can't!" She glared at me, or tried to. It's difficult to glare and smile at the same time. "Free all next weekend, though."

"That's great," I replied, and I meant it. I was looking forward to a weekend together. Lesley and I had been flatmates since I'd moved to London; she'd introduced me to one of her closest friends, Alex, and the three of us had been pretty much inseparable for the last three years.

Living with Lesley was just perfect. I had a habit of forgetting to take care of myself, and so she fussed over me, made sure I ate regular meals, bought me Lemsip when I was ill and put up with my constant chaos. In exchange, I *entertained* her, or so she always said. I made her laugh and kept things cheerful.

6

I've always been good at doing that, even when I don't *feel* cheerful at all.

I met Lesley the summer before moving to Aberdeen to study English at Uni, one of those seemingly unimportant encounters that end up being of huge consequence. I'd gone to visit my Aunt Mhairi in her cottage on the loch shore. It was pouring, but of course, me being me, I had forgotten my umbrella. Actually I hadn't seen my umbrella in months.

While I stood at my aunt's door, getting soaked and calling her name to no avail, I saw a group of people walking towards the neighbouring cottage, a holiday let. They were clearly tourists. If a six-foot-tall man with skin the colour of black coffee and a full head of dreadlocks – Lesley's brother Kamau, I was to learn – had been living in the village, I would have known. The impossibly tall man was accompanied by a group of young men and women, and among them there was a startlingly beautiful girl with her hair in cornrows. The group stopped in front of the cottage, occasionally looking at me, but too polite to stare. They exchanged a few words that I couldn't hear over the noise of the rain, and then the girl with braided hair walked towards me.

"Hello, we are just . . . um . . . We are staying at Heather Lodge there, and you're getting soaked, so we were wondering if you wanted to wait inside, you know, out of the rain. For whoever you're waiting for." She had a pleasant London accent, with a touch of something else – I thought it was French, but it turned out to be the West Indies, not an easy mistake, but one I would make. I was touched by their concern. "Thank you, it's okay. I'll just walk back to my house. It's not far."

"Oh . . . Then take this," she said, offering me her bright-red umbrella and lifting her hood up, negotiating the mass of braids.

"Don't worry, I'm used to getting soaked! You need it anyway," I said, and put my hands up.

"Not really. Look," she said with a smile, rummaging in her backpack. "I've got another one!" She produced a tiny polka dot umbrella and handed it to me.

I laughed. "Why do you have two umbrellas?"

"Just to be on the safe side." She shrugged. That was Lesley in a nutshell.

I took the polka dot one and walked away under the pouring rain. I remember turning back and seeing Lesley standing there, framed by her scarlet umbrella like a shiny exotic flower, still looking at me – she waved with a smile and turned back, following her friends inside. Little did I know then that she was to become my best friend, in spite of the distance and the fact that we came from two different worlds.

The next day I returned to the cottage to give back her umbrella, and we ended up chatting for hours. When she went back to London we kept in touch and emailed nearly every week. Slowly our friendship deepened, and after ... after my life in Scotland fell apart, I moved in with her. She saved my sanity.

"So why the hard day?" she asked now, hanging her coat up and taking off her shoes, lining them side by side as she always did. Beside her things, on a wicker chair, was a messy pile of jackets, hats, mismatched gloves and the odd sock, mixed with various rubble: that was *my* corner.

"I'm stressed!" I sighed.

"It's hard to be a writer!" she teased, walking on the wooden floor to the kitchen in her bare feet, her braids bouncing on her back.

"It's hard *not* to be one," I replied, truthfully. I was fast losing hope of ever writing for a living. And writing had been my ambition since . . . since forever.

"Right. The werewolf thing not going as planned?" she asked, switching the kettle on. "Want some coffee?"

"No thanks. The werewolf thing . . . not good. I don't know why this kind of story works in other people's books, but when I try to write it . . ."

Lesley took her sip of her milky coffee. "Maybe it's not *your* story. I mean, the story you're supposed to tell."

"Maybe." Was there a story for me to tell at all? I'd always thought so, but I was beginning to wonder if that was the case, or if I was just deluded. If my saying 'one day I'll be a writer' was the equivalent of a five-year-old girl declaring, 'When I grow up, I want to be a ballerina.'

I sighed. "Anyway. Better go get ready . . ."

"Do you have time for a curry?" Lesley asked me.

"A takeaway curry or a Lesley curry?" I enquired hopefully. Lesley's family was Jamaican, and her curries were out of this world . . . while I barely managed spag bol. Lesley had renamed my signature dish spag bog, which I suppose says it all.

"A Lesley one, my dear!"

I was sorely tempted, but I didn't want to be late for Alex. "Can you leave some for me? For when I come home?"

"Maybe . . ."

"Oh, go on!"

"All right. But you must eat something. To line your stomach."

"Yes, *Mum*!" I laughed.

I went back into my room and saved the Cassandra file,

though I was tempted to just delete all I had written that afternoon and start again later.

I slipped on a pair of jeans and a jumper – I wasn't going to dress up. It was Alex, after all, not a date. But then casual didn't feel right, and I decided on a black dress and a pair of bright-purple tights. I tried my best to brush my hair into submission – there was *so much* of it – and then looked at my reflection in the mirror. It's the weirdest thing, when you don't really recognise the person looking back at you. A girl who looks like you – the same mass of wavy hair and Scottish snowy skin – and still, who is she?

I sighed and started hunting for my handbag among the mounds of discarded clothes. I had no idea how it happened or why, but pretty much everything in my life seemed to have become difficult all of a sudden, and a strange, subtle restlessness had crept into my days and nights. It was like I had lost something very important, something I was desperate to recover. Something I used to have, someone I used to be . . . someone who went by the name of Inary, and who wasn't the girl sorting out other people's books and writing about werewolves. Who wasn't the girl I just saw in the mirror.

I looked around me, at my little London room – messy, tiny, but mine: the wardrobe I'd painted light blue and silver, rows of dresses peeking from its doors, one haphazardly hanging from its left handle; the pile of books on my bedside table; the corkboard covered in tickets from gigs and plays; the desk overflowing with paper and magazines and books . . . The debris of my life, a happy life – a life I'd built from nothing after everything I had, everything I knew, crumpled.

So why the restlessness?

Maybe because everything looked and felt so mundane. I

used to be able to see *beyond* all this, beyond the little things of everyday life, beyond our reality. I used to be someone with six senses, and not five. But not any more. And still, the thought that my life was somehow meant to be different was rising inside me and would not let me be.

I spotted my handbag's strap hanging from underneath a pile of manuscripts on my desk. I walked through the room to retrieve it, and my eyes fell on the Glen Avich picture once more. There it was again, the chill running down my spine. I slipped the bag around my neck and rested my hand on the framed photograph of my sister sitting just beside the computer. Even when my room was at its messiest, Emily's photograph was never hidden, its silver frame shiny and polished.

I was due to visit in a few weeks, and I was conflicted about it, as always – I couldn't wait to see Emily, but I dreaded seeing Logan, and I dreaded his silences and recriminations . . . As I was thinking of them, the silver frame of Emily's picture grew icy under my touch – I shivered and took my hand away. I looked at my watch – was there enough time to give her a call? But I was already late. I'd call her from the pub, I thought, and ran out with a quick goodbye to Lesley.

The London night was full of noise and people, as it always was, its sky lit with orange – so different from the still, black nights back home.

Why did I keep thinking of home? I often did, but not as much as tonight. I tried to focus on the here and now and stepped into the pub, dribbling clusters of men and women clutching their drinks and chatting loudly over the music.

Alex was there already. I wish I could say my heart didn't jump at the sight of him, but it did – another of the things

11

that have been unsettling me recently. I was beginning to look forward to seeing Alex a bit too much; I was starting to notice how solid his hands looked, and how good it felt when they somehow ended up on me – on my shoulder, casually, or grabbing my fingers as he led me through a busy club . . . I spotted the top of his head – a mop of black hair – and there it was again, that little *oh* I felt inside whenever I saw him.

Not good.

"Hey!" He was waving at me, his fingers stained with ink from a Pantone marker, as they always were. Alex has had Pantone-stained hands since he was old enough to hold a pen. He was a graphic designer, and fanatical about his job. It was his livelihood and his passion, and he certainly was a lot more successful at it than I was at my writing.

"Hiya, how's things?" I said, sitting beside him. It was a miracle we got a table the place was so crowded.

"Aye, good. Busy. You?" Alex had lived in London for years, but he still used *aye* instead of *yes*. It always made me smile. I suspected that keeping his Scottishness was a point of principle for him.

"All right, I suppose."

"What's wrong? Wait, I'll get you a drink, then you'll tell me. The usual?"

I nodded, and I watched as he glided through the crowd – he was a lot taller than most people there, and far from making him awkward, it seemed to command attention wherever he went. Female attention, especially, I thought as I spotted some pretty girl eyeing him approvingly. I rolled my eyes. I didn't want to admit to myself that it annoyed me. The good thing was that Alex never seemed to notice, or to act on the attention anyway. How someone like him could be single, I had no idea. He'd broken up with his long-term girlfriend three years before, and there had been no one else since.

"So. Tell me all," he said on his return, sliding my drink towards me.

"Well . . . Oh, nothing." How could I put into words how strange I'd been feeling recently? How my skin felt tight on me, how nothing felt quite right?

"Come on, tell me. I'm listening."

"It's my writing," I blurted out. Well, that was part of the problem, at least. "It's not really working out." I took a sip of my drink. "Lesley says that maybe what I'm writing now is not my story to tell . . ."

"The Cassandra one? I just can't believe you won't allow me or Lesley to read anything of yours. I'm sure it's great . . ."

I felt myself blushing and shook my head. "No it isn't. Believe me."

"You'd say that. I find everything I do complete rubbish, as a rule. When things fall into place at the end of a project I'm always kind of surprised."

I laughed. Anything Alex did seemed quite wonderful to me, but I knew what he meant. I worked with writers and I knew how they were usually full of every kind of insecurity. But there was more to my dismay than insecurity. My work just didn't *feel* right any more.

"You seem to be doing pretty well, for someone whose work is regularly rubbish . . ." I said.

He laughed. "Well, maybe it isn't, but often it feels that way. That's what I'm trying to say. You feel down on your work, but everyone else thinks it's good. It happens a lot. Thing is, you won't know if you don't let anyone read it . . . Hint, hint."

13

"I will give you something of mine to read, I promise! Just not yet."

"Has anyone ever read your stuff?"

"Only my sister. Nobody else."

"Emily? How is she?"

"She's been doing okay . . ." As I mentioned my sister, my mind wandered to Glen Avich again. A sudden longing nearly made me gasp – I needed to hear her voice. I needed to hear her voice so badly it hurt.

I shook myself. Alex was still talking. ". . . maybe it's just a dry spell. You know, no inspiration, feel depleted . . . that kind of thing. It happens."

"Oh . . . yes. Yes. I hope so," I replied, and took a sip of my vodka orange. "Sorry Alex, I just need to make a quick call . . ."

"Sure. Is everything okay?" he asked. I probably looked worried. I certainly felt it.

"Yeah, all fine," I said, and jumped up without bothering with my jacket. I negotiated my way out of the pub, squeezing myself between warm bodies. I stepped outside between two wings of smokers freezing and puffing, and the cold air took my breath away. No reply on my siblings' home phone. I tried Emily's mobile, and then Logan's – they were both switched off. They were probably out somewhere, maybe at the cinema in Aberdeen. I made my way back inside, elbowing through the Saturday night crowd.

"All okay?"

"No reply. I was phoning my sister."

"It's Saturday night. They're probably out painting the town red. Painting the village red, as it were."

"Ha ha."

"By the way, did I log that?" he asked, pointing at my purple tights.

"My legs?" I smirked, but I knew what he meant. Just like I collected owls, Alex collected colours – he took pictures of things, and logged his findings in a special database he was building, called Chromatica. It was some sort of colour bible or something that would change the graphic-designing world as we knew it, or so he said. Yes, that was Alex. At the moment, he was working on the endless shades of the colour purple.

"Not sure, did you?"

"Don't think so. Wait," he said, and slipped his phone out of his pocket. He took a picture of my knee under the bewildered gaze of our next-table neighbours. "Thank you. Oh, before I forget . . ."

A blast of loud music exploded from the speakers just above us, drowning out the last of his words. We went to that pub all the time, but recently they seemed to have upped the noise to an unbearable level.

"Has it always been this noisy?" I said, massaging my ear.

He laughed. "That, or maybe we're just growing old! Do you want to go to mine?"

My stomach tightened a little. Now, after three years of spending evenings together on the sofa watching DVDs, and crashing in each other's spare rooms, and dropping by uninvited at the weekend for an unscheduled lunch thrown together using anything we could find in the cupboards . . . after all this, an invitation to go to his house shouldn't have disquieted me. Or thrilled me. Or disquieted and thrilled me all at the same time. But it did.

Nonsense. It was just nonsense. We were just friends. Weren't we? Okay, sometimes things got a bit ambiguous

15

between us. But we'd never crossed the line, and I was sure it'd stay that way. If I tried hard enough. I had my reasons not to get involved with Alex, or anyone else. I just wasn't ready.

And still, recently I'd felt so confused . . . No point in agonising over it now, though. It was just another night between friends, like many before.

"Sure," I said, and gathered up my handbag and my jacket.

We walked into the freezing February night, and twenty minutes later I was sitting on the rug in front of Alex's fireplace, a whisky in my hand. A *Talisker* in my hand, to be precise. Not many places in London have a real fire, and for me, raised on peat fires, it was wonderful to have found one. I lost myself in the dancing flames.

"Inary Monteith, you're the only woman I know who appreciates a good whisky. My sisters hate it."

"Oh no, there are a lot of us. You just don't know many women, Alex," I teased.

"Yes, it's probably that!" He smiled and sat down in front of me, crossing his long legs. The fire made his blue-grey eyes shine and played on his features – he looked so familiar, like I'd known him forever, and not just three years.

"So, I tried to tell you in the pub, but I happen to have something that will cheer you up," he said, and slipped a little box out of his pocket. I could guess what it was, and I smiled in anticipation.

I opened the silver ribbon and lifted the lid – it was, like I'd guessed, an owl statuette – iridescent blue and no bigger than a marble. "It's beautiful! Thank you . . ."

Years ago, my mum and dad went to a pilgrimage to Lourdes together, and they brought me back a terracotta owl – instead of the usual religious statuettes, I suppose. I loved it – for some

16

reason, I always felt an affinity with owls – and that's how my collection started. Once I mentioned my collection to Alex, and ever since he'd taken to bringing me owls from wherever he went. He was a graphic designer who worked on large campaigns for companies all over the world, and because of this he travelled a lot. He got me owls from Oslo, San Francisco, Beijing, Kuala Lumpur . . . and the best one, my favourite: a little one made of whalebone, from St Petersburg.

"You're welcome. I got it in Madrid in this amazing covered market . . . I'll take you there one day," he said and looked away, into the fire.

"That would be nice," I scrambled, trying to ignore the implications.

"But seriously, Inary . . . what's up? You've been strange recently. I don't know . . . not yourself. Is everything all right at home?" He started playing with the metal tongs, avoiding my gaze.

"Yes. I don't know . . . Just . . ." I shrugged. "I don't know." I took another sip of my whisky. I couldn't explain the way I'd been feeling. I could never tell Alex the way I used to be, the things I used to see, and how it stopped when I was twelve. And how I just didn't feel whole.

"Whatever it is . . . you know I'm always here for you, don't you?" he said, and looked straight at me. At that moment a little Catherine wheel started spinning in my heart. It was a physical effort not to kiss him there and then – I was used to it, I was used to stopping my arms from wrapping themselves around him, stopping my mouth from looking for his. I could do that once more. But something betrayed me.

Maybe it was the warmth from the whisky, maybe it was the fire reflected on his face, or maybe the strange feelings I'd had recently – of not knowing who I was any more. Because another me, another Inary, reached over and kissed him. And then it was like gravity, the way we were pulled towards each other again. He put one hand on the nape of my neck, and entwined his other hand with mine. I was still for a moment, my face against his – I freed my hand and wrapped my arms around his neck, drawing him closer.

His lips tasted of whisky and honey and home and it felt right, like it should have happened a long time ago. But all too soon his mouth left mine and I felt suddenly dizzy at the loss of him.

His breath brushed close to my ear. "I'm not sure how to say this, but . . . I think I've fallen for you," he whispered into my hair, and immediately a cold knot of fear twisted my insides, snapping me momentarily back to reality.

What was I doing? What were we doing?

I had sworn . . .

But it was too late. It was done. Those words were said; they couldn't be unsaid. They hung between us and echoed in both our minds. "Inary," he whispered, and he said it *right*. Like we say it at home. My heart was winning the silent battle with my head. It usually did.

He stood up and took my hand, and led me into the bedroom, into another world.

I remember every minute of that night. I remember the way he locked his eyes onto mine and the way he said *you're so precious to me*. I remember how I could think of nothing, wanted nothing, needed nothing but him and me together, at that moment.

*

18

The morning came and I found myself in his bed, naked and defenceless, and I felt afraid as the reality of our previous night hit me.

Alex was sleeping, his long, black eyelashes casting soft shadows on his skin, one arm around my waist. I didn't know what beauty was, but I knew he looked perfect in my eyes. Like I'd known him forever, even when I was a little girl, as if the features of my soulmate were encoded in my blood, in my genes.

Still, I looked at him and I imagined the moment he'd wake up. I imagined the moment after, and the one after, and the one after that. Hundreds and thousands of moments that would add up into days and weeks and months where I loved him, and trusted him, and made him the centre of my life. Until *that* moment – when he opens his mouth to speak and I think it's something harmless, something or other about our life, about our family or the weather or some new book he's read, and instead he tells me we're not going to be together any more.

I imagined all that and it was easy, because it had happened to me before.

And I couldn't let it happen again.

I got up as quickly as I could, wrapping a sheet around me, and started gathering my clothes scattered all over the floor. I heard him call my name from the bed, his voice sleepy, full of warmth. Full of contentment.

"Inary . . ."

"It was a *mistake*," I said without turning around, before *he* could say it, now or next week or in six months, because I knew that sooner or later he would. "I'm sorry, Alex," I began, each word a drop of blood dripping on his plush cream carpet.

I rummaged in my bag looking for new contact lenses – my eyes stung. "We shouldn't have . . ."

"What do you mean?" He sat up, shock painted all over his face. I felt a spasm of guilt. Those words could never be taken back . . .

I emptied the contents of my purse onto the floor, looking for the lenses' blister, when I caught a glimpse of my phone. Again, that sinking feeling from the day before, the same sensation I'd felt when I looked at the picture of Glen Avich, invaded me. There was a little red icon in the corner of the screen – I lifted it up to check what it was, and all my words died in my throat. Fourteen missed calls. All from Logan.

"Oh . . ."

"Inary?" I heard Alex calling, from somewhere far away.

The room was spinning and I felt like I could double over with pain – I didn't know why, I didn't know what this searing ache in my heart could be. And then the phone rang, and I saw my brother's name flashing on the screen, and at once I *knew*.

I could barely tap the green button, my hands were shaking so much. I listened to Logan say that our sister's time was nearing its end, that the new heart she was waiting for, if it ever came, would be too late. I had to hurry back, or I might not see her alive.

2

I loved her since forever

Alex

She's gone. The wall doesn't protest as I pound it over and over again.

A *mistake.*

That's what she called our night together, and then her mobile rang. There were broken words and tears, and I didn't know if I was too furious to even look at her or if I wanted to hold her in my arms and comfort her and tell her it'd be okay, that I was sure her sister would be fine, that whatever happened I would always, always be in her corner. Always be there for her.

But I said nothing. I stood there, too conflicted to speak or move.

And then she finished getting dressed. Her face was strewn with tears – she was about to step out the door and, I feared, out of my life – and I grabbed her hand and turned her to face me. "Whatever last night was, Inary, don't call it a mistake. Don't call my feelings for you a mistake."

She said nothing. The door closed behind her, and she was gone.

★

I've loved Inary since forever, or at least it feels that way.

The first time I saw her she had paint all over her. Even her lovely auburn hair – somewhere between red and brown, a warm, coppery hue that I'd only seen in paintings – had strands of purple in it. I'm obsessed with colours, and to see that girl crowned in purple and red and blue, like she'd just walked out of a Chagall masterpiece, took my breath away.

I was helping Lesley move into her new home. She'd hit me with a van full of stuff, and another few bin bags and boxes to pack my car with – she owned enough to fill two houses. She had also given me a set of keys, and I was about to try and extract them from my pocket while keeping hold of the box when I realised the door was ajar. I made my way in, and there she was. Inary. I'd heard so much about her, Lesley's best friend from up north, but somehow we'd always missed each other.

"You must be Alex," she said, smiling that sunny smile she has.

"You must be Hilary," I replied.

"Inary," she corrected me with a smile. "No H or L. N in the middle."

"Oh, sorry . . ."

"Don't worry," she smiled again. "It happens all the time. My mum found the name in a book of Scottish fairy tales, never heard it anywhere else. Is that Lesley's?" she asked, gesturing to the big box I was carrying.

"Yes. Yes. Not long to go. There are only another twenty-seven of these. We'll be done in a week or so."

She laughed. That's good, I thought. I made her laugh.

"There's a few bin bags as well. Oh, and Lesley is on her way with the van."

"Oh no!" Inary swept a lock of hair behind her ear. She kept talking, and I could hear her words, but I couldn't quite make them out. I was somewhere else, somewhere windy and beautiful, somewhere I had been as a child and long forgotten. "I knew Lesley was a bit of a hoarder, but I didn't realise she had so much stuff! Come, I'll show you her room. At the end of the hall, there. Alex?"

I shook myself. "Yes. Yes, sorry."

"You're a man in need of a cup of tea!" She laughed again. She was so . . . alive. Beside her I felt grey, like she had all the colours I'd ever need.

"That would be great. Thank you." I put down the box in Lesley's room and followed her into the kitchen, desperately thinking of something else to say. "So, Lesley said you're Scottish too . . ." I said.

"Not that I have an accent or anything . . ."

I smiled. She had a soft, musical Highland lilt. "Whereabouts?"

"Glen Avich, not far from Aberdeen. You probably won't have heard of it, it's tiny. You?"

"I was brought up in Edinburgh . . ."

"Hello!" Lesley entered, carrying another box. She dumped her burden on the floor with a sigh, her mane of tiny braids falling over her face.

"Hello! I already started painting!" Inary said.

"I can see that!" Lesley replied, taking in Inary's paint-sprayed clothes. "So you met Alex. At last! I've wanted you two to meet for ages . . ."

I went to University with Lesley's brother, Kamau – that's how Lesley and I met. There was never anything more than a friendship between Lesley and me, though I often wondered

23

why. We got on so well. Still, it never happened. Once it was clear to everyone involved, including us, that we would only be friends, we became very close. It didn't stop Kamau trying to set us up though, even if by then I'd had a girlfriend for a while, Gaby.

And then I met Inary, covered in colours like a little earthed rainbow. Everything about her – her small body, the sound of her voice, the way she smiled – was so full of life, she made me come alive too.

I could sense Lesley looking at me looking at Inary, and I knew she would guess what I was thinking. She knew me too well. I almost ran out of the room, mumbling something about twenty-seven boxes and a van to unload.

The rest of the day was a blur. Lesley's insane amount of stuff made its way from the van to her flat, bit by bit, while I caught glimpses of Inary painting, making tea and singing along to the music Lesley put on. We finished the day with fish and chips, our plates balanced on boxes – there were no sofas or chairs yet – and then we walked to a pub in Battersea, not far from my house. It was dark already, and we hurried on to get out of the cold. I went to order a round of drinks while the girls sat at a table.

As I was leaning on the counter, waiting my turn, I felt a presence beside me. I turned to see that Inary had followed me; she was standing very, very close, our arms touching.

"It's okay," I said. "I'll get the drinks."

"I know. I just thought I'd keep you company."

Tenderness came to her as easily as breathing. She was unafraid, unashamed, wearing her emotions like a crown.

A few weeks later I broke up with Gaby.

Now three years on, after an endless will we/won't we, she'd

24

finally spent the night with me. And then she'd called it a mistake, and it hurt like hell.

She'd gone back to Glen Avich, swept away from London by the horrific news about her sister. I couldn't believe that Emily was dying – Emily, as vivid and cheerful as a little windmill, one of those brightly coloured ones that people put in their gardens. Emily, five feet of spark and cheekiness and love of life.

The first time she came down – she only visited twice; the journey to London was exhausting for her – she and Inary didn't stop chatting for a week solid. They were like sparrows, chirping and twittering to each other, so happy to be together.

I couldn't quite believe it.

I wanted to be there for Inary – I *had* to be there for her. But the question was, could I keep doing this to myself? Was I some sort of crutch she used and then discarded? I didn't deserve to be treated like that. Her fears and doubts didn't give her the right to use me that way.

*

I went to work feeling like a zombie and waded through it as though through a field of mud. No word from Inary. The stupid phone went all day with messages and emails and stuff I didn't care about, but none of them were from Inary. She clearly meant what she said.

As soon as I got home, I drowned all my thoughts in a glass of whisky, and before I knew it, it was dawn. She was in Glen Avich by now. She might as well have been on another planet.

Why, why did she say it was a mistake? Why, as she said those terrible words, did she look frightened? Frightened of me, of us?

25

My fingers, clumsy with alcohol and sleeplessness, started composing a text. And then I deleted it. I lay on my bed, studying a crack on the ceiling. It was then that I spotted something on the floor near the window. It was an enamel daisy chain – the necklace Inary was wearing last night.

I sat on the window seat and stayed there for a long time, weaving the necklace between my fingers, looking out to the London skyline and thinking of home.

3

The last word before silence

Inary

I went back to my flat and stuffed a bag with random clothes and my laptop, the taxi still waiting downstairs to take me to Heathrow. As soon as I got to the airport I called Rowan, my boss at Rosewood Publishing, to say I wouldn't make it to work on Monday and that I needed extended leave. And then I called Lesley. I was falling somewhere deep, bottomless – a dark well – and I needed her to drag me back to the surface.

"Oh, Inary, I'm so sorry . . ."

"Yes. Yes. Well . . ." I was struggling not to cry. "We sort of knew it could happen, but we always thought she'd get the operation and she'd be fine . . ."

"She might be okay in a few days. It might just be a false alarm . . ."

"I hope so," I said, and I did, against all the evidence, in spite of what Logan had told me. I did hope so, with all my heart. Miracles, after all, do happen. And that was what we needed: a miracle.

"If you need anything, just call me. Any time, day or night," she said, and she sounded so kind, so Lesley, that I couldn't hold the tears in any longer, and I had to finish the conversation quickly. After I put the phone down, a text from her came through – the image of a little green clover for good luck. I realised she hadn't asked me why I hadn't come home last night. Just as well. I just couldn't discuss that now, anyway.

It was like a nightmare, one I couldn't wake up from. All of a sudden, my life had been turned upside down. Again. Things were pretty messed up before – losing my mum and dad in the accident, and the Lewis thing, and now this: my Emily . . .

Maybe I'd known for a while that something wasn't quite right with Emily, I'd just refused to see it. In the last few weeks there had been a brittle, forced cheerfulness in Emily's voice. I'd meant to ask Logan if something was up, but I was due to visit the following week for a few days anyway, so I thought I'd see with my own eyes. It would save me from having to speak to Logan more than was strictly necessary. My brother had never forgiven me for having moved to London, and he didn't make a secret of it.

And he was right. I left Emily, and now she was dying, and I'd been away for three years. Away from her, away from Glen Avich, away from Logan, who was left shouldering it all.

Tears started streaming down my face again. Thankfully from where I was sitting nobody could see me. I slipped on my iPod, trying to get a grip of myself.

I wanted to speak to Alex so badly. I craved his voice. But it was all too much; I just couldn't deal with all that too. Spending the night with him had been a bad decision on so many levels. As if I could let myself be in *that* situation again. Let myself be broken into pieces again.

Three years ago I was engaged to be married. Although Lewis came from Kilronan, a village down the road from mine, our orbits had never collided until we both enrolled on the same course at Aberdeen University. I bumped into him

– literally – in the cafeteria, and his scalding coffee burnt my arm. I still have the scar, a white, discoloured patch on the inside of my arm, where the skin is softer, more fragile. How symbolic.

So yes, we ended up in A&E, with him even more upset than I was and apologising over and over again. A few months later we were living together. I'd never felt that way about anyone before – it was like stepping into a new world, a new solar system where he was the sun. We moved to a house in Kilronan and he insisted we get engaged. It was like his life depended on it. Soon after, the venue was booked and the wedding dress was hanging in my wardrobe, cocooned in thin white fabric. I wore his grandmother's wedding ring.

Then one day, eighty-nine days before our wedding – yes, I counted – he changed his mind.

Just like that.

Maybe it was cold feet, maybe he realised he had fallen out of love, maybe he'd never actually been in love. But I suspected he was scared. Scared because in a moment when the intimacy was complete, in a moment when I wanted him to know everything about me, I told him about my gift – and since then things had never been the same. He probably thought I was some kind of freak.

I moved back home with Logan and Emily, but I couldn't bear to walk the streets of Glen Avich any more. People kept looking at me that way – you know, the *poor thing* look. I kept bumping into his mum and brothers everywhere. I had to drive past our former house to get to the bloody supermarket. It was torture. Everywhere spoke of him and the life I was supposed to have, everywhere I looked there were memories of us.

29

Not long after, in a haze of grief, I went to see Lesley in London while I figured out what to do next. I had introduced her to Lewis once when she was up in Glen Avich for a visit. I'd sensed she didn't like him much, although she never said. I wish I had paid more attention to her moods around him.

In one of those weird moments of serendipity, Lesley told me that her housemate was going to teach English in Singapore and that she was looking for someone else to share a new flat; and an old University friend emailed me to say that Rosewood Publishing was looking for an editorial assistant. It was the perfect opportunity, a new life laid out for me to seize. I had the chance to leave Lewis and what he did to me behind.

I was moving to London without plans to ever live in Scotland again.

A few days before I left, Emily came into my room as I was finishing my packing. We were just back from a farewell meal in the Green Hat with Aunt Mhairi and our cousins. It had been bittersweet, the end of an era for me, for us all – Kilronan was twenty minutes away from Glen Avich, but London was another planet.

"Take this," Emily said, offering me something sheer and weightless, the colour of Loch Avich in the summer – something between aqua, turquoise and blue. She'd made it as part of her project in college – they'd even had a small fashion show with all the graduates' work showcased. Emily's collection was the best, of course. I was so proud of her.

"Hey, no . . . That's yours, I can't take it."

"You're going to need dressy clothes a lot more than me, Inary! With all those glamorous gigs Lesley will take you to!"

She smiled her breezy smile. Emily and I had this in common: we tended to be cheerful most of the time.

"You'll have nights out too. You don't plan to always be stuck in the house with Logan, do you?"

She sighed, and I remember that for a second her face had looked nearly other-worldly, translucent – as if she were there with me, in my room, but at the same time she was far away already. Like her presence in this world was only transient.

"I want you to have it, and I want you to go and be happy and not look back. I want you to live for me. To do all the things I want to do but can't."

Live for me. Her words cut too deep. I couldn't speak for a moment. It was as if she had given up on life, and that wasn't the plan. We were supposed to prove the doctors wrong. Emily would outlive us all, I was convinced of that.

And there I was, my bags packed, abandoning her.

"Maybe this is a mistake . . ." I agonised.

"It's not a mistake. Don't let Logan convince you of that. You must go, Inary! You must build a life for yourself, and you will. I can't just now, but you can and you will. Away from . . . everything that happened." She didn't mention Lewis, but his name hung between us, unspoken.

"Logan is furious. He's barely said a word to me."

Emily rolled her eyes. "He doesn't want you to go because he's worried I'll get mortally ill on him, but I won't. Besides, there's a good chance I'll be on the heart transplant list soon. We'll be fine," she said, and laughed. "Logan's just forever looking for a reason to sulk!"

"He has a point."

"Yeah, well." She shrugged. "You'll be the London branch of our family. You'll do us proud. Look . . ." She smiled again,

31

resting her hand on the pile of manuscripts sitting on my desk ready to be packed, all lovingly tied with ribbons to keep the sheets together. "You've been working on your books for forever. Giving up sleep, spending all weekends in your room, typing away . . ."

"Because I'm a geek, really . . ." I laughed.

"Yes, you are!" She laughed too. "But also because you are so dedicated. You have never wanted anything else, have you?" I shook my head in response. She was right. Ever since I was a little girl I had never really wanted much else but to write. "You've got to go and make your dream come true."

"It's not that simple . . ."

"It is really, Inary." She twisted a lock of my hair around her finger, in one of those little affectionate gestures of hers. "All you need is determination . . ."

"And talent . . ." I said, my voice dripping with self-doubt.

"Yes, talent, and you have it. I know you have it and I know you'll make it. Whether I'm here to see it or not . . ."

"Don't say that, Emily. You'll get on the list and you'll get a new heart and everything will get better." To hear her talk this way was like a stab to my heart.

"Oh, don't worry," she laughed. "I still have a bit of life left in me! I'll come and see you in London and go for nights out with Lesley's crazy friends . . ."

"Exactly! Which is why you need your top . . ."

"Tell you what. Hold on to it for me, I'll wear it when I come and see you."

"Deal."

She didn't really keep her part of the deal, though. She could only come to see me twice, and a night out with Lesley's friends would have been too much for her. Soon even the car journey with Logan was out of the question – it would have been too tiring. And I didn't keep our deal either; I still didn't have a book to my name, and I didn't even know what I was supposed to write any more.

I fell into a fitful, restless sleep, and I only woke up when we were about to land. I saw from the window that while I slept, England had turned into Scotland's soft hills and moors at last, a million shades of brown and purple shining in the light of dawn.

My head and my eyes hurt as I waited at the station for the first train to Glen Avich, drinking a double espresso that managed to wake me up and bore a hole in my empty stomach. I couldn't phone Logan to come and get me – it was nearly two hours round trip from Glen Avich to Aberdeen, and I didn't want him to be away from Emily for so long. Finally I boarded the train, a tiny two-carriage. It was just a couple of pensioners, the conductor and me. From the train window I could see the landscape I've known forever, the place I'd called home for the first twenty-odd years of my life.

As I stepped onto the platform in Glen Avich, my heart soared for a moment, in spite of the exhaustion and worry. I took a deep breath, inhaling the sweet smells of pine trees and peat fires. I could see a cluster of pink clouds over the hills where the earth was kissing the sky, the air was chilly and pure, and there was a sense of peace, of calm all around. I was home. Funny that I should still call our Glen Avich house home, even after a few years of living away . . .

I nearly ran from the station to our house, a few hundred yards away, keeping my head down in the hope of not having to stop and chat with anyone. I just wasn't ready to talk about Emily. My feet were heavy as I walked through the back alleys, avoiding the faster route through Main Street. I stopped across the road from our house, a whitewashed cottage that stood at the foot of St Colman Way. I took a deep breath, clutching my overnight bag. The lights were on in the windows upstairs, in the cold, grey gloom of early morning.

I crossed the road, each step agony. I didn't know what I would find; I didn't know what I would see once I stepped into Emily's room.

I stood in front of the heavy wooden door and knocked lightly, my hands shaking. A woman I didn't know, in a nurse's uniform, let me in.

"You must be Inary," she said.

I nodded, too anxious to speak, and I stepped in.

My brother was standing on the landing, conferring with Aunt Mhairi in a low voice, their heads bent towards each other, with Logan towering over her. My heart broke, because as soon as I saw my brother's face I knew all was lost. I knew for sure that the doctors weren't wrong like I'd always thought they would be. I knew for sure that Emily's days were really coming to an end.

Despair is a weird thing, the way it can come over you in a scarlet wave, making you scream and sob and curse the world; or it can just freeze you on the spot, deprive you of all the energy and purpose, tear your soul away from you and leave an empty shell behind. That is how I felt when I saw my brother's stricken face and I realised death was in our house, waiting for the right time, and that time would come soon.

"Oh, Inary! Thank goodness you're here!" Aunt Mhairi smiled at me, her face lined and exhausted. She hurried down the stairs and enveloped me in a warm hug. Logan followed

34

her, but he didn't throw his arms around me, like I hoped. He stood in front of me and fixed his eyes on mine, as if he were pleading, as if he were drowning and only I could save him – but how could I save him when I was drowning too?

"You're here," he said, as if he were surprised. There was an accusation in his voice, and guilt clawed at me once more.

"Emily . . ." I whispered.

"She's sleeping. Best not disturb her now."

For a moment the air hung heavy between us, full of all the words we weren't saying. Then Aunt Mhairi said she would put the kettle on and make some breakfast, and to come and warm myself by the fire, and those simple, everyday words about tea and toast and what a cold morning it was, and how lovely it was for all three of us to be back home together, broke the spell I was under and forced me back to the land of the living.

Emily was dying upstairs, and still, time would not stop, and we would keep going. But nothing, nothing would ever be the same again.

★

While Aunt Mhairi was making breakfast, I stepped into Emily's room as quietly as I could and sat by her bed. She was ashen, and her lips had a blue tinge. There were dozens of medicine bottles carefully lined on her bedside table, and her sewing machine sat unused on its table in the corner, together with samples of fabric piled on top of one another. She'd been working on something, I noticed, before she was forced to stop; it was still under the needle in the sewing machine. Something in a deep plum colour, with tiny flowers all over . . .

My eyes returned to Emily, and I froze. That broken doll

35

couldn't be my sister. My sister was full of life and shining from the inside, happy and rebellious and strong. I noticed that her nails were painted bright green; it was such an Emily touch . . .

I was grateful that she was sleeping, because I had to step out and escape to my room. I screamed silent screams into my pillow, with Logan hovering on the doorstep, heartbroken and awkward. And then I dried my tears, I shaped my mouth into a smile, and I decided I would not cry again until . . . Until it was time. I decided I would be strong and never, never show upset in front of Emily. I decided I would bring her joy until her last moment. In a way, my parents' death being so sudden was a blessing – I know it sounds strange, but at least they didn't have time to be afraid, to suffer. But for Emily, it was going to be a long agony, a tunnel with only more darkness at the end of it.

I went back into her room, and she was waking, her eyelids fluttering, like she was still wandering in a dream. I took her in my arms – she'd lost weight, she was like a little bird – and instead of breathing in her lovely, sweet Emily scent, I breathed in illness and medication, and my heart sank once more. But I kept my resolution.

"Hey, sweetheart . . ."

"You're back . . ." she murmured.

"Of course. I'm here to drive Logan mad."

"You always do that," she said, and laughed a small ghost of a laugh.

"She does that all right," said Logan from the door. He looked at me, and there was a weird mixture of bitterness and relief in his eyes.

Yes, I was back, and I would not go anywhere.

4

The other half of me

Logan

So the prodigal daughter has returned. For longer than a weekend, it seems.

Emily had a good day – seeing Inary cheered her up. Inary is good at cheering people up, always has been. But she's also good at running away when things get tough and leaving people in the shit.

That's what she did to me.

Everybody is asleep now, and the bottle in front of me is nearly gone. This is worrying. I can't remember starting it. But it seems the only way to get through the night. Once the whisky has done its job, I'll be able to close my eyes and stop aching inside. Sleep and forget, for a few hours.

It hasn't worked yet, but it will. Islay whiskies, you can trust them to take the edge off. Thing is, Emily's picture from her college graduation is sitting on the mantelpiece across from me, and that makes it all the harder. She's looking at me while I drink. I'm not crying, obviously. Not even a little. Maybe later, when I'm drunk enough.

When Emily was born I was ten years old. All I knew was that there was something wrong with the baby, that my mum had to stay in the hospital with her and she wouldn't be back for a while. When Mum finally returned, bringing Emily with her, I didn't even want to look at my sister. She'd turned our lives upside down and she'd taken my mum away for what seemed like an eternity. For days I refused to have anything to do with her.

One evening, though, I went into my parents' room, alone. I hovered around Emily's cot for a while, and then I couldn't help wanting to catch a glimpse of her, this little creature who had something terribly, terribly wrong with her heart. She was tiny – had Inary and I ever been that tiny? I touched her cheek as gently as I could, and her downy hair. She was sleeping, but when I touched her she opened her eyes, and I gasped – was she going to scream and cry? Had I upset her? Had I hurt her? I held my breath as I listened for my parents' footsteps, waiting to be scolded . . . But Emily didn't cry. She smiled, a tiny, gummy smile.

Knowing what I know now, I think she was too young to actually see me, and babies don't really smile as early as that anyway. But at the time I was sure she did. I held her hand, and she clung on to me with her wee fingers.

Suddenly, I realised that someone was standing behind me – my mother.

"You're her big brother. You need to look after her," she said, and those words stayed with me forever. Emily was still clinging to my hand. She didn't want to let me go. And I didn't *want* to go.

Things pretty much stayed that way. My parents died in a car accident – I know, when bad luck was handed out, our family must have been first in the queue. I was twenty-three, Inary was nearly sixteen, and Emily thirteen. We kept going. Me, looking after my sisters; Emily, in and out of hospital; Inary, in a world of her own, with her stories and books and dreams of writing. We were a good team. Aunt Mhairi, our dad's older sister, helped, and my parents left me enough to buy the Welly, the town outdoors shop, and it did good business. Enough to pay someone to work in it when Emily needed me. We muddled on.

Even when Inary went to study in Aberdeen, she was still there for Emily. And when she got together with Lewis – that pathetic excuse for a man – she was around at ours a lot, helping. I don't know what I would have done without her, with my work, and the house, and the hospital appointments, and the constant worry and care and stress.

And then that bastard left her, and she was crushed. I'd never seen Inary like that, not even when our parents died – like a light had gone out of her. Or maybe everything had hit her all at once: our parents' death, and Emily's illness, and now this. Maybe it was the last straw. She moved to London, and I was left looking after Emily. Alone.

What can I say? I did it. What choice did I have? Don't get me wrong, I'm not a saint. Sometimes all that kept me from imploding was going out into the garden and chopping logs for hours at a time. There were days when I could have driven down to London just to shout at Inary for having landed me in it.

I should have done.

Yes, there were a few shit times. But I raise my glass to you, Emily. Because for all the days and nights I spent looking after you, with or without our parents, with or without our sister, I wouldn't change a single one.

5

The long goodbye

Inary

And so the wait started. The doctors said a week; my sister's heart beat for another three. The longest, hardest three weeks of my life.

Day followed night that followed day that followed night again, and we kept going, on autopilot, dazed and exhausted and hungry but too upset to eat or sleep. It was like life was draining away from us too. The nights were the worst. Emily slept for a few hours only, and the rest of the time we took turns keeping her company. There were two nurses who worked on shifts, as Emily had to be watched constantly, but we wanted to be with her too. I told her stories of my life in London, and read to her, and we watched late-night programmes together. When I finally hit my bed I was too tired to sleep and my face was sore from smiling.

Often Logan's steps would linger in front of my door, the floorboards creaking, and I would know that he needed company. Things weren't good between us, but still he looked for me, for some reason. I'd get up and we'd spend hours drinking tea – or in Logan's case, whisky – in front of the living room fire, watching some mindless programme and exchanging a few words about everything and nothing. I did most of the chatting, in my endless attempts to keep everybody upbeat. I failed, of course. Logan carried the weight of the world on his shoulders. Sometimes he was so low he didn't have the energy to speak; sometimes he was full of anger, against the genetic lottery that had misshapen Emily's heart, against our parents for having died young. Against me, for having left. I could feel it, the resentment seeping out of him like vapour. I could feel his sorrow, and I was afraid for him nearly as much as I was afraid for Emily.

As for me, I sank into a silent, deep loch made of tears. Somewhere beneath its still waters I was floating, trying to come to terms with this new, strange, painful world. We'd been through the sudden death of our parents, and it had been worse than I could ever say . . . But somehow, as cruel as it was that they should go, it was still the order of things – grandparents go, then parents. Not your twenty-three-year-old sister, with her whole life ahead of her.

Lesley phoned every day. I clung to her voice like a lifeline, but every day I felt she was drifting further away, and my life in London was like a distant dream. I had stepped into a dark land alone, and as I travelled deeper and deeper into it not even my best friend could follow me.

★

"Read me something you've written, Inary." Emily was lying curled up, her white hands under her cheek. I'd just given her a few spoonfuls of soup, and even that had exhausted her.

"Oh . . . Well, I'm working on this story . . . *Cassandra*. It's about a werewolf, but it's a bit rubbish."

"I don't believe you. You know I love your stories."

"You won't love this one . . ."

"Why don't you write something about life here? In Glen Avich?"

"Funny you should say that. Lesley told me the other day that I had to look for my story to tell . . ."

"Maybe your story is here," she whispered. I'd woven her hair in one braid on the side of her face, so it wouldn't bother her as she lay. Her hair was so lovely, fair with a hint of red – she was the perfect strawberry blonde. I wondered if Alex had that particular shade logged into Chromatica . . .

I stroked her cheek, and she closed her eyes.

"Maybe," I said. "Anyway, I'll go and get my laptop. I bet it'll send you to sleep . . ."

"Don't be silly," she murmured, smiling. I was about to step out when she called me back. "Inary?"

"Yes?"

"I was thinking of leaving my music to Lesley," she said. My heart tightened. I didn't trust myself to speak. I just stood there, all the air knocked out of my lungs. "Will you give it to her, when I'm gone? It's all there . . ." She gazed towards her pea-green iPod on her bedside table.

"Don't talk like this, Emily . . ."

"I might as well sort out my things . . ."

She was right. It killed me, but she was right. "Of course I won't give it to her. I'll sell it all on eBay and put it towards a jacuzzi for Logan."

She laughed. It was my favourite thing, to make her laugh.

I sat on her bed, reading from *Cassandra*. After a while I could see her eyes struggling to stay open.

"Great, my book *is* sending you to sleep," I said with a smile.

She smiled back, and then her eyelids fluttered, and she was asleep.

★

I tried to get out of the house once in a while, to get some fresh air and clear my thoughts. Glen Avich had welcomed me again, as if I had never left. Walking its streets didn't feel like it did when I was only up for the weekend, or for short holidays. Back then I was always somewhere between Scotland and London, my head torn between two places. Now, there were no other thoughts but thoughts of Emily. Tomorrow didn't exist, and I had no plans, no desires but making Emily as comfortable as she could be. Whenever my mind wandered to my life in London, to Alex, I tethered myself back.

I walked through Glen Avich like I belonged again, and in the here and now, I did. Every expedition out of the house involved stopping every few steps to chat with someone – everybody was friends or family. It wasn't easy to live in a goldfish bowl, where everyone knew about me and everyone knew what we were going through, but sometimes it was a comfort. I never felt alone. The whole village was rooting for Emily, rooting for us.

I often went to Peggy's shop for groceries – anything to tempt Emily's dwindling appetite. Peggy is a distant cousin of mine – like most people in Glen Avich, I must admit – and her shop was one of the beating hearts of the village. It sold just about everything, from food to magazines to souvenirs, and even babies' clothes, knitted locally and arranged in a little display on one side of the counter. From bleach to clothes pegs to coloured pencils, from buckets to homemade tablet to string – you'd find it there. Also, it was *the* place to catch up on everybody's lives.

Peggy was a bit like a doctor and a priest and an agony aunt all rolled into one; everybody talked to her. If you were in need of a private consultation, she'd take you into the little kitchen in the back, give you tea or juice and sweets – depending on your age – and you could unload your heart. I remember sitting there many times, as my granny chatted with Peggy and her sister Flora – and I also remember asking myself, as we were all McCrimmon women (on my mother's side), did they have the gift my granny and I had? I never had the nerve to ask. Now I couldn't help wondering what Peggy would say about me and Alex if I confided in her . . .

I was there one morning, stocking up on reading materials for Emily – she loved fashion magazines, which we read snuggled up together in her bed – when my cousin Eilidh came in. I had heard she had moved back to Glen Avich and was living with Jamie McAnena, a blacksmith and artist and an old friend of my brother's, but I hadn't bumped into her yet.

"Inary! Oh, sweetheart," she said, and held me tight. She smelled of green apples. "I'm so sorry . . ."

I never liked people feeling sorry for me, but on that occasion, somehow, it felt different. I hugged her and hid my face in her hair, and when we released each other I could feel my eyes welling up.

"I wanted to come up to the house, but Logan said that Emily is just too ill for visits . . ."

"Yes. She can't really see anyone." I took a deep breath. "And how are you, Eilidh? I haven't seen you in years!" I was quite amazed when I looked into her eyes. I'd forgotten how

44

alike they were to mine – the same shape, the same shade – aqua blue. You could see we were related, though she'd been spared the red hair – I prefer to say auburn, but let's face it: it's red. Eilidh's was the colour of chestnuts and rested in lovely waves on her shoulders.

"I'm good. I'm back in Glen Avich now. I have a son . . ."

"Yes, Aunt Mhairi told me. Congratulations . . ."

"And he's such a bonny baby!" Peggy jumped in.

"I'm looking forward to meeting him. Say hi to Jamie for me . . ."

"Will do. Listen . . ." She put her warm hand on mine. I looked down. I didn't trust myself to look into her kind, open face and not burst into tears. "I'm only up the road. If there's anything you need just call me or drop by."

"Thank you."

"There's a new coffee shop a few doors up, did you see it?"

"Oh, yes, La Piazza. I only saw it from the outside."

"If you fancy a coffee, one day . . ."

Suddenly, the door opened and a gust of cold wind blasted us. "Hello, Inary," said a voice I knew. A voice I knew well.

I turned around, and there she was. Anabel. Lewis's mum. On some church-related errand, no doubt.

We hadn't spoken in three years. I was bound to run into her, sooner or later. I forced myself to look at her, though I knew how that would make me feel. She was a tall, broad woman, with a booming voice and inquisitive eyes.

"Hi, Anabel." My heart was hammering against my ribs.

"And how have you been?" she asked, with that slightly condescending tone she'd always had with me. Like I wasn't too bright, I wasn't too beautiful, I didn't go to their church, but I was her son's choice – for a while – and she had to put up

45

with me. Once, she said that the McCrimmon women were a bit odd; Logan never spoke to her again. Emily called her Cruella, because she bred dogs and she was convinced she made coats out of them. She had liked to joke that Anabel would turn up at my wedding in a Dalmatian coat.

"Good. Yes," I replied. How have I been? Had she not heard? Strange. Everyone knew everything about everyone, around here.

"Lewis told me about Emily . . ." Oh. She *did* know. I gazed at her face, and I was quite astonished to see that she looked genuinely upset. "But Emily was always sickly, wasn't she . . ." She made it sound as if it was Emily's fault, somehow. The tainted McCrimmon blood, I suppose. In other words, she was back to her usual charming self. I cut her short.

"Well, it was nice to see you, Anabel" – it wasn't – "Thanks, Peggy," I said quickly and practically ran out of the shop, my cheeks on fire. I stood outside and inhaled as deeply as I could. There was a question stuck in my throat: *how's Lewis?* The question I just couldn't ask, because I didn't really want to hear the answer. In case he wasn't well, and it would upset me; in case he was happy with someone else, and that would upset me too. And I wasn't supposed to care, anyway.

All of a sudden I realised that I was holding a stack of magazines that hadn't been paid for. I had to go back in . . . and try not to thump Cruella. But just as I was about to open the door, Eilidh walked out.

"Those are on me. Nice woman. Come," she said, and slipped her arm in mine. "Let's head off before she comes out."

"Thanks. Yes, she was always a charmer." I swallowed.

"You had a lucky escape with that lot," said Eilidh.

46

A gust of wind mixed with rain hit my face, and I fastened the collar of my jacket. The sky was heavy, laden with pewter clouds. Eilidh and I walked towards St Colman's Way in peaceful silence. I was grateful that Eilidh wasn't asking questions – even the easiest of enquiries brought on painful thoughts. Like *how long will you stay for?*

Until . . . and then the thought I couldn't think without my heart breaking in two: *Until she goes.*

"So where's your baby today?" I asked, trying to steer my mind towards happier grounds.

"At the soft play in Kinnear with his dad and Maisie. I'm doing some spring cleaning. My life is so exciting!" she joked.

"Spring? You're an optimist!" I said, raising my eyes to the stormy sky.

"Spring will be here soon," she said.

Yes. And Emily will not be here to see it.

We said goodbye with one last hug and the promise to meet soon, and I stepped back into the house – and with that step, I knew I was walking into the limbo between life and death, a no man's land where all I could do was wait and hope against hope.

6

Girl in a white dress

Alex

"Going down to the cafe, do you want something?" one of the other designers, Sharon, asked in her soft voice. A freezing rain was falling on London, three weeks to the day since Inary left. I was trying to forget about her for a few hours the only way I knew how – working. Lesley was due to come to the office soon, to discuss the redesign of the website of the company she worked for, which cheered me up a bit.

"Alex?" Sharon was looking at me, waiting for an answer. I realised I had forgotten to reply.

"Sorry, I was distracted there. No, no thanks. I'm not that hungry."

"No lunch today again?" She folded her arms in mock reproach.

"Maybe later." I smiled.

"No, no way. You are going to eat with me. I'm going to buy you a . . ." – she raised her eyes to the ceiling, trying to remember what I like – ". . . chicken mayo sandwich, wasn't it?" I nodded, smiling. "And a cream cake too. I won't take no for an answer!" I opened my mouth to protest, but she stopped me again. "Right, I'm off!" she said and looked straight into my eyes. I noticed how the muted light made her brown eyes darken to near-black, like two pieces of obsidian.

"Thank you. Tell me how much I owe you . . ."

"My treat," she said, and disappeared through the door.

Sharon had been working with me for two years. It took me a long time, and some help, to figure out that she was interested in me. I just hadn't noticed. I never fail to see the patterns and colours of people's clothes, the shapes of buildings and flowers and every shade painted in the sky in every hour of the day . . . but people's behaviours are a bit of a mystery to me. In the end, Gary, my colleague and friend, had to spell it out to me.

"You sure she likes me?"

"Oh yes. Did you not see how she looks at you?"

"Not really."

He rolled his eyes. "Wake up, Alex. You'd be a fool to let her go."

I avoided talking about Sharon from then on. I avoided Sharon herself, as much as I could in a small office. Don't get me wrong, she was beautiful, and kind, and funny. She was everything a guy would want.

She just wasn't Inary.

She seemed to keep her distance for a while, maybe hurt over the fact that I didn't seem to respond to her interest. But after a while things seemed to settle down again, like she had understood and accepted my choice.

One day Inary came to see me at the office. She walked in like a ray of sunshine, smiling, chatting happily, the way she always did. I could see Sharon watching her long and hard. Even I realised that Sharon's smile was forced and that she was sitting rigid in her chair, just waiting for the moment Inary would leave. Sharon had figured it out; she knew how I felt about Inary. Well, no biggie, everybody around me knew.

49

And everyone at some point had tried to make me see sense. Except for Lesley, who was convinced that Inary and I were made for each other, that she just needed time to get over this guy who had left her.

One night, when the two of us were alone at my house, I was given a glimpse into Inary's old life.

"Did you know I was about to get married?" she said, pouring herself yet another glass of vodka. She was curled up on my sofa, her bare feet folded underneath her, her head on the cushions. Inary is usually a happy drunk, you know, the kind that dances and laughs and tells everybody they love them. Not then.

"Were you?" I was astonished. I knew there had been someone in her life, but not that it'd been so serious. Inary, engaged?

"He didn't want to just live together," she said, waving her glass about. "No. His mum and dad would not approve. People would talk. People from that bloody church of his. No, he wanted. To. Get. Married."

"Right," I replied soothingly.

"So I went and bought a dress. Emily helped me choose. It was lovely, you know? Sort of strapless, like that . . ." Half the contents of the glass ended up on the cushions as she showed me the shape of her wedding dress. "And then he left me!"

"I think you've had enough to drink, Inary . . . Come here. Have this . . ."

"Oh, thanks. What is this? Why are you giving me *water*?" she grimaced.

"Drink up . . ." I insisted, and sat beside her.

"No."

"Come on. If you drink up, tomorrow I'll make you a cooked breakfast," I tried to bribe her like you would a child.

50

"Okay then. Crispy bacon and scrambled eggs please." Had she not been so upset about her ex-fiancé, I would have found it funny. She leaned her head on my shoulder. "Oh God, I'm so tired . . ."

"Right. Time for bed." I lifted her up and carried her to the spare bedroom. As I was helping her to the bed, she mumbled something.

"What was that?"

"I said I never want to love anyone ever again!"

"Oh. Okay . . ." I said, slipping the duvet over her. Part of me was amused at her drunkenness, but there was a sad note in her voice that made me nervous, made me wonder if she meant what she was saying.

"You know what was the thing?"

"What was the thing?" I asked.

"Lewis hated my gift."

"Did he?" I said, covering her with the duvet. She had panda eyes and her hair was damp around her forehead. She looked very young and very vulnerable. "What gift was it?" I asked, thinking she must mean some present she'd given him. Bit of an odd reason to leave someone just before the wedding. But I never got my answer; she was sleeping already.

The whole thing was very un-Inary – I'd never seen her like that before or after that night, and I never knew what she meant by Lewis hating her gift.

Inary's refusal to date anyone, and not for lack of offers – I lived in fear of the writers she worked with – had lasted three years already, and didn't seem to pass. I knew that the guy she was engaged to broke her heart, but was it really her disappointment, her fear that kept her away from me? Or was it something else, something a lot more final – she just wasn't

51

interested in *me* – and when she was finally ready, she'd find someone else. One of those literary types she worked with, for sure. I'd torture myself picturing her with some Swedish short-story writer who'd whisk her away on a cruise around the fjords. Okay, fjords are in Norway, but you get my point. Every time she mentioned someone at work, dread settled in my stomach in a cold, hard lump. I wanted to believe Lesley's theory; I wanted to keep hoping that one day she'd change her mind about us. But what happened three weeks ago – the pain she'd caused with just a few words – it slayed me.

Sharon's return interrupted the chaos of my thoughts; she was back with a delicious-smelling parcel in her hands. I made coffee and we ate together. Without warning, she leaned over and brushed my cheek with her finger, very close to my lips. Her hair smelled rich and deep, of some dark-noted perfume. "You had cream on your cheek . . ." she said, smiling, and lowered her eyes at once.

She knew what she was doing. Even *I* knew what she was doing.

At that moment Lesley came in, and sure enough, she knew too. She never mentioned anything, not even when Sharon left and we were alone in the office, but I was sure she would, sooner or later.

She sat beside me at my desk and subtly started to straighten things and align things, and generally give my stuff the Lesley treatment.

"You really are messy, aren't you?"

"No, it's you being freakishly tidy," I replied.

"Shut up," she laughed.

"So . . . have you heard from Inary?" I forced myself to sound casual as I brought the work in progress onto the screen.

52

"Yes. She called a couple of times. It's just terrible, Alex. She sounds worse every time. Emily is in a bad way . . ."

Suddenly, I felt horribly selfish. Here I was, agonising over our night together and my feelings for her when her sister was dying and she must be going through hell.

"I can't imagine how it must feel . . . Emily is only twenty-three . . ." I said.

"I can't imagine either. If I lost Kamau . . . Anyway. I just hope a miracle happens. I wish I could be there for her, that she wasn't so far away."

"Me too."

"Have you spoken to her?"

"No."

"You haven't spoken to her at *all*?" Lesley looked astounded. So Inary hadn't told her about us . . .

I shook my head. I couldn't bring myself to discuss what happened between Inary and me. I just couldn't.

"Maybe you should give her a call . . ."

I took a deep breath. "I think she needs space."

"Maybe," she replied, and looked at me curiously.

I just couldn't take that conversation any more. "Let's get to work, Lesley," I said, and desperately tried to concentrate.

★

That night I took the broken daisy chain and slipped it into a drawer, which I closed with a little more force than I should have. Out of sight, out of mind. Maybe forgetting Inary was like trying to stop smoking; it wouldn't work the first time, but you'd try over and over again and fall off the wagon once, twice, three times, until, if you were lucky enough or determined enough, you made it. Inary was like any other addiction, sweet and eventually destructive – I couldn't live without her, but ultimately she stopped me from living.

It was time to stop this coming close and then being lost to each other again. It was time to stop it. But how could I, when Inary was going through all that grief? And was I ready to live my life without her, not only as a girlfriend, but as a friend as well? Without Inary at all.

I wasn't sure how I could face it.

7

A wall between us

Inary

I could sense it from the way he was closing and opening drawers, from the way he was sighing while making coffee, going through Emily's pill bottles to check I don't know what, wrestling with the tea towels as if they were a nest of snakes. I knew he was spoiling for a fight.

Part of me wanted to keep out of his way, avoid the confrontation I knew was coming, and part of me wanted to face it head on and tell him all I'd had in my heart since I'd moved away. How I resented him for having punished me constantly, incessantly. How I never chose to have my life broken into a million pieces, forcing me to leave. How I hated the way he always had a chip on his shoulder . . .

"Inary! Whatever it is you're making, it's burning," Logan yelled. I shook myself and removed the soup from the stove. "That's all we need. The house going up in flames! Can you just focus, for once? Can you keep your head on what's happening here and now? Or do you have a million more important things to think about, as usual?"

There. It was bound to happen. My hands were shaking with anger as I swept my hair away from my face, trying not to shout back. But he wouldn't let me be.

"Can you tell me where your head's at, Inary? Can you tell me?"

He was standing very close to me – too close. I looked up at him. My brother was a tall man, and strong; he towered over me. But I wasn't afraid of his anger; I was *furious*.

"My head is here with Emily," I whispered angrily. "Where it's always been, Logan. My thoughts were always with her. And keep your voice down . . ."

"So all the time you were in London your thoughts were with Emily? She didn't need your *thoughts*, you know? Your *thoughts* didn't make sure she took her pills every day, didn't take her to the hospital every four weeks, up and down to Aberdeen, and it was always bad news. Always. I never heard 'things are looking good', never. Every month it was a professional smile and a shrug of the shoulders when I asked when is the new heart coming? Is she getting better? Is she going to live?"

I hated myself as I felt tears streaming down my face. I tried to open my mouth, but he wasn't finished.

"I haven't slept a whole night in years. I always wake up to go and check on her. Like Mum used to do when we were children, remember? Or maybe you never noticed. I haven't slept one whole night in years for fear of finding her dead in the morning. And there was no telling you the truth, Inary, it just would not sink in . . . Every time we tried to tell you she would not live unless she got a new heart, you just wouldn't listen! You were always convinced a miracle would happen . . ."

I sobbed, a hand clasped over my mouth.

"Maybe it was to your advantage, to think that way. So you could allow yourself to leave. Because Emily would be fine. But she's not fine, she's *dying*. And you were away from us for three years. You left me dealing with it all . . ."

56

I couldn't take it any more. I couldn't stand there and listen any more.

Because he was right.

I wanted to run away, run out into the street and up to St Colman's well, and cry in peace.

Instead I slapped him.

He froze and just looked at me, eyes blazing. For a second I thought he'd strike me back – I braced myself – but he didn't. He turned around and punched the wall so hard I heard a crack. He held his injured hand in his good one, wincing.

"Can you keep it down, please?" The nurse Lynda's face appeared through the door. "Emily can hear you. She's upset. Whatever it is, go sort it somewhere else!" she hissed.

"I'm sorry," I said, drying the tears that were still flowing down my face.

"You can never make it right, Inary. Whatever you do. You can never undo what's been done. Live with it," Logan said in an angry whisper, leaving the room and the house.

★

I let myself cry at the kitchen table for a bit, then I went upstairs to see Emily. I'd promised she wouldn't see me cry, and I intended to keep that promise. I sat on her bed and smoothed the covers down around her.

"I'm sorry we were shouting. You know us. Cat and dog."

"Yes. Is Logan giving you a hard time?" she whispered. I could never get used to how blue her lips were, how troubled her breathing sounded. I wanted to breathe for her.

"Not more than usual." I tried to smile.

"He doesn't understand you."

"Nah. He's right. I should never have left you . . ." I hated myself. At that moment, I truly hated myself.

"He doesn't need to live the way he does, Inary."

"What do you mean?"

Emily took a deep breath – as deep as she could muster. "I'm his excuse."

"His excuse?"

"While I'm around, he needs to look after me. He can't leave Glen Avich, he can't have a serious relationship . . ."

"Why not? I mean, he could have a girlfriend . . ."

"Exactly," she murmured. Her breathing was becoming even more laboured. I had to leave her be, talking was too hard for her. "Like I said, I'm his excuse."

"Enough talking now, honey. Can I get you anything?"

"Can you read me another chapter of *Cassandra*?"

I smiled. "Sure. So you'll find out if she managed to run away or not."

"Poor Cassandra . . ." she whispered.

I nodded. "Women werewolves have it hard. Imagine when she needs to shave her legs . . ."

I'd made her laugh. I squeezed her hand and winced a little, my palm tender from where I'd hit Logan.

8

Spirit be free

Inary

One afternoon, three weeks to the day that I arrived, Emily fell into a deep sleep, suddenly, like an exhausted child. It wasn't the fitful sleep she'd had for weeks, the medication-induced oblivion that came in short bouts and left her more tired than before. It was deep and peaceful, and it brought the colour back to her face. She was breathing steadily, her eyelids still and not fluttering; she looked like Emily again, her cheeks rosy, her expression serene. The sun was setting in orange splendour above the hills, its rays dancing in Emily's hair and turning it to honey.

Logan and I sat with her, and as the hours went by and she still wasn't waking up, we knew she would never wake up again; we knew that the fight was over.

Darkness fell. Emily's chest kept rising and falling for a while, and then her face changed. Something imperceptible, something intangible – whatever made Emily herself – vanished. She was gone. Just like that. No last words, no solemn conversations – only sleep, peace, silence. It was three in the morning, the deadliest hour, when many ailing souls give up their fight and let themselves be carried away.

My eyes were dry with shock as I lowered my face to Emily's, and no breath, however slight or ragged, came to meet me. I could hear my brother sobbing as I got up and opened the window and the door wide; I was following the Highland tradition of letting the dead soul fly away. The freezing air of winter swept the room and filled it, and filled our lungs.

I wanted Emily's spirit to be free.

I wanted Emily to be free and no longer trapped in that treacherous shell that had been her body, her strength ebbing slowly, betraying her soul, hungry for life.

The smell of sadness and medication dissolved as the scent of the Scottish night swept the room, and a wave of relief ran through me. My beautiful sister was free.

In the grief-laden silence, I sat on her bed. I held her cold hand and undid the clasp of her charm bracelet. The silver swallow had its wings extended, free in flight, like I wanted Emily to be. I tried to tie it around my wrist, but my hands were shaking and Logan had to help me.

My brother and I stood looking at each other, bewildered. I wanted to give him words of comfort, those words that soothe more for their tone than for their meaning, like humming soothes a crying baby. I raised my eyes to him and opened my mouth to speak, to tell him I was there for him, that I was so sorry I'd left . . . But as my lips parted, I caught a glimpse of Emily lying lifeless on her bed, her fine hair scattered across the pillow, her eyes closed forever. One hand uncurled at her side, the other resting on her chest, the shape of her slight body under the sheets, that body that I had held so many times, that I had washed and dressed in her final days . . .

Images of Emily exploded in front of my eyes. Emily as a little girl, running along the loch shore in a yellow summer dress; the two of us playing hide and seek in our grandmother's house; sharing a bag of sweets on the way home from school; puddle-jumping on a wet day . . . And a still frame: the special place we had in the room we shared, between the chest of drawers and the desk, the nest-like nook where we sat and made ourselves small and cosy and safe and I told her stories I'd made up, just the two of us in the world.

And now she lay with no more life in her.

Something broke inside me, in my chest, as sudden and sharp as a crack in a mirror. It was so real a feeling I could almost hear it. My mouth was poised and ready to speak, but the words were stuck in my throat; the crack had absorbed them all. Nothing came out. I tried again and again, but where there should have been words, there was only silence.

*

Logan and I sat in the living room and watched the slow-burning peat, both silent, both stunned with grief. I still hadn't shed a tear.

As dawn rose on the hills around Glen Avich, its grey light filling the room, I got up in a daze and went to fetch the scissors from the cutlery drawer. I stepped into the bathroom upstairs and looked at myself in the mirror. Again, I didn't recognise the face staring back at me. A face full of pain, eyes red-rimmed and dry – who was this woman?

I wavered for a moment – I didn't know what I was doing – and then, as if I'd split into two people, I watched my hair fall on the tiles snip after snip, in soft little mounds. My head felt light and strange.

I let myself fall to the floor too and I just sat there, staring at the tiles on the opposite wall. There were tufts of hair entangled in my fingers. I couldn't feel my arms and legs, I couldn't feel my body – as if too much suffering had caused me to leave it. I could only sit there, hugging my knees, soft red clumps in my hands.

After a while – I'm not sure how long – Logan came in. He wrapped an arm around my waist and lifted me up. I closed my eyes and went to lean my head on his chest, but he held me at arm's length.

"Your hair . . ."

What about it? Oh yes. I cut it off.

"Come on," he said, and led me into my room and onto my bed. He lay me down and covered me with the duvet. Only then did I realise how cold I was. A long, painful shiver travelled through me. I was so cold, I was sure I would never feel warm again.

There was a voice – Lynda. "Logan, a minute . . ."

"Just rest now, Inary. I'll be back," he said. His eyes were wide, like he couldn't believe what had happened. Like he couldn't believe that death had just visited our family again.

I waited until I heard his steps down the stairs, then I got up, ignoring the cold and the way the room was spinning around me. I switched the laptop on and opened the folder marked *Stories*. Everything I was working on, nearly everything I had ever written, was in that folder. One by one, I deleted all the files, until it was empty. Cassandra's story didn't exist any more. None of my stories existed any more. It was like I had never written them. I felt like I should open the window again, like they too should go free and follow Emily's spirit in her flight.

My heart was frozen, my eyes dry, my soul empty. A sudden bout of panic gripped me, so intense that I started shivering again. I thought I would go the same way as Emily, the same way as my stories, dissolved into air.

And then it happened.

My hair stood on the back of my neck, and all my limbs started tingling, a faint drone singing softly in my ears. A strange, unnatural chill spread over my shoulders, and I knew at once that I wasn't alone – there was someone behind me. I turned around slowly, trembling, and that's when I saw her, sitting at my dressing table. I blinked in the darkness, my gaze fixed on the shadow; I tried to remain perfectly still and perfectly silent, without even breathing.

Emily?

I called her in my heart, and called and called, willing the shape to take form, willing the mute, slender figure to turn around and show me her face, her beloved face. But it didn't happen. Her edges started fading quickly, and before I knew it she was gone.

Please come back. Come back to me, I kept imploring, staring at the space where the spirit had been, trembling with fear and longing and awe. My gift was back. It had to be back. So I could see Emily again.

"Inary?" It was Logan. He helped me up, and I held onto his hand tightly, for him to keep me on this side of reality, this side of the living.

After that, I don't remember a thing.

9

The end and the beginning

Inary

A few hours later I woke up on one of the sofas. Logan had wrapped a blanket around me, I realised gratefully. From a gap in the curtains I could see the bleak winter light seeping through – I realised it had to be late morning already. We'd sat up until dawn, but weariness must have won me over – I couldn't remember falling asleep. I couldn't remember anything from the night before.

Emily was dead.

Nothing else mattered, then.

But life is always stronger than despair. Thoughts of the present grabbed me and made me sit up. My head felt strangely light.

My *hair*! I'd chopped my hair off. Shit. Why had nobody stopped me? I ran to the bathroom and looked at myself. My hair wasn't too bad – it was my face that looked terrible. I grabbed the first brush I could find and smoothed down my chopped waves. No longer weighed down, the ends were curling up already. I washed my face in icy water and sucked my breath in with shock. After that, I felt a bit less dazed.

My brother was sitting at the kitchen table, clutching a steaming cup. He looked terrible too, blue shadows under his eyes, dishevelled in his ancient woollen jumper, jeans and bare feet. He was bent over the table, under the weight of his loss. My heart went out to him.

He sensed my presence and composed himself. "Inary. Want some coffee?" he asked, getting up slowly. He was stiff, like he'd been sitting there all night. He probably had. The knuckles on his left hand were blue where he'd hit the wall a few days before.

I opened my mouth to accept his offer of coffee, but no words came out. In an instant I remembered what had happened just after Emily died. The way my voice seemed to have gone, all the words stuck in my throat.

I tried again, and again, mouthing "yes" many times under Logan's bewildered gaze. Nothing. I felt panic spread in my chest and brought my hands to my throat.

"Inary, are you okay?" Logan came to stand beside me. I locked my eyes on his as I tried to speak once more, but again nothing came out. It was as if my vocal chords had frozen. So it wasn't just a momentary shock.

I shook my cropped head, hoping to dispel whatever was clutching at my throat and stopping me from speaking; the sudden movement, coupled with the lack of sleep and food, made me dizzy. I grabbed a chair and sat quickly, leaning my elbows on the table.

"Inary?"

I was in two minds whether to try to speak again. I decided to leave my next attempt for when I was alone, and I nodded instead.

"On you go upstairs and lie down. I'll bring you some coffee. I'll take care of . . . everything. They'll be here in half an hour." He sounded almost tender, almost like he still cared about me.

65

I knew who he meant. The undertakers. Coming to take Emily away. I nodded again, my eyes heavy with exhaustion and a sudden bout of grief renewed. I went upstairs slowly, negotiating every step. I walked past Emily's door; silence seeped through it as loud as a scream. Had I walked through that door, I would have seen my sister dead on her bed. I felt all that was left of my energy leaving me, leaking from me and evaporating in the air with a soft hiss, like when air seeps out of a balloon. Will my heart stop too, now? Like Emily's, I wondered. Why was I still alive, when my sister lay with no more life in her?

But that wasn't my sister. That was just her body, I reminded myself to numb the pain a little. She wasn't dead. She was free, like the swallow on her charm bracelet, the one that was clasped around my wrist now.

I leaned against Emily's door, resting my forehead briefly against the wood.

Come back, come back to me, I found myself pleading with her. *Let me see you again, Emily ...*

★

Hot, nearly scalding water enveloped me and soothed me a little.

Dressed in clean jeans and a jumper, my hair wet and my feet bare, I sat on my bed, the door closed. I took a deep breath.

I am Inary, I tried to say, wrapping my lips around each syllable, willing my vocal chords to vibrate.

Hello. Hello. I am Inary.

Nothing. No sound came out. I mouthed the words but nothing happened, nothing louder than a sigh or a breath.

66

Again I brought my fingers to my throat, trying to feel what was wrong there . . .

I must have caught something. The flu, or laryngitis, or something of that sort. I had neglected myself in the last few days of Emily's life, forgetting to eat, to put on a jacket when I went to the shops, and it was so cold outside. Glen Avich in March was still freezing. So that was my answer. I needed paracetamol and throat lozenges and I would be fine.

I was relieved for a few seconds, but then my heart sank again. I felt my forehead – fresh and cool. No pain in my throat at all. My chest wasn't heavy. I wasn't ill.

My heart started pounding with panic again.

I can't speak. I really can't speak.

I checked myself, taking more deep breaths. If ever there was a bad time to have a panic attack, it was now. Logan couldn't possibly deal with that as well, and neither could I. I had to keep it together. It was just a temporary thing, after all. It had to be.

As I focused on trying to slow my shaky breath, voices and noises from outside made me jump. I closed my eyes briefly, bracing myself for what was about to happen. They were here, the funeral director Mr Clarke and his sons. They had taken care of my granny when she died. And now they were here for Emily.

I was shedding loved ones like a tree sheds its leaves; one by one they were going, and I felt bare and barren like the black branches outside my window. All gone, but for Logan and me.

I forced myself to walk to the door, each step heavy, as though my legs had turned to lead. I made my hand turn the handle, and I looked. There they were, dressed in black like a murder of crows. And there was Logan, his eyes distant,

67

unbelieving – weird how such a strong, tall man could suddenly look so small and lost, like a little boy.

I went to stand beside him; I had to be with him. I had to, like I hadn't been when he and Emily had needed me the most.

For a second, it crossed my mind to scream at the top of my voice and rip Emily from the undertakers' hands, to throw them out of my house and shout at them to leave us alone. My chest heaved with anger and hatred for the only people I could hate at that moment, the ones who were taking Emily from us. A sob escaped my mouth, and Logan stepped closer to me, his arm touching mine. All my anger ebbed away, and the tears started flowing.

At last.

"I'm so sorry, Inary," said Mr Clarke, an elderly man who always spoke quietly and had been to nearly every home in the village in their darkest hour. He'd seen grief in all its forms.

I nodded, ashamed of the fury I'd just felt. I wondered if it had happened to him before, being the object of anger from people who had nobody else to be angry with, who were angry at the universe, at life itself.

We wanted to go with Emily, but Mr Clarke said to stay at home, that they would think of everything. To go down at lunchtime for all the arrangements. The door closed behind them, and they were gone. Emily was gone.

My lungs tightened and I couldn't breathe – it was time for my mantra again. *Emily won't be a prisoner of her body ever again. Emily won't be buried. Her soul is free.*

★

"I'm having a drink . . ." Logan's voice sounded funny, like he had to work so hard just to form words and sentences, when all he really wanted to do was cry. I could see it in his face, could spy the tears pressing behind his eyes, gathered in a silent torrent that would flow as soon as he could allow himself.

I took hold of his arm and made him look at me. *I can't speak,* I mouthed.

"What do you mean?"

I tapped at my throat and shook my head. My chest was tight with panic.

"Is your throat sore?"

I shook my head again.

"You must have caught a chill or something . . ."

A knock at the front door – Aunt Mhairi, her eyes heavy with crying and the sleepless night. She held me tight.

"Dearie, your hair! What happened?"

I shrugged. Logan shook his head swiftly, as if to say "don't mention it". I was grateful.

"Have you two had any sleep at all?"

"Not really," Logan replied. I couldn't answer. "Inary caught a chill; her voice has gone," he explained.

"Oh, sweetheart. Do you have anything in the house? No? I'll run up to the chemist for you."

I realised I'd always counted on Lesley's medicine stash. I never bought anything, really. Aunt Mhairi was out of the door before I could protest, returning a short time later with assorted medicines, plus a tub of vitamins – "to build you up a bit". I took anything I could – Lemsip and lozenges and a vitamin pill – and then, at the bottom of the bag, I spotted two lollipops. I held them up, raising my eyebrows.

69

"Mr Talbot gave me these for you and Logan," Aunt Mhairi explained. "He must think you're still ten years old." I smiled, in spite of myself. The sight of those Chupa Chups was strangely moving. "He said he'll come down later with Nuala."

Of course. The whole village was 'coming down later'. My stomach twisted. Of course people would come and see us, make sure that we weren't left alone, that we were all right. They'd bring covered dishes and offer precious words of comfort. I was grateful for that, I needed to feel we had family and friends all around us, but how could I explain my silence? Hopefully everything would be back to normal soon.

As soon as I'd formed the thought, dismay filled me again. Nothing would ever be back to normal. My voice might come back, but Emily wouldn't.

The next few hours tumbled over each other, with us in a daze. We saw Mr Clarke, talked about Emily's funeral, went home. People came and went. I just wanted night to fall, so we could be alone. I also wanted Logan to get some sleep. I was so worried for him and kept following him around, trying to make sure he wouldn't drink too much when he was so tired, and slipped glasses of water into his hand every once in a while.

I managed to convince everybody that I had a throat infection. Nobody seemed to doubt my explanation for my silence: nobody but Logan. I could see him looking at me when he thought I couldn't. People were telling me to wear a scarf, to wrap up; to have tea, an orange, a hot toddy, a vitamin drink; to lie down for a bit, to go for a walk, get some fresh air. And on and on, their bits of advice and concern chipping away at my sadness, just a little. My grief was an ocean and

70

people's kindness only took a few drops away, but it was better than nothing.

In between rounds of tea and sandwiches and neighbours dropping in with shepherd's pies and apple crumbles, I realised in shame I hadn't told Lesley that Emily was gone. I slipped upstairs to my room, relishing the solitude, and switched my phone on for the first time in three days.

At once I was flooded with missed voicemails, all from Lesley. Nothing from Alex. It hurt, but what did I expect after the way I'd treated him?

Instinctively I went to tap Lesley's number – I wanted to hear her voice so badly – but then I remembered that I couldn't speak. I had to text her instead.

Emily died last night. I can't speak today – which was true, though not for the reasons she probably thought – *will phone soon.*

Or at least, I hoped I could.

The reply came at once. I was sure she'd been waiting by the phone for news from me.

I'm so sorry. Do you want me to come up?

Oh God, yes. You have no idea how much.

Please. It would mean the world to have you here. The funeral will be the day after tomorrow.

Stay strong honey. On my way xxxx, she replied.

71

I closed my eyes briefly and exhaled. The idea of having her beside me at the funeral made everything just a little more bearable.

But I didn't even know if I'd be able to speak to her, no idea when my voice would come back. In an hour? By tonight? By next week?

I wondered if I should tell her about my voice before she arrived, but I decided against it. It would have alarmed her even more. But what if my voice didn't come back, how would I explain . . . My thoughts were all jumbled up and my head was pounding. I curled up on the bed and lay my cheek on the pillow, fresh and soft against my skin. I needed to rest, but my thoughts would not stop leaping and swirling over each other.

As I considered the chaos of my situation, a sudden need to tell Alex hit me so hard I was nearly breathless. I said to myself he needed space, but I couldn't help it – I sent him the same message I'd sent Lesley, then I dragged myself downstairs to join Logan.

After another hour of keeping an eye on my brother as he tried to make small talk with people, I heard my mobile ringing, just once.

I slipped into the kitchen and looked at the screen. It was a missed call from Alex. When we couldn't speak and didn't have time for a text message we would phone and make it ring just once, so that the other person knew that we were thinking of them. We called it *trilling*. I can't remember who came up with the word. The trills could take many different meanings – goodnight or good morning, a favourite programme coming on TV, the end of the tea break at work, or simply a flying thought.

I stood leaning against the kitchen table and looked at my

phone for a long time. *Missed call from Alex* – a thought from him to me, floating above us somewhere between London and Glen Avich. A little spark of comfort ignited in my heart, making everything seem a little less dark, a little less cold.

Alex

What could I do? I couldn't just disappear. Not after all that was happening around her. Talk about bad luck – her family's story was full of tragedy. First her parents and now Emily. It killed me to think about what she was going through.

After what had happened between us, she probably didn't want me at the funeral. And I didn't think I was ready to face her. I decided it would be best if I kept away, but I'd let her know I was there for her.

I was still angry after what she'd said, after what she'd done, but I couldn't bear the thought of her in pain. I grabbed my phone and called her, only to end it before she could answer. A trill, just to say *I'm here*.

10

A party for the dead

Inary

Lesley arrived on the morning of the funeral, a bright, sunny morning, so uncommon for early March in Glen Avich – a prelude to spring. I wasn't sure if it was a blessing, a sweet goodbye for Emily, or a way to mock us.

I stood in the street waiting for Lesley – she'd texted that she was only ten minutes away – drinking in the beautiful light and breathing in a new season and new life in the air, while knowing that my sister was about to be buried. That she would never breathe in air again, she would never feel the wind on her face again, or see everything in bloom around her . . .

When I saw Lesley's little red car appear at the end of the street, my eyes welled up with relief. I ran to meet her.

"Oh, Inary," she whispered as she got out of the car. "I'm so sorry . . ."

I held Lesley tight for a long time, and I didn't want to let her go. We looked at each other, and I couldn't reply. I hadn't told her about my voice – I kept hoping it would come back any moment. I took her into the house by the hand; Logan was waiting on the doorstep. "Thank you for coming, Lesley."

"Of course. I'm so sorry, Logan," she said, and enveloped him in a hug, which he returned stiffly. "Is there anything I can do . . . ?" she said, looking at me. I couldn't answer.

"Inary lost her voice," Logan explained. I nodded and touched my throat.

"Oh . . . have you taken something? Just what you need now! Do you have a temperature?" She rested her hand on my forehead, and I closed my eyes. I was soaking up her tenderness. "You feel quite cool . . ."

"She's going to the doctor after the funeral. It's just a throat infection or something, but better to have it checked," Logan said for me.

"And you had your hair cut . . ."

I glanced to one side. Lesley took the hint.

"It looks lovely. You are so brave, Inary. Come here," she said, and held me again. I wished I could just stay in her arms and never have to face what was ahead of us.

★

We desperately wanted a small family funeral, but the church was full. We couldn't stop half of the village – nearly the whole village, I suppose – from turning up. Alex wasn't there, and I felt his absence as keenly as a missing limb – but I understood why he'd chosen not to come: me. I couldn't blame him.

Emily's friends and classmates were seated near the back, wide-eyed, incredulous that something like this could happen to one of them – young people don't die, do they? David was among them – he'd been Emily's boyfriend for a wee while. He was pale and hunched over with grief. He was there with his mother. Afterwards, they both came up to us, heads bent, and offered condolences.

"We were so fond of her," whispered his mother. Her eyes

75

were bright with tears. "Such a lovely young woman. I'm so sorry, Logan, Inary."

David said nothing. He shook Logan's hand for a split second and looked away at once. My heart went out to him.

So many people were in tears. I was one of them, my arm linked with Lesley's, repeating my lifesaving mantra over and over in my head: *She is not there. She is not in that coffin. She is not being lowered into the ground now. The earth is not closing over her head. She's not in darkness.*

Emily is free.

I watched as they lay her next to our mum and dad. Three graves, one after the other. Logan and I were all that was left of our family. I looked for his hand and I clung to his fingers like a lost child. He gave me a brief squeeze, then took his hand away, and I stood alone.

*

We went back to the house for food and drink. This tradition had always baffled me. It's like a party for the dead, really. I suppose it helps the bereaved, as they're not forced to go home to an empty house just after the funeral. It did help me, but it was overwhelming as well. Lesley stayed by my side through it all, yet there were so many people, so many bunches of flowers everywhere, and platter after platter of sandwiches brought by our neighbours ... All those bodies and voices were beginning to twirl into one and my head was starting to spin, when I felt a hand on my arm and I smelled a sweet, fresh-apple-scented perfume. It was Eilidh. I hadn't seen her since our chance encounter in the shop, having spent all my time ... with Emily.

76

Emily.

I breathed in as deeply as I could and regained my composure.

Eilidh was holding her baby, cute and snuggly in a blue babygro and a knitted blue cardigan. She gave me a one-armed hug and waved to Lesley.

"Logan told me you lost your voice . . . Grief does strange things to people," she said simply, looking at me with those clear blue eyes, exactly the same shade as mine. I was a bit startled. Nobody had mentioned my silence in those terms up till then, not to my face anyway. Everybody had pretended to buy the throat-infection theory.

"But you know, it does get easier . . . Even if it doesn't feel possible now," she added in that sweet, soothing voice of hers.

The room wasn't spinning any more. I had regained some sort of calm. Eilidh had something about her that enfolded people like a warm light – a kind of serenity, a bit like my mum. Eilidh's words had comforted me, maybe because she had spoken aloud what everybody suspected and nobody said – that it had been the trauma of Emily's death that had taken my voice away. Or maybe seeing how much we looked alike had reminded me how deep my ties with Glen Avich were, how I was somehow related to half the village. How I belonged somewhere, even if I'd wanted to escape from it.

"Inary! I'm so sorry . . ." a familiar voice said, coming from behind me. Eilidh said goodbye discreetly and walked away, and I turned around to see Torcuil Ramsay – Lord Ramsay – my mother's second cousin. He had holes in his jumper as usual, mud on his shoes and hair that looked like he hadn't seen a comb for months, but he wore his 'special occasions' kilt.

Torcuil was one of the kindest people I'd ever met. He enveloped me in a hug, and as I looked in his eyes memories of us playing together as children came rushing back. I half-smiled, remembering the tree house in the Ramsay grounds and him helping Emily up, so she wouldn't strain herself . . .

"Come and see me, Inary. It's been so long," he whispered – he always spoke very quietly – and he held my hands for one last time before walking away.

I felt somebody touching my arm lightly – it was Lesley. I'd forgotten she was there.

"Just nipping upstairs for a minute," she said. "Will you be okay?"

I nodded.

"Inary . . ." Next it was my old school friend Christina. I briefly looked at her face, just for my eyes to be drawn to her enormous bump. She read my expression. "Yes, I'm six months gone. Not long to go, now." I looked at her, not sure what to do. I couldn't say congratulations; it just seemed too difficult a word to mouth or mime. I waited for her to keep talking, and she did. "I was so sorry to hear about your sister, Inary. Poor Emily. I wish I could find the right words . . ."

I stared at her. Words weren't my forte either, at that particular moment, so I nodded, my standard reply.

"Inary, are you okay?" she asked, her face full of concern. And then it dawned on me. She didn't know that I had lost my voice. Unbelievable: somebody in Glen Avich didn't know. Was the grapevine not working as well as it had when I used to live here?

I gestured to my throat, shrugging and opening my arms wide, feeling a bit like a French mime. For a crazy second, I pictured myself climbing an invisible set of stairs, wearing a stripy black and white jumper and white gloves, a red carnation pinned somewhere. The thought made me laugh silently, in a way that was completely incongruous with the situation. Slightly hysterical, I suppose. Christina was still looking at me, bewildered. She probably thought I had lost my mind. Maybe I had.

"Aw, you have a sore throat? Well, hope you get better soon. Like I said, I'm so sorry about Emily. Better go, Fraser is waiting for me." Oh yes, Fraser Masterson, he was in our class too. We actually snogged once – try miming that. My goodness. Married and pregnant at twenty-five. But then, that probably would have been me, if . . .

The room swayed as the thought I had just formed seemed to jump out of my head and take on a life of its own. I felt my heart skipping a beat – Christina had just turned into the ghost of What Could Have Been.

He was there. Lewis was there. And he was holding another woman's hand.

They walked across the room to me. My ex-fiancé, and our former coursemate – pretty, petite, giggling Claire McKay. Before I could say anything, Claire hugged me, murmuring her condolences. I stood rigid, unable to wrap my arms around her.

I wondered if she knew what he'd done to me. I wonder if she knew he hadn't just left me – he'd left me three months before our wedding. Did she know that I'd had to take my wedding dress to Oxfam? I left it in a bag on the shop doorstep and ran away before they could see me. I couldn't have borne the humiliation of them saying *thank you for this – what a lovely dress – you must have looked beautiful in it – was the weather kind to you on the big day?*

Maybe something had happened between Lewis and Claire while we were still together. Maybe that was why he'd left me so suddenly. The thought cut me like a knife. I bled, and kept bleeding silently as they both stood in front of me.

"I wanted to come and say how sorry I am," Lewis said.

Sorry about what? My sister dying? Or breaking my heart?

I took in his face, those features I knew so well. All the mornings I'd woken up in our bed, and his face had been the first thing I saw – his long, fair eyelashes, those lips I couldn't get enough of, his dark-gold hair tousled and soft on the pillow. *Good morning, sleepyhead*, he used to say.

I expected a wave of pain, and it came.

I expected the intense, hungry need for his presence I'd had since we met – and it didn't come.

Instead, a bone-deep cold seeped into me, the memory of how I felt when he'd left me. When he told me it was over and went, just like that, saying it was better for me to be alone for a bit, that he needed time to think, that he'd phone me later to check I was okay. I'd spent hours sitting at the kitchen table in our home, stunned, unable to speak, unable to move, not quite believing what had just happened. For the first three weeks, I pleaded with him to see me. We had to talk, it couldn't just end this way . . . but he refused. After a while, it was his turn to ask to see me – he wanted to explain. I realised that I couldn't bear to lay eyes on him. Six weeks later I left for London; we hadn't seen each other since.

And now here he was.

I suppose I had just realised that Lewis was out of my heart, that my love for him had died. What he'd done to me still hurt, but I knew that already; part of me was still sitting at the kitchen table at our home in Kilronan, with dry eyes and trembling hands.

"I wish I'd known her," said Claire, absurdly.

I nodded and looked down. I didn't know what to do next. I just wanted him to go and take Claire with him. I hoped they'd be happy. Or maybe I didn't, maybe I hoped Lewis would suffer as much as I had . . . No, I wouldn't wish unhappiness on anyone; I just didn't want to be that kind of person.

"Well, glad to see you're well. Time to go now," said a voice behind me. Aunt Mhairi materialised at my side, standing squarely in front of Lewis and Claire, all five foot of her. Her head barely reached his chest.

"Oh. Oh. Yes, of course . . ." he stumbled.

"Bye," she said unceremoniously, a hand on his back and one extended to show him the way towards the door. She escorted him and Claire out with a face like thunder, and came back to stand beside me. I was still standing in shock. Numb.

"You all right, pet? I could strangle him!" she hissed. I swallowed. For a second, my cardigan-clad, woollen-skirted aunt had looked pretty scary. "The cheek to show his face, and with his fancy woman!" I nearly smiled at the expression – but not quite. "I swear, if he comes near you again . . . Oh, there's Lorna. She's having terrible problems with her Derek." She lowered her voice dramatically. "You know, her youngest. Peggy told me he doesn't have an inch of skin left on his arms that's not tattooed. The tribulations . . . Will you be okay?"

I nodded.

"Oh, here she comes . . ." She rolled her eyes and went to greet Lorna.

My eyes surveyed the room, looking for whisky; now *that*

would help. As I made my way towards the nearest bottle I could spot, somebody stood between me and my Laphroaig.

A man.

A man with a tanned face and smiling eyes, and a bunch of white roses in his hands.

"You must be Inary. I'm Taylor, a friend of Logan's," he said, holding out his hand. He had an American accent – New York, I guessed. Who was he? A newcomer, a very *new* newcomer. He must have moved here in the last few months, because I'd never seen him before. "Logan said you lost your voice. Don't worry, you don't need to say anything. Just . . . I brought these for Emily. I'm so sorry . . ." He offered me the bunch of roses.

I nodded for the thousandth time that day.

Suddenly, I felt weary. I just wanted to be alone.

"You must be desperate to be alone," he said, reading my mind, "so I'll go now. But I just wanted to say, I work at the dig . . ." What dig? What was he talking about? "Logan and I go out on the loch once in a while. Maybe sometime you can come . . . if you like. With Logan, of course . . ." he added quickly, probably in case I thought he was chatting me up at my sister's funeral. I didn't care either way. I looked down, and he took the hint. "So, yes. I'll see you. And again, I'm so sorry." He turned away and made a beeline for Logan.

I sorted the white roses in a vase, and finally I managed to pour myself a drink. I'd settled for a cup of sugary tea. Logan was drinking enough whisky for both of us. I took a couple of sips and felt a bit better.

But I was still reeling after Lewis's surprise appearance, with Claire in tow. Thank goodness Logan hadn't spotted him. Even if my feelings for him had been wrangled out of me, he still had the power to make me feel as alone and bereft as an abandoned child. And I hated myself for it even more than I resented him. I should have never depended on him like I had – no man or woman should have their lives revolve around someone else, only to be empty and lost when they leave. Or maybe that is the nature of love, to become so dependent on one person. Which was why I never wanted to love again.

In a way, I thought confusedly, I wished Claire luck. That she would not get hurt like I did.

The bitch.

I took another sip of tea, and suddenly, Lesley was back at my side. "So, Lewis."

I nodded.

"I never noticed before. He has bow legs."

Incredibly, unexpectedly, I laughed.

★

At last, it was finished. We cleaned up with the help of Maggie and Liz, two of Aunt Mhairi's friends from the parish. We were not to worry about a thing, they told us cheerily; they were a dab hand at funerals and wakes, and they'd have everything clean and tidy in no time. Good skill to have, I thought, and I smiled a feeble smile.

Funerals were complicated affairs, I'd just found out. When my parents died I was too young to be given any real responsibility, but now things were different. Funny thing is, I don't remember anything about my parents' funeral – where my memories had been there was now a big gaping hole. A few snippets remained – sleeping at Aunt Mhairi's; my new cream brogues I kept staring at, too frightened to look around me; my then boyfriend, Ally, sitting in the kitchen, silent and awkward.

Feeling like the sky had fallen.

I was grateful to Maggie and Liz, the kind of practical, unsentimental, energetic women you want around when there's a lot to do and a broken heart to do it with. When they went – one last hug, a few words of comfort – Logan, Lesley and I arranged all the flowers we had been given into vases and displayed all the sympathy cards nicely on the window sills. Emily would have been happy to see how many people loved and cared for her and for us. She would have liked the white roses best – who left them? Oh, yes, the guy with the boat. Emily loved white roses . . .

Before I knew it, my tears were flowing again on a bunch of chrysanthemums. Lesley was beside me at once, holding me close and patting my back. I had to face the fact that it was finished. Face the fact that there was nothing left to do, except wait for the flowers to wilt and for the right time to put the sympathy cards away in a box to be kept somewhere we wouldn't see it every day, but not too far either. And except clear out her room, I said to myself desolately. But I couldn't think of that, not yet.

So it had really happened. It wasn't a bad dream. Emily was gone for real.

Lesley had wandered upstairs, and I didn't notice Aunt Mhairi leaving too, though she must have said goodbye; all of a sudden Logan and I were alone in the kitchen, surrounded by a sea of flowers and cards and silence.

And I fell, I fell.

And then I remembered myself. I knew we needed to keep some kind of normality. I knew we had to keep going. All I could think of was lying down and crying, but there were still things to be done. I opened the fridge door and took out some covered dish or other that one of our neighbours had brought. I put it on the table and rested a hand on my brother's shoulder, gesturing towards the food.

"I'm not hungry, Inary. I'll have a drink."

My heart sank. Logan had been drinking all day, and on an empty stomach.

I shook my head and went to switch the oven on.

"I said I'm not hungry, Inary! Are we playing house now? Because there's not much point in that. You'll be gone soon."

Logan's words wounded me deeply. But even worse was the look in his eyes as he spoke to me. I'd seen him angry, worried, upset, but never before had I seen him this way. His eyes were *empty*.

11

Ice and chocolate

Alex

One night three years ago, not long before Christmas, I took Inary skating. She'd only been living in London for a few months, and I was hoping to find a good moment to ask her out – properly.

London was at its best: everything shone. *Everything.* The ice glittered, the museum was ablaze with lights, and Inary's eyes were full of sparkle. It was perfect. We slipped the skates on, Inary's head bobbing in her bright-blue hat. I stood up and offered her my hand – hers felt small and delicate in mine. I took off slowly, making sure that Inary stayed on her feet.

"You're good! It's not fair!" Inary was holding onto me for dear life.

"Skating is a bit like riding a bike. Once you learn, you don't forget. I used to go ice skating in Edinburgh as a child every year in December. Ever been?"

"No, but I've always . . . ooops!" She lost her balance and did a little trying-to-stay-on-my-feet dance. I held her up.

"Thank you," she said, and took refuge against me as a group of expert skaters whizzed past us. I draped an arm around her waist, and we glided on tentatively. "I've always wanted to go to Edinburgh for my Christmas shopping," she said. "Never quite made it . . . Always stuff on."

"It's great . . . Edinburgh is beautiful in every season, but at Christmas it's just stunning. The lights and the panoramic wheel turning, and the piping in the background . . ."

"To deafen you if you get too close . . ."

"They do, yes! Maybe we can go, one year."

"I'd like that. Emily could come . . . my sister. She'd love it," Inary said and smiled, sliding determinedly, frowning in concentration as she put one skate in front of the other.

"Older or younger?"

"Younger. I also have a brother, older than me. Logan. You?"

"I have three sisters."

"Oh . . . Should I commiserate you? The only boy? Or is it a good thing?"

"It's a good thing, really. They all look after me like mother hens. Though they say that my mum thinks I'm the golden boy who can do no wrong!"

"That'd be Logan, yes!" she laughed.

"You having fun?"

"I'm loving it!" she replied, and let go of my hand. Hesitantly at first, she skated away, then a little bit further. She laughed, full of Inary-happiness. "Look! I'm doing it!" She was like a child learning to cycle.

"Brilliant!" I kept an eye on her blue hat, among hats of every colour and shape. "Keep going!"

"Uh oh . . . Alex!" She was wobbling.

I reached her and held her hand tight, steadying her. "You have a strong arm," she teased, her eyes twinkling.

"Couldn't think of a better compliment. My granny always said that about me."

We skated on, with Inary becoming more and more

ambitious. She was doing great until a little girl changed direction suddenly and Inary had to brake fast to avoid crashing into her. She lost her balance and toppled over.

"Ouch . . ."

"That looked sore," I winced, taking both her hands and lifting her up.

"It was. But I do not regret a thing!" she said dramatically. "It was worth dislodging a vertebra or two just to enjoy the moment. You know what I fancy?"

A kiss, I hope? But I didn't say that. "You fancy a hot chocolate with cream and marshmallows."

She laughed. "How did you know?"

"I just know." I grinned.

We ended up in a little café not far from Oxford Circus, full of Christmas shoppers trying to take the weight off their feet. There were silvery fairy lights all over the walls, like a Santa's grotto, and Christmas music played in the background. Our hats, scarves and gloves lay on a chair beside us in a colourful bundle. Steam curled from our mugs of hot chocolate; Inary's cheeks were rosy and so was the tip of her nose, after skating for an hour in the freezing cold.

Okay, it was time. I would just ask her. Would you like to go out for dinner with me? Just the two of us?

I took a deep breath and prepared myself.

"I was won—"

"Oh, look at those lights! I love winter in London," she said. "It sparkles. Glen Avich in winter is dark and quiet."

Argh. Missed my chance! "Dark and quiet can be beautiful too," I replied. Do you see yourself ever going back?" I waited for the answer with my heart in my throat. I didn't want her to go anywhere.

"For good? I don't know. I miss Scotland, though. I never thought I would leave. Then . . . stuff happened." She glanced to one side. "Would you go back?"

"I'm not sure. I miss Scotland too, but . . . I don't know if I'd go back."

"Your parents are in Edinburgh, aren't they?"

"And my sisters, yes."

"What are you doing here all alone, then?" she laughed. "Maybe, the same as me . . ."

"Why, what are *you* doing?" I smiled back.

"Forgetting," she said, and licked some cocoa-covered cream off the spoon. "Mmmm . . . this is gorgeous."

"What? Forgetting what, I mean? Sorry, I don't mean to pry . . ."

"No, it's okay. Forgetting someone." She shrugged.

"Oh . . . I'm sorry," I replied, hoping to God that this guy was out of the picture.

"Better this way. Taught me a lesson. I just want to get on with my life." She sighed and smiled a brittle smile. "I'm done with all that. Never again, I'm telling you."

Oh.

"Sorry, I didn't mean to depress you! Are you seeing someone?" She tilted her head to one side.

"Not at the moment, no. I was. Not any more." I took a long sip of my hot chocolate and scalded my lips. Better not say that the break-up with Gaby had a lot to do with meeting her.

"What brought you to London in the first place?"

"Originally work. But I love London. Five years here last November."

"You haven't lost your accent."

"I don't intend to."

"Me neither," she said, and laughed. "I feel like we should burst into song, now . . ."

"Some sentimental song about missing Caledonia?"

"That. Or 'Rudolph the Red-Nosed Reindeer'."

And then I thought what the hell, I'll ask her. What's the worst that could happen? That she says 'no, I just told you, I'm done with all that'? If I don't try, I'll never know . . .

"Inary. I was thinking . . . Maybe we could go out for dinner sometime . . ."

"Sure! Why not tonight?"

"Oh . . . Yes. That's great . . . I can book somewhere . . ."

"Lesley should be here any minute; she said she was in the mood for Indian . . ."

Right.

As if on cue, a well-known voice interrupted us. "Hey! How was the skating?" It was Lesley, laden with Christmas shopping. She let herself fall onto a chair at our table. "I need a cup of tea!"

I leaned back in the chair, deflated.

So that went well.

"Hello! I'll get one for you," said Inary, and got up at once.

My face was frozen in a smile. It was the first time since Lesley and I had met that I actually wasn't happy to see her.

"It's bloody freezing outside! By the way, you'll be excited to know that your Christmas present is in one of these bags. But which one?" she teased emphatically. I looked at her, trying to muster a smile. "Alex?"

"Yes?"

"You all right?" Lesley arched a brow.

"Yes, why?"

"Inary texted me to say you were here, and I was just around the corner in the Candle Company, and . . . Do you mind me joining you?"

She must have read my expression. I felt terrible about it and tried to recover myself.

"Not at all! Sorry. Are you hungry? Do you want to get something to eat?"

"Oh," she said, and her lips opened in a slow smile.

"Oh, what?" I asked.

Her eyes twinkled and her grin grew wider. "You *like* her. As in . . . you *fancy* her. Inary," she whispered, turning around briefly to check that Inary was out of earshot and then leaning in towards me. "Oh my God!"

"Yeah, well . . ."

"Oh my God!" she repeated, a little louder. She was beaming. "Just like I planned!"

"You *planned*?" I began. I couldn't believe it. My sisters, Gary, Kamau, now Lesley. Did I have "looking for my soulmate" written on my forehead? Why was everybody trying to set me up?

"There you are!" Inary was back. She placed a steaming cup in front of Lesley. "To warm you up a bit. I got you some cake as well. What's wrong?" she said, looking from me to Lesley, then back.

"Nothing," Lesley said quickly. "Alex was telling me how much he loves skating. You really enjoy it, don't you?"

"Yes." I nodded. I suspected that my cheeks were scarlet, like a ten-year-old sent to sit beside his first crush.

"So do I! As from today!" Inary declared, and took a sip of her hot chocolate.

"You've got to take Inary out more often," said Lesley, smoothing her ponytail of braids. "You both look so happy."

12

Looking for Emily

Inary

I didn't go upstairs until the small hours. Logan was in his room – the drink had knocked him out – and Lesley and I sat watching something or other on TV and not really paying attention. What mattered was not being on my own, not having to go to bed, close my eyes and think terrible thoughts. We were on the verge of falling asleep on the sofa when Lesley dragged herself up. I gazed at my watch – two in the morning. Again. I was living on no sleep.

"Off to bed," she announced, and squeezed my shoulder. "Will you be okay?"

I nodded, though the truthful answer would have been *no, I won't* – but I knew Lesley needed rest, and so did I. I followed her upstairs and she disappeared into her room with a whispered goodnight.

In the back of my mind was fear and longing mixed together, that what happened the night of Emily's death would happen again, that I would *see* her. Part of me was hopeful; part of me was frightened. All of me was longing for Emily. Would it happen again?

After seeing the apparition at my dressing table, I'd spent hours staring into the darkness, half longing, half terrified. I'd willed my limbs to tingle, the hum to start in my ears.

I'd willed the air to turn electric, the hair on the back of my neck to stand up, a sudden chill to grip me. But there was nothing. I'd lain awake in my bed, rigid with frustration, my tears turning icy in the cold of night, torturing myself with thoughts of Emily.

And still, if it turned out that my Sight really was back – that thought was frightening too. The reason why I'd lost my gift when I was twelve was too terrifying for me to recall. I'd done my best to forget.

Now, as soon as I stepped through the threshold of my room, I froze. The air was thin, charged, like right before a storm; it felt different from the rest of the house. I looked around me and took an uncertain step in, reaching for the light switch. The light illuminated every corner, and I surveyed the room. There was nobody there – and still, I could feel *something*. Something in the space around me. Something in myself.

I washed and dressed for bed quickly, teeth chattering in the damp night air. I switched the light off again and lay, still shivering, under the duvet. I just couldn't get warm, and although I wanted to cry, to try and release some of the grief, I was all cried out. I lay there curled up like I was sixteen again and I'd just been orphaned, hugging the pillow and hoping dawn would come soon. Another sleepless night.

All of a sudden, something travelled through the air and burst into the room like a lightning bolt – a rapid rush of static, filling my ears with a low sound and touching each and every one of my nerves, like a bow on fiddle strings. My limbs started tingling, the hair on the back of my neck stood up and my skin puckered into goose bumps. I sat up and stared into the gloom, panting hard.

Emily? I mouthed. And then: *Emily, is that you?* No sound came from my lips, but I knew it wouldn't make a difference to her.

Nobody answered. The darkness didn't stir.

Nobody.

Disappointment filled me again and turned into rage, angry tears finally rolling down my cheeks. Was this some kind of cruel trick my senses were playing on me? Some horrific side effect of grief, hope given and taken away, to break me even more than I already was broken? I slapped my open palms against the wall over and over again, enjoying the release of pain, small sounds escaping my mouth like the yelps of a little animal. Then I remembered myself, and stopped at once – had Logan and Lesley heard me? The last thing Logan needed was to see me like that. I pricked my ears in the darkness – nothing.

I lay back on my pillow, feeling utterly alone, utterly lost. Suddenly the darkness felt heavy around me, squeezing air out of my lungs. The four walls of my room were closing around me and I was sure that I too was about to be unable to breathe, like my beloved sister.

I leapt out of bed and opened the curtains and the window, gulping in the icy air, staring in wonder at the beauty in front of me: the ink-black sky dotted with stars, shimmering through the blanket of clouds, a claw-like white moon, and Venus glimmering cold and silver.

Where are you? Please come to me. Come back to me, I pleaded, touching the little swallow that hung from Emily's bracelet. *Where are you? Where will I find you?*

I had to get out and breathe. I had to go and look for Emily.

I threw some clothes on and tiptoed downstairs as quietly as I could. I slipped on my boots and grabbed my coat, taking off before anyone could notice I was gone.

The night was full of wind and pervaded with the scent of wet soil and moisture – the smell of the Scottish night. The relief of being outside was immense. Darkness never scared me; I felt at home in it. When I was a wee girl I often tried to stay out after sunset, because the chances of Seeing were higher. It seemed strange to me then, but before that horrible day on the loch, the day I lost my Sight, I used to seek out spirits. Far from frightening me, I welcomed the physical signs that it was about to happen, the whispered thoughts that didn't belong to me – and then the apparition, surprised in whatever they were doing in the moment, frozen in time. A woman with flowing skirts carrying a baby across the play park, walking straight through the swings and the roundabout; two girls standing beside the graveyard wall, hair in buns, wearing long dresses with full skirts and giggling about something only they knew; an elderly woman walking on the side of the road, hair covered by a handkerchief, a sickle in her hand . . . Every time it happened – and they weren't many, they were rare and magical – I felt a little bit stronger, a little bit richer. The Sight was a part of me, a part I cherished.

Until I went onto the loch with my father, and the shock of what I saw took my gift away. For years I'd felt like I was missing a limb. But now the old feelings, the old sensations had returned, to my relief – and to my terror as well. But what mattered most of all was seeing Emily again.

Please, let me see her, I pleaded as I strode up St Colman's Way towards the well.

I passed Eilidh's cottage, black and silent, and Jamie's workshop, and then the houses started getting sparser as the well came into sight. There was no noise but the occasional hooting of a tawny owl, the distant barking of foxes, and the sound of my boots against the pavement. I stepped through the gardens, their solar lights dotted all around, giving out a spectral glow. From up there I could see the whole of Glen Avich spreading out like a patchwork quilt with its white cottages and its terraced houses along the main street, and the river cutting it in two. And beyond Glen Avich, the hills with their ragged edges smudged into the sky, black against black.

I dipped my fingers in the water that gathered at the bottom of the stone basin, gasping at how cold it was, and feeling the soft, tiny algae clinging to the stone. A sudden gust made me shiver, and I pulled the collar of my jacket tighter around my neck. I looked up to the sky and saw that the clouds were closing over my head. The Scottish sky can change in a heartbeat, and before you know it the heavens have opened and you're drenched to the bone. But I couldn't go home, I just couldn't – better getting soaked than holing myself up again. Emily was somewhere, and I would find her.

I strolled around the gardens some more, peering into the shadows, hoping and watching and searching – but there was nobody, and I couldn't feel anything. I looked around me. With my mind's eye I could see Emily, with her maroon school uniform on, sitting on the low stone wall bordering the gardens, reading *Harry Potter* . . . A memory of her, one of many, each of them a knife to the heart.

I walked down St Colman's Way again, stepped onto the play park and sat on a bench for a moment. Here the darkness was broken by the orange glow of street lights. I checked myself. Still nothing. No tingling, no buzz, nothing. The tawny owl's call resounded in the air again, echoed by another call from the woods, while the foxes had stopped barking. The flapping shape of a tiny bat, smaller than a sparrow, darted above.

How many times had Emily and I sat on those swings, first as children and then as teenagers, chatting in low voices and telling each other everything we didn't want to speak about at home, where our parents or our brother could hear us? There, just there, she had told me that David was a good kisser, but had terrible taste in music. How she was planning to get a tattoo of a dolphin on her wrist, as soon as she could convince Logan that it was a good idea. How when she grew up, she wanted to be a fashion designer . . .

Oh, Emily. I miss you, I miss you, I miss you.

I stood up and walked past the hairdresser – here you came to have your hair pinned up for the prom – past Peggy's shop – here we used to go and buy pocket-money sweets after school – and past the new coffee shop – no memories of you here, we just didn't have time to make them. You were too ill to come here with me. Down to the Green Hat, dark and shut, no music or voices seeping through its doors – here you used to have a sneaky shot of vodka added to your orange juice, even if you knew you weren't supposed to, because of your medication. "What's the point of being alive if I can't do anything?" you used to say.

Memories of my sister were everywhere, inside and outside of me. I felt my eyes stinging again. These memories – they were so intense now, but would I forget in time? Even if I loved her so much, as time went on would I forget her voice, and the scent of her skin, and all her mannerisms? Like sweeping her hair away from her face with both hands every time she was thinking hard about something, or calling everything *absolutely mind-blowing* in that passionate, fervent way she had; like curling up her nose when she laughed; or singing along with every song that came on the radio, even if she didn't know the words.

I remember when she saved a ladybird – she must have been about five – and christened it Polly, and every ladybird we saw after that was a *polly*. I remember how she dyed her hair blue for her fifteenth birthday and Logan went crazy. I remember when she adopted a litter of kittens, all completely black with white paws, and called every single one of them Murdo, even the female ones. Glen Avich is still full of Murdos.

I remember my sister. I remember you, Emily.

I was crying again, without shame or restraint, my face cradled in my hands. I hurried away from the streets and towards the woods, calling to her with every step I took. Suddenly, I saw a heart-shaped face looking at me from a branch, and I froze – it was the owl I'd heard call earlier. I walked towards it, carefully, silently, so as not to startle it. But it opened its wings and flew off, perching itself on another branch not too far from me. I switched my phone light on and followed it, and just as I was about to reach it again, it flew, this time a bit further away.

It kept beckoning to me for a while, perching itself on trees further and further away, and I followed, branches hooking my hair, twigs snapping under my feet like brittle bones. Dawn was breaking – I could see a hint of grey in the east – but it was still pitch-dark. The sky was black and shimmering with ghostly clouds edged with steel. The trees seemed to whisper all around me, their branches shaking and creaking in the rising wind. All of a sudden, the owl took off again and disappeared for good into the darkness.

I stood there, lost. I'd thought the owl would lead me to

Emily. I really had. But as I turned, there was silence and solitude. I was alone. Really, completely alone. There was nothing left for me to do but go home.

Suddenly, the dim light of my phone illuminated something – a pine tree, a section of its bark white where it should have been brown. It was graffiti, made in relief so that the letters would stand out instead of being carved in. I walked closer and placed the phone just in front of it, so I could read the words.

The graffiti said: *Emily, I love you. D.*

David. The good kisser with terrible taste in music, the boy who'd come to the funeral with his mother.

I felt the first few drops of rain on my hands and my face, and then the downpour began.

13

She came softly in

Inary

When I got to my house I looked – and felt – like a wet kitten. I swept my soaking hair away from my forehead and walked across the threshold.

It hit me immediately.

My hair stood on end, and there they were again, the signs that a spirit was near – the tingling; the hushed, continuous sound vibrating in my ears; the goose bumps. I almost felt dizzy with relief. Of course. Of course. I'd gone looking all over the village when she was here all along. Where else? I ran into the kitchen – *Emily, Emily, Emily*, I called, surveying the kitchen cupboards, the stove, the table. I turned back and strode into the living room – the sofas, the fireplace, the bookshelves, half hidden in the gloom – nothing.

Emily! I strained to call. My throat hurt with the unspoken words. I ran upstairs, nearly stumbling at the last step, such was my desire to see her. I was still prickling all over, so much so that it was nearly sore. Static was crawling over my skin. I went straight for her room. My heart was in my throat as I pushed the door open . . .

The yellow glow of the streetlight in front of our house, the same I could see from my window, seeped through a gap in the curtains. I surveyed the room – her bed, carefully made, untouched; her desk, her dressing table with her perfumes and medicines all lined up; her sewing machine; the cosy space between the bed and the wall where we used to sit, where I used to tell her stories.

There was nobody there. Emily wasn't there.

A sob escaped my mouth. *Where are you? Why are you hiding from me?*

And still, I could sense her presence. I even had the eerie feeling that my hair was actually beginning to stick up, like after you brush it too hard and static makes it fly. By now my heart was ready to jump out of my chest. I ran into my parents' old room, but the second I walked in, disappointment hit me like icy water – the tingling was subsiding, and so was the feeling of static around me. There was still a low sound in my ears, but it was feeble now. The air felt nearly normal again, and not charged with electricity. She was going . . .

Emily . . . No! Not before I see you! I mouthed so hard that a strangled whisper came out, like a ragged breath. I opened the door of my room and stepped into the dark.

And then I saw her.

There was a shape sitting at my dressing table, the same womanly shape I'd seen before, her back to me. For a second, terror blinded me – the memory of what I'd seen years ago, of the horrible vision that had taken my Sight away flashing before my eyes. But it was just a moment; this apparition felt different. It *had* to be my sister. It had to be Emily.

I blinked again and again in the gloom. The spirit's hair was dark, and not strawberry-blonde like Emily's. But still it didn't register. Of course it was Emily. Who else could it be?

Her hair was gathered in a loose bun at the nape of her

neck – Emily never wore her hair like that. Her slender frame was draped in a blue woollen nightgown – Emily hated nightgowns.

And then she angled her face slightly, and I caught a glimpse of her profile.

I couldn't deny it any more. It wasn't Emily.

Disappointment wrangled my heart. I'd been cheated.

And still, in spite of the renewed grief, in spite of the wound of my sister's loss open and bleeding again – I could see a spirit.

My Sight was back, after thirteen years – I was sure now.

I was too entranced to move. In the silence I could hear my shallow, rapid breathing and the thumping of my heart. The girl was smiling, and a light suffused her face, a light of happiness. Her slender fingers were holding an old-fashioned fountain pen; she was writing a letter. I stood as still as I could, trying to stop myself from shaking and my teeth from chattering. I was drenched, and freezing cold.

The girl's voice filled the room, resounding in my mind and in my heart, as if she were speaking from inside me. I'd heard spirits' thoughts echoing in my mind before, but I never heard them actually talking. She was special. Stronger. More real than anyone else I'd ever seen.

"Please, Robert, come back to Glen Avich soon," she said, murmuring each word as she wrote. "You know I'm counting the days, you know I can't find peace until you return. I am forever yours, all my love, Mary." She drew a long sigh, while in the meantime I was holding my own breath so that I wouldn't miss a word she was saying. I was filled with fear and wonder. I couldn't make a sound.

The girl called Mary clasped her hands over the letter and

raised her head to look at the grey sky outside. I let myself slump on the carpet, in perfect silence, and I watched her lovely face in profile, her bare feet tucked under the chair, her hands moving gracefully as she slipped the letter into an envelope. I sat there, on the cold wooden floor, my hair dripping onto my shoulders, and watched in awe at the girl who had come to see me on the worst night of my life. I was broken with disappointment, but still, there was comfort in her presence, like a reprieve from loneliness.

Suddenly, a knock at the door interrupted our silent intimacy.

"Inary, are you okay?"

It was Lesley. I moved my gaze to the door briefly, and when I looked back Mary was gone.

★

Half an hour later, my hair was dry and I was back in bed. I was so disappointed at not having seen Emily, I felt like my heart was battered and bruised; it hurt with every beat. But I was also full of amazement at Mary's visit.

Mary in her happiness, while I was so full of grief. Writing a love letter and sighing for joy.

All of a sudden, out of nowhere, came an overwhelming desire to speak to Alex. But how could I keep looking to him after what had happened before I left? He wasn't at the funeral. That had to mean something.

I looked at the time: 4.34 a.m. It was a completely uncivilised hour to call someone, and I couldn't *speak* anyway – I would have just breathed down the phone without talking like some sort of stalker. My fingers scrolled for Alex's number, and

103

before my brain could tell me to stop, I touched the *call* button. I fumbled about to stop the call, but the phone fell to the floor, and it was too late. I grabbed it as quickly as I could – I was expecting the voicemail message I knew by heart – *Hi, it's Alex, I'm not here but tell me all and I'll call you back* – but to my horror I realised that the phone was ringing, the display all lit up in the darkness. I finally managed to tap the end button. My heart was beating in a crazy rhythm. What was I thinking?

I didn't even know myself. I just had to make sure he was there. That he still *existed*.

All of a sudden, my phone made a deep DONG that seemed incredibly loud in the silence of the house, and I jumped. That would be the second time I'd woken Lesley, I thought contritely. It was a message from Alex.

Do you need to talk? Do you want me to call you?

Yes. Yes.

My stomach twisted at the intensity of my need to hear his voice, that voice I knew so well. I wanted to tell him everything, about Emily, about Mary even, although it was hard to explain and hard to believe. But I couldn't speak, I remembered, touching my throat.

So sorry I woke you. I lost my voice. I can't speak. It's not an excuse, I promise.

The reply came at once, the light at the side of my phone flashing in the gloom.

I'm worried about you. Emailing you now.

I got up and switched on my laptop. When I saw an empty space where the shortcut to my writing folder used to be, I felt a jab of regret. All my stories were gone. I sucked in air as I saw that the email Alex had promised was already in my inbox – we were among those rare types who just couldn't get into Facebook. We both hated the lack of privacy, the invasiveness of thousands, millions of users who muscled into your life.

From Alex.McIlvenny@hotmail.co.uk
To Inary@gmail.com

What is this thing about your voice? I'm so sorry I wasn't at the funeral. I wasn't sure what you'd want. I hope you understand. Are you okay?

Not really. I couldn't think of anything that was okay in my life.

From Inary@gmail.com
To Alex.McIlvenny@hotmail.co.uk

Dear Alex,
Sorry for not speaking to you for so long. I lost my voice. We are telling everyone it is a throat infection but I don't think it is. I lost it the night Emily died. Everything feels strange and wrong now that Emily's gone.
Inary

The reply came after a few minutes.

From Alex.McIlvenny@hotmail.co.uk
To Inary@gmail.com

Dear Inary,
I'm sure you're just in shock and that your voice will come
back soon. I'm so sorry about your sister, so sorry for you and
for Logan. I wish I could be of more help to you both.

All of a sudden, I felt my eyes closing. All that had happened
that day – and night – fell on my shoulders at once, and I was
crushed under the weight of it. My body was falling asleep
without consulting me first.

From Inary@gmail.com
To Alex.McIlvenny@hotmail.co.uk

Talking to you is helping . . .
I have so much to tell you. I'm about to fall asleep any
second, it's been such a long night, but I'll email you soon.
Inary

PS: I'm sorry.

I let myself fall onto the bed and curled up under the duvet.
I was supposed to avoid him, and there I was, going to him
again.

I knew it was my fault. I should have not let it happen –
that night between us, that night that had been so glorious, so
tender; it just hurt too much to remember. When I told him
it'd been a mistake I don't know which one of us was more
devastated, but I couldn't allow him or anyone else to get that

close to me. Nobody would ever have that sort of power over me again. And the way Alex had held my heart in his hands, that night . . .

Never. Never again.

And still, I couldn't stop thinking about him.

I was too tired to be angry at myself. My consciousness started ebbing away at once, just as I thought I'd heard Mary whispering again; I tried to listen, but I couldn't stop myself precipitating into darkness. I fell asleep with her voice in my ears like a murmured lullaby.

14

A thought from me to you

Alex

I was in a restless sleep when I woke up with a jolt – a noise somewhere: my phone, ringing. I looked at my watch on the bedside table – four-thirty in the morning.

I grabbed my phone – fearing bad news like you always do if somebody phones you in the middle of the night – and I saw Inary's name flashing on the screen for a moment. Inary was trilling me. I blinked, trying to wake myself up.

Yes. *Missed call from Inary*. I hadn't dreamt it.

I didn't really think about it – I just texted her. If she'd trilled, it meant she couldn't speak at that moment, so there was no point in calling her. I was still furious after what happened, but there was no way I could ignore her. I had to make sure she was okay.

Her reply came after a few seconds – she'd lost her voice? Maybe she'd caught a bug. But it didn't sound right. It didn't sound like a bug. My gut told me it was something a lot more ominous. I got up and switched my laptop on to email her – nothing too intense, just a few lines to try and gauge her state of mind. But her replies were so vague, I couldn't make out what was going on. *I'm sorry*, she'd said.

My stomach churned.

I was still angry. Whenever I thought of what she'd said the morning after – oh, whenever her words came back into my mind, my chest tightened again. She'd been so unfair. And still.

It was Inary. Her sister was dead, and she couldn't speak.

I had to defend myself – but Inary was my weakness, my addiction. Stopping it would have been a lot more painful than giving in. I knew already that if and when she contacted me, I would always reply.

15

Voices from long ago

Inary

Aunt Mhairi turned up at our door on Sunday morning, dressed in her best. I knew what was coming.

"I'm going to Mass. Will you come with me?"

"Count me out," Logan called from the kitchen. He was getting ready to go hillwalking.

I hesitated. I hadn't been to Mass in a long time. All of a sudden I felt a longing for the little stone church and all the times I'd been there as a child with my mum and my granny. Apparently when I was around three I became convinced that church was the place to sing, and I used to burst into random songs in the middle of the celebration . . . Father McCroury used to think it was hilarious (thankfully for my mum) and would thank "little Inary Monteith for her lovely singing". I still cringe remembering it.

Yes, I would go. I nodded, and Aunt Mhairi's face broke into a smile. She was delighted her lapsed niece was still in for a chance at salvation.

We walked up to St Colman's, the church, under a fine drizzle. Every ten steps we met someone we knew – just like when I was a wee girl, and all my Sundays revolved around Mass and meeting friends and family there.

Except Emily was always with us.

Not any more.

It was bittersweet to walk with Aunt Mhairi and feel Emily's presence so strong, so real, hanging between us in every conversation, at every step.

The chapel was a lot smaller than the Presbyterian church, but beautiful, with its stone walls and a simple cross on the top. We were about to step inside when Maggie, one of Aunt Mhairi's friends who helped us at the funeral, appeared at our shoulder.

"Oh, Inary! It's good to see you here, dearie. How are you?" she said, concern in her eyes – I suppose it could have irritated me, but I felt her worry for me and her sadness for Emily were real.

I nodded – all I could do. "She still can't speak," explained Aunt Mhairi. And then it happened.

Maggie had begun to talk – I could see her mouth moving, and I could see Aunt Mhairi nodding – but I couldn't hear what they were saying. All of a sudden, my limbs were tingling all over, and a low drone had drowned out every other sound. My heart started pounding – it was like I was somewhere deep underwater, far removed from everything around me. I closed my eyes briefly, overwhelmed with fear and the sense of unreality – and when I opened them again I was somewhere else.

The church was still behind me, and there was Glen Avich, spread at the foot of the small hill. But Aunt Mhairi and Maggie were gone; everyone was gone.

I could feel a fine drizzle falling on my arms and shoulders; I could feel the breeze in my hair and smell the wet soil. Suddenly, a line of people started streaming out of the church. Their clothes were strange – the women in long dresses and stiff felt hats, and the men in woollen trousers and shirts, all

111

in muted colours. Fear streaked through me. Nothing like this had happened to me before. I saw spirits in *my* world – but I never saw the world *they* came from. I'd never been transported somewhere else – to some other time . . .

I jumped. Someone had appeared beside me – a priest, standing to greet his parishioners after Mass. I looked at him, waiting to see if he saw me, if he sensed me – but he took no notice of me. I was there, and yet I wasn't.

I stood watching face after face, men and women and children walking out of the church doors, exchanging a few words with the priest – Father Hall, they called him.

Finally there was a face I recognised. Mary, walking beside an older woman . . . I did a double take, and a sudden longing filled my heart: the woman looked just like my mum. At her side there was a little girl with long black braids.

"Mum, I'll just wait for Leah," said Mary. "Oh, there she is . . ."

I forced myself to leave the older woman's face and followed Mary's gaze towards a tall, full-figured blonde girl, rosy-cheeked and giggling, smiling at a young man in a tweed jacket. The man walked off to join a small group of women standing on the grass a few yards from the church.

"See you in a moment," whispered Leah, who ran to catch up with the young man she was chatting to. Mary was watching them, a smile on her face.

My gaze returned to Mary, who all of a sudden seemed far, far away, removed from the group, removed from everybody, in her own world. She was standing still, looking over at something – someone – a man who was watching her in return, their eyes locked. It must be Robert. He was smiling, but he looked bewildered too. Like he wasn't expecting what had just happened.

My head spun a little as I felt Mary's emotion sweep over me, so intense that it was almost physical, nearly painful. I clutched my heart as Mary's consciousness exploded into mine.

And then a woman with a beautiful face and poised expression, dressed in an exquisite woollen coat and a velvet cloche, came to stand beside Robert and rested a hand on his arm. The gesture said *he's mine* – and the silent bond between Mary and him was broken.

Suddenly, the contours of the scenes started to blur, and it was like looking through a window in the pouring rain – everything melted and smudged before my eyes, until I could see only black. Nothing – and then my eyes snapped open and Maggie was talking.

"So I said to Father McCroury, if we can't find another catechism teacher before the spring, I'm going to have to step up . . ."

"Absolutely. Unless she tells us for sure if she's coming back . . ."

The world was spinning around me, and the sky and the ground were about to swap places. I tapped Aunt Mhairi lightly on the shoulder and gestured towards the church door. "Sure, on you go, dear," she said, unaware of what had just happened to me. I stepped inside and let myself fall on a pew, breathing heavily to calm my heart. I was sure I'd just witnessed Mary and Robert's first encounter, and I couldn't wait to see what would happen next.

16

The days between winter and spring

Inary

Lesley left the day after. She couldn't have taken more time off work at such short notice. As I watched her car disappear I felt like my old life was finished, and a new one was starting. One without Emily, and without Lesley beside me every day like I was used to. It was so hard – and still, I knew I had to face it. I had to live my days and nights and be grateful for each of them, as difficult as it was.

It does get better, even if it seems impossible now, Eilidh had said. I had to believe her.

Aunt Mhairi offered to sort out Emily's things for us. To see what could be given to charity, what could be gifted, and what was going to be thrown out, she'd said, her voice trailing away at once as she saw my and Logan's horrified faces. She didn't mean any harm, we both knew that, and we both knew that some kind of sorting was actually needed – but to throw out some of Emily's things, anything of hers, anything – even old magazines, a half-used bottle of nail-polish remover, the used bus tickets in her bag, the debris of her life – just seemed too cruel.

And there we were, in Emily's room, me sitting on her bed, freshly made – I couldn't bear to see it stripped – and

Logan on the carpet, his back leaning against the wall. Neither of us was showing any signs of wanting to move. For a moment grief overcame me again and my eyes welled up. All of a sudden all the details of the room – the piles of clothes folded neatly on Emily's bed, her books, her perfumes, the photographs that Logan had lovingly taken, printed and framed for her – were such an unbearable sight. Everything spoke of absence. The plum-coloured shirt she'd been making was still in the sewing machine. I didn't have the heart to remove it. It was as if she'd come in at any moment and sit there to finish her work . . .

Suddenly, I couldn't take the silence any more. I had so many thoughts in my head, so many emotions overflowing in my heart that could find no outlet, no relief, in the spoken word. I couldn't find respite even in the simplest conversation. Silence was devouring me. I ran to my room, under Logan's perplexed gaze, and opened a drawer in my desk, and another, until I found some paper and a pen.

Do you want me gone? I wrote, leaning on my desk. I went back into Emily's room, sat on the floor beside Logan and showed him my note, my hands shaking.

"*Do you* . . . Don't be stupid." He gave me a look, a *Logan* look – then got up and leaned against the window. "But you're going to go anyway."

I stood up too and took hold of his arm, forcing him to look at me, and then I shook my head.

I don't want to go back, I wrote. I was furious at myself, because I felt tears stinging my eyes and I didn't want to cry in front of him. I showed him the notebook. The writing thing felt good. Not as immediate as talking, but at least I could communicate.

115

"You don't want to go back? Why, what's wrong with London now?" he said, taunting me.

What could I say? I don't want to go because you need me? Because we need each other? I could imagine what he'd reply to that. That it was too late. That the damage was done. How could I explain how all this had poisoned me from the inside so that my life just didn't feel right, ever, since I'd gone away from Glen Avich and from my brother and sister?

There was only one thing I could say.

I'm sorry I left, I wrote, and handed him the notebook. My hands were trembling. His eyes flickered across the page, and handed it back without looking at me. I dried my tears with my fingers and took a deep breath.

"It was bloody hard, Inary," said Logan. His face was dark.

For a moment I thought that there was no hope for us, that the wall between us would never come down. And then, suddenly, he turned towards me.

"Do you still have a pair of wellies here?"

What? I mouthed.

"Wellies. It's soaking on the hills this time of year."

I nodded, bewildered.

"Good. Otherwise I was going to run to the shop and get you a pair. Let's go."

Where are we going?

"I need some fresh air. I'm going on the hills with my camera. Come with me?"

You want me to?

"Ach, yeah. It's not like you're going to bother me with endless chatter," he said, perfectly deadpan. His joke was so surreal, given the situation, that I couldn't help laughing. There was so much sorrow around me, and still a little spark

116

illuminated the dark. There would still be a time for laughter, even amidst our tears. As I slipped my boots on, thoughts of hope blossomed in my mind and surprised me.

★

We walked in silence, our breathing the only sound. Out there in the winter woods, silence felt peaceful and completely right. The sky was pewter and steel overhead, and a soft drizzle had begun to fall. We had warm, waterproof jackets from Logan's shop, so the rain didn't bother me. Everything was too beautiful for me to mind the weather anyway.

It had been a mild winter, and red unshed leaves covered the trees. It was too early for blooms, too early to see little shoots breaking the soil, but somehow, though I couldn't see any, I could feel them. They were curled up inside the branches and under the earth, like babies in the womb, waiting for the right moment. The emptiness of winter was about to end and the air was full of the scent of things to come, whispering and quivering and dreaming dreams of life.

Every once in a while, Logan stopped and studied a shot, silently considering the light and the frame that would satisfy him. I stood beside him, taking in the peace of my surroundings, letting it enfold me and loosen all the knots in my soul. The more I was in the woods, the more serene I felt.

After a couple of hours we sat on Logan's waterproof cloth, wrapped in our high-tech jackets, dunking digestives in brightly coloured melamine mugs. Logan loved his equipment. He would have taken a compass to go to Tesco, just for the fun of it. He carried a fire kit everywhere he went, even to the

117

cinema – in case he got stranded between there and home. Sooner or later he'll end up mistaken for an arsonist.

"I saw you chatting to my pal Taylor, at Emily's funeral." The words *Emily's funeral* were like nettles brushing against my skin. I nodded. "He's from San Francisco," he continued. "Here for the dig on the loch."

San Francisco? Not New York? I was really rubbish at accents. I made a face as if to say *what dig*?

"They're digging a crannog out of the loch. You know, those houses on poles, built right into the water. He's an archaeologist . . . pass me the chocolate ones. Thanks. He's based in Edinburgh but he'll be here for a few months. We go for a drink once in a while."

Right. Why was Logan talking about Taylor so much? Was he trying to set me up with the guy? It couldn't be. My brother, a matchmaker? Impossible.

"So, yeah, he said he'd like to take you to see the dig. I wasn't sure, I mean with you not liking the loch much . . . But I thought I'd leave it with you. I've been to see the crannog. It's quite amazing, took lots of shots."

I wasn't sure I wanted to go back on the loch – I had avoided it for the last thirteen years, especially on misty days. I brushed biscuit crumbs off my jacket and took out a crumpled piece of paper and a pen I'd brought with me. I peered at Logan as I did so, and as I'd guessed, he looked completely cool and unconcerned, as if our conversation about Taylor had been no important matter. He was more concerned about the biscuits. I breathed a sigh of relief. There had been no conniving between my brother and the American archaeologist (A.A., I would call him) to try and cheer me up or distract me. Or find me a boyfriend.

You been seeing someone? I wrote on impulse, knowing I was stepping on thorny ground. Logan didn't seem to do that well when it came to relationships. That made two of us, I suppose.

"Ach, just people, you know. Nobody important." He shrugged.

Logan seemed to only do casual relationships. He didn't find it hard to meet people; he was a handsome man, with sharp features and an intense look in his eyes, that "*I'm in charge*" look women seem to love. Yet he'd spent all these years with Emily, caring for her; he never seemed to want to work on any kind of a romantic relationship. I used to think that that was the way he wanted it to be: occasional relationships, nothing too deep. But in the last few years I'd come to wonder if it was enough for him.

"Time to get back," he said, gathering the remains of our picnic. I got the message – no more talk about his love life. But I still had something to ask him.

You still didn't tell me if you want me to go, I wrote.

"Do you really want to stay?" he said, busying himself with our flasks.

I nodded.

"Stay, then." He tried to sound unconcerned, but I knew him too well not to detect emotion in his voice. I inhaled deeply. It was the closest thing to a reconciliation we could have at this time. It had to be good enough. Maybe it was the right time to tell him about Mary. He knew everything about my granny and me, how we had the Sight, and how I lost it years ago. My parents thought that it was better if Logan and Emily were aware of it, especially if the gift ever turned up in their children.

The Sight is back, I wrote.

119

"The Sight is . . . Oh . . . And how do you feel about it? I mean . . ." He stumbled. His eyes were full of worry, and I could guess why. I never told anyone what I saw that day on the loch so many years ago, but my family easily worked out that something very frightening had happened. My mother and my grandmother tried to find out – they asked me gently but persistently, and they grilled my father, who'd taken me out that day. But I never said, and my dad hadn't seen, of course. To put it into words would have been too terrifying, too real.

Not sure how I feel about it yet, I wrote.

"Who . . . Who did you see?" he asked, glancing down at his hands.

A girl called Mary. In my room, I wrote, nodding at each word for emphasis. Those days I was nodding so much I was worried I would get a neck injury.

"Who was she?"

I'm not sure. I shrugged.

"Right. Are you sure you're okay?"

I can handle it, I wrote, truthfully. *Actually, the girl kind of kept me company. It was good to see her. I know it's weird . . .*

Logan sighed. "I don't know if it's weird. I mean, I don't know how I'd feel if I could see what you see. Sometimes I wish I could, so maybe I could see our parents. And Emily . . ."

I sucked in air. Logan wasn't one to talk about his feelings much, and I'd never imagined he wished to have the Sight.

"But who knows how it would be to actually see them . . . dead."

I bowed my head. I lost the Sight before my grandmother and my parents died, so I had no idea how I'd feel if I saw them as spirits. I knew I would give anything to see Emily.

120

"Inary . . ." my brother whispered, leaning against the tree once more. I knew at once what he was going to ask. Not a premonition. Just human nature. "I wonder if you are going to see *her*." There was no need to ask who he was referring to.

I hope so, I scribbled.

A pause. And then Logan shifted slightly, imperceptibly, closer to me.

We walked back, the damp ground soft under our feet, yielding like a mossy carpet – the scent of wet earth and of the wide, wide sky over our heads. Many generations of my family had walked these woods. I could feel Glen Avich running in my veins, and again I asked myself how I could stand to ever leave.

17

Little fire

Logan

My sister has always been a law unto herself. Once when she was in primary school, she forgot to come in after the interval bell rang. Just like that – she forgot. After twenty minutes her teacher realised she wasn't there and panicked – Inary was found crouching in a corner of the playground, feeding some starlings. She hadn't even noticed that everybody else had gone in and she was alone in the playground. Another time, she went to school in her slippers. I'm not making this up.

She always lived on Planet Inary, which could be a mixed blessing. Things didn't really seem to upset her. She was always happy, lost in her own head or in a book. It was me who had to stomach enough reality for the both of us.

When our parents died, she changed. It was like a spell had been broken. She didn't live in an enchanted place any more – now she looked life hard in the face, like I'd always done, and what she saw terrified her.

When Lewis came along, it was like having the old Inary back for a while. It was such a relief to see her smiling again. I liked the guy. He was decent, and he was in for the long haul, or at least I thought so. I, on the other hand, didn't seem to be able to have a relationship that lasted more than six weeks, but hey, that's my own fault.

And then Lewis left, and Inary was shattered. That's the only way to describe it. Not everyone noticed – actually most people thought she took it quite well – but I did. Little bits of Inary floated in her old self, but the Inary I knew was gone again.

She doesn't know that I went to see Lewis, and that it took all my self-control not to pummel him black and blue. When I finished having a chat with him, even if I didn't lay a finger on him, he was scared enough.

So yes, Inary was in pieces, she couldn't stay, she couldn't see him around, and that awful mother of his, and blah blah. So she upped and left. But I couldn't accept that. Not moving so far away, not with Emily needing us so badly.

Not with me needing her, for God's sake. Selfish? Maybe. You try it, to be in charge of a sick girl on your own. Because Emily had been sick and dying for years now – Inary was the only one who believed it would be okay. Maybe I should have spelt it out to her.

But I couldn't.

I've been angry with Inary for so long. Three years. I never told her I missed her. But I did. Today, for the first time in a long time, I felt I could reach her, and she could reach me.

There's still a long way to go between us, but we'll get there.

We must. We're all that's left of our family.

★

Taking long walks by myself always helped me deal with everything at home. In the last few days of Emily's life, I needed the woods desperately. I needed to go out and feel the wind on my face and the wide sky above me. But I couldn't leave her, not even for half an hour.

On a particularly low, lonely day a couple of years ago I went to Aberdeen and, on impulse, I bought myself a state-of-the-art camera. I swear it changed my life. I even enrolled in some photography classes – the first thing I'd done for myself in years. When I was out looking for shots in the woods, on the loch shore, on the moors – it was the closest I ever felt to peace. And I came home with beautiful images that captured the moment forever. A gallery of beauty that I printed and framed, filling my house and my shop with nature, bringing the outside in.

Let's face it: I'm a solitary bastard. I'm happy by myself, without speaking to anyone. But this, like Inary living on her own planet, can be a mixed blessing too – it's fine to a certain extent, then it just gets very cold, and before you know it, you're bloody freezing. I think Emily sensed that. She was worried about me being alone.

One day I came home from a night camping to find a little drawing held up on the fridge by a sheep-shaped magnet: a bear waving its paw, beside a little tent, with a caption beside it – *I am Logan!* It made me laugh, but I knew there was a lot of truth in Emily's drawing.

So that was my life. Still frames of a stag, its horns outlined black against the sky; the black waters of Loch Avich the moment night falls; lightning in a stormy sky, a lonely boat moored among the stones, faces in the bark of an ancient tree. The stories I want to tell. Snippets of the huge wide world, of which Glen Avich is a tiny, perfectly beautiful corner.

But all I loved, all I knew, was kept together by Emily. Now she's gone, and nothing seems to make much sense.

The night Emily died, Inary opened the window wide, to let our sister's soul go. I could see that above the hills, the sky was full of stars. Ancient navigators didn't have radar or satellites or sophisticated instruments; they could only rely on constellations to show them the way. I had spent all my life following one star, and never letting anything else sway me or change my course. I had followed what was for me the true North. And now my guide was gone, and I had no idea where I was or where to go next. Without Emily I was lost.

I don't want to tell Inary how black inside I really feel. She's fighting her own battle. I don't want to tell her that I feel just as dead as Emily.

18

Scenes from a Scottish village

Alex

I turned the keys in the door, stepped over a little mound of envelopes and leaflets the postman had delivered while I was away, and went inside my house. It was freezing. A cold snap had hit England, but I'd forgotten to turn the heating on. Since what happened with Inary, since she left, I kept forgetting things, big things and small ones. Things that suddenly didn't seem to matter any more – my work, the people around me – but that were the pieces of the jigsaw of my life. I felt like the world around me didn't really exist, it only pretended to exist, like some sort of dream – persistent, but still just a dream.

I had a good job, and it wasn't just work to me, it was my passion; I worked with great people who depended on me; I had friends, and a family that was far away but very loving. But everything seemed like an illusion not quite worth pursuing.

I suppose the real question now was, will this feeling of unreality fade with time? Was I going to get better – like Inary was some sort of illness I'd caught and couldn't shake off?

I opened the fridge door, more out of habit than anything else. I wasn't hungry, and anyway it was nearly empty; I'd only come back the night before after two days in Krakow. And yes, I did find an owl for Inary there. I couldn't help it.

I know, I know. What can I say? Old habits die hard. And as

hard as I tried to forget her, I found she was always on my mind.

I started the fire as quickly as I could, then sat on the rug in front of it, waiting for the flames to rise. On impulse, I switched on my laptop and googled the words *voice loss trauma.*

A ribbon of websites unfolded itself in front of me: voice loss, post-traumatic stress, find your voice with Dr Whateverstein, a long list of useless rubbish in which a few little truths were swimming. After a while, I'd figured out that what Inary had was called psychogenic dysphonia, or loss of voice through trauma – yes, that much I knew, apart from the fancy name. What I really wanted to know was if there was a cure.

There wasn't, obviously. Not as such. No magical pill to make you speak again. Like most illnesses of the soul, the road to fix it would be long and arduous. Psychotherapy, apparently, and, if you were so inclined, a whole lot of other therapies from the plausible to the absurd – swimming with dolphins, anyone? Dream therapy? Dance therapy?

Inary was heartbroken. That was it. She lost her voice because she was so full of pain, she didn't know how to deal with it and she shut down. What she needed was someone to help her through the trauma, someone who could guide her. I was sure that she could find a good psychotherapist somewhere close to her . . . maybe in Aberdeen.

But that would involve Inary opening up about all that she had gone through – the loss of her parents, and Lewis, and now Emily – with a stranger. I just couldn't see it happening.

On impulse, I typed *Glen Avich photographs*, and a tapestry of squares and rectangles appeared on the screen. So that's where she was. That was Glen Avich.

Most of the pictures were breathtaking – the loch, grey and still under the steely sky, and the hills, in a thousand shades of heathery purple. Some were funny and sweet, snippets of village life. Someone winning a knitting competition (a Mrs Edna Boyle, 84 years old), the first coffee shop opening up in Glen Avich (proud owners standing in front of a silvery-blue door, grinning), a girl taking part in the Mod in Paisley (her hair freshly done, her face somewhere between a woman and a child).

I searched on, paging through pictures of Glen Avich streets – the river with its stony bridge, and the main street with its little shops. Apparently, there was a sacred well on the hill that overlooked the village, St Colman's well. It was supposed to aid fertility. Had Inary ever mentioned it? Because the name sounded familiar. Oh, yes, she had; she'd said she used to go there after school with her friends and with Emily . . .

Photograph after photograph, Inary's life in the village seemed to take on a life before my eyes. Now I could visualise where she was, where her family was. This soothed me a little. The wonders of Google . . .

Dear Inary,
I did a search on the Internet, and apparently what you have is called psychogenic dysphonia, or voice loss because of trauma. Here are a few links. Most people get their voice back after a wee while. Some seem to take medication and follow some sort of therapy. I don't really see you doing that, but maybe you should consider it.

I looked at pictures of Glen Avich. It's beautiful, like Lesley always said. And please pass on my congratulations to Mrs Edna Boyle for her knitting trophy.
Alex x

PS. I put something in the post for you.

19

The chemistry of grief

Inary

"Inary . . . I'm so sorry about Emily."

I looked into Dr Nicholson's kindly face. She'd known the three of us since we were children, and I trusted her. But I was sure that being there was a waste of time. I was sure that a doctor couldn't help me get my voice back. Alex's email had given me a clearer idea about what was probably wrong with me, and I felt less apprehensive about what Dr Nicholson might say.

Thank you, I mouthed.

She took a breath. "Inary. I think both you and I know that this is not a throat infection or anything like that. But just to be on the safe side, I have to check you over."

I nodded. She shone a light down my throat, in my ears and my eyes; she checked my heart and my breathing; she actually hammered my knee, which was something I'd only seen done in films.

"You're in perfect health, but I think you knew that already."

I nodded, buttoning up my shirt.

"I've done this job for a long time. And I've seen grief do the strangest things to people," she said, echoing Eilidh's words. "What I need to know, Inary, is how you feel in yourself."

How do you think I feel, I wanted to say. *My little sister has just died. I feel like I should die too. I feel like my heart should stop at any moment.*

I shrugged. *I'm in bits*, I wrote. I couldn't be more eloquent than that.

"I know, sweetheart," she said, and put a motherly hand on my shoulder. "It's been hard for you all. I remember your mum and dad, and all the worry they had . . ."

It was a physical effort not to cry. I frowned and looked down. I *couldn't* cry. If I started, I'd never stop.

"Are you sleeping these days, Inary?"

I nodded. It was the truth. I was sleeping, though not so well and not for long.

"Good. Are you eating okay?"

I nodded again.

"Inary, you have to promise me. If you feel it all gets too much, if you feel the sadness is unbearable . . . if you can't eat or sleep and if you cry constantly . . . you need to come back and see me."

What will you do then? Nothing can bring Emily back, I wrote. I didn't mean to be rude to Dr Nicholson, but I truly felt she couldn't help me. It was some mysterious chemistry of grief that had taken my voice away from me, and there was no way to know if and when it would come back.

She was unfazed. "We can discuss our options. Maybe look into medication."

I looked at her, eyes wide. She wanted to give me antidepressants? Some chemical compound that would artificially take the sadness away, like Emily didn't deserve to be mourned? Like it wasn't only right that my heart should be broken . . .

I shook my head.

"Well, if that's something you'd rather not consider, let's

130

leave it at that for now. But if you feel worse, please come back and see me."

I nodded. I wouldn't.

"Promise?" she said.

I nodded again, and again I lied.

She looked at me, her head slightly tilted, like she was studying me. A doctor for thirty years, a mother of four and a grandmother of six, she *knew* I was lying. She knew I wouldn't come back.

"Right. And how's Logan?"

My heart skipped a beat. Now, that was something that needed to be talked about. Maybe she could help him, like she couldn't help me . . . *Not good*, I wrote. *I'm so worried about him. He's just—*

I shook my head. I couldn't put it into words. I couldn't explain how he was . . . broken. As simple as that.

"I see. Will you ask him to come and see me? I think he should."

I'll try, but it'll be hard to convince him.

"Well, let's see what you can do, anyway. He's lucky to have you looking out for him."

Really? I felt so powerless. I nodded again and made my way to the door. Aunt Mhairi sprang up when she saw us coming out.

"What is it, Shona?" she whispered to Dr Nicholson. The surgery was empty but for the practice nurse, who tactfully closed her door, and Mrs Boyle – one of the Boyle sisters, the infamous knitters of baby clothes – who was stone deaf.

"I think it was shock, with all that happened . . . but Inary will be back to see me, and we'll see what we can do. Won't you?"

Another half-hearted nod.

131

"Mhairi, I think Logan needs to come and see me," the doctor continued. "Inary says he's not doing that well . . ."

"Oh, he won't come. He'd rather walk through fire than go to the doctor! His dad was the same and so was my husband . . ."

"I know, I know. But see what you can do."

"We'll do our best. It's all that drink . . ." She shook her head. I felt ill. Thinking that Logan had a problem was bad enough; hearing it spoken aloud was just horrible. "Thank you, Shona . . ." my aunt continued.

"No problem. And thanks for the picture," said Dr Nicholson, gesturing towards her office. From where I stood, I could see her desk, and there, in its white card frame, the picture of Emily we'd sent to our family and friends. Weird, I hadn't noticed it when I was inside. It was one we'd taken the night of the fashion show – she was smiling, wearing a light-green silk shift dress she'd designed herself, her hair loose on her shoulders and her nails painted bright green too.

Emily.

Aunt Mhairi and I walked back in silence. The strange, sudden joy I'd felt during my walk on the hills the day before had seeped out of me. Only grief remained. Again. It was to be expected, I suppose. Good days, bad days, is that not the way grief is meant to go?

Where was the green silk dress? I wanted to keep it forever. I wanted to wear it and have Emily with me, like she'd never left.

★

I was barely in the house when Lynne, our neighbour, knocked at the door. "A courier left this for you," she said, and handed me a small parcel.

132

There was nothing written on it, no sign of a sender, only my address and some foreign-looking stamps – but I knew who it was from. Inside, like a set of Russian dolls, there was another box, small and velvety. I lifted its lid – nestled in the velvet there was a little china owl and a minuscule note folded into four.

Here's the first of the Glen Avich owl family. A.

Sellotaped on the statuette was a tiny Polish flag, glued on a toothpick and coloured in with felt-tip pens.

A tiny, uncertain smile made its way from my heart to my lips.

From Inary@gmail.com
To Alex.McIlvenny@hotmail.co.uk

Dear Alex,
I got your owl! Thank you so much. It sits on my desk in my old room. Also, thank you for your email with the links about what's wrong with me. Calling it psychogenic dysphonia makes it sound quite scary. I saw the doctor, but she said there's nothing I can do. To just wait. I'll be staying here for a while. Rowan will send me work. Everything feels strange these days . . . I deleted all my stories, I don't even know why. It's like I'm in a bubble. I miss Lesley and I . . .

. . . I miss you, I wanted to write. But I decided against it. It just wouldn't be fair on him.

I shouldn't be writing to him at all – I had promised myself I would not keep doing this to him, I would not play with his feelings.

133

. . . I'm having weird dreams.

Can I tell Alex about the Sight? Would he understand?

. . . I mean, visions about the past. I see the past. As in, dead people.

Nobody but my family knew the true extent of my gift. My family, and Lewis. Who'd been completely freaked out. He said it scared him, and it made him wonder what was going through my head. Code for 'it made him wonder if I was mad'. I suppose you don't get to be brought up by two bigots for nothing – Anabel would have thought I was possessed by the devil.

I didn't think Alex was like that, but I was still wary. I deleted the whole sentence.

> . . . I miss Lesley, and I'm trying to help Logan through this.
> I hope you're well, and thank you again for the info on lost
> voices. Weird. It's the kind of thing that always happens to
> someone else, until it happens to you . . .
> Inary x

My fingers hovered above the keyboard. I was opening the conversation between us again, and the way things worked between Alex and me, soon we'd be emailing every day, and we'd be back in the same situation we were in before.

I went to press 'discard'.

Instead, I pressed 'send'. Obviously.

I was so angry with myself, and still so relieved to keep speaking to him . . . the usual Alex-induced chaotic feelings. I got up and paced the room until I heard the laptop beeping again.

From Alex.McIlvenny@hotmail.co.uk
To Inary@gmail.com

Inary,
You deleted your stories? That's pretty radical . . . but then,
all your life has changed now, and it's not like you to stay still.
You made room for the new. There's so much inside you just
waiting to come out, and it will.
Take care,
Alex

He always had all the right words.

Strange, I thought. I'd done my best to lock my heart, and I'd done such a good job I couldn't find the key any more. And a locked heart can feel very heavy.

I slipped into Emily's room, and I opened her wardrobe. A dull ache filled me as her scent enveloped me – something between Miss Dior, her favourite perfume, and her own, individual Emily scent. I closed the wardrobe at once – if I opened it, her scent would be lost in the air, I could never, ever smell it again. It would just disappear. And would I be able to recall it? Next week, next month, yes – but next year? In ten years? Would I be able to recall the exact chemistry of my sister's skin, of her breath?

A sob escaped my lips. It was inevitable. It would happen. Even if I kept her wardrobe closed forever her scent would fade anyway, the memories would fade, until one day I'd be gone too, and Logan. And everybody in this village, this whole generation.

But before that happened, I was here, I was alive, and I was remembering my sister. I slowly opened the wardrobe door again, and stroked the rows of dresses and shirts and jackets, until I noticed a flash of light green. There it was: her college graduation dress.

I lifted it out of the wardrobe and buried my face in it, my eyes closed.

I would wear Emily's dress. Inside me, Emily was alive.

★

That night my skin was prickling again, and there was a soft, low drone in my ears. I wasn't surprised when in the middle of the night, in the darkest hour, some inner ripple woke me, and Mary was by my window again. I lay still with my eyes wide open, perfectly awake; I didn't move, I didn't make a sound, I even held my breath as long as I could, in case she disappeared. It was as if a light was shining on her, or from inside her, because I could see her clearly. Her hair was down around her shoulders in dark, silky waves, and she looked so young and fresh and radiant. I could see she was happy. Her lips were moving; she was talking, but I couldn't hear her . . . and then, as I became attuned to her presence, I began to make out her words. She was talking to someone, a black, shapeless shadow that I couldn't quite make out.

"I never thought I could feel that way about anyone," she was saying. "It seems forever I have to wait for him to come back. I know he has to speak to her, sort everything out, but I can't wait. I just want him here with me." A pause as the other shadow spoke – a low murmur that I couldn't unravel. "I think my mum knows, yes. I never told her, of course, she wouldn't approve, but you know the way things work here. You just can't have secrets. I will tell her myself as soon as he's free from his engagement. She won't be able to say anything against him then. And Robert will win her over anyway."

I felt utterly intrigued. Mary's life was being revealed to me bit by bit. I couldn't wait to see what happened next. But with my disappointment, I saw she was starting to vanish slowly already. She was still talking, but her voice was fading, her words lost to me. I wanted her to stay just a little longer, but I couldn't stop her.

A few minutes after she'd gone, I was already falling back to sleep, a thought whirling again and again in my mind – would Robert keep his promise and return to Mary? But my heart went also to the woman on the other side of all this, the woman he was engaged to. I was sure it was the lovely-looking woman at his side in the vision I'd had of his and Mary's first meeting.

I knew how she'd feel when he told her.

20

Remedies

Inary

Aunt Mhairi's tablet was heavenly, just like everything else she made. I was attacking a second square and sipping a cup of tea. We were sitting at her kitchen table, a notebook, already littered with conversations, ready beside my mug.

I'd figured that Aunt Mhairi might know who Mary was – her clothes and hairstyle told me that she would have lived in Glen Avich in the late nineteenth century, which was her grandmother, my great-grandmother's, generation. Aunt Mhairi might have stories about Glen Avich from when her gran was a little girl. Maybe some about Mary herself? I was going to try and find out something about her without explaining why I wanted to know. Aunt Mhairi had no reason to know about the Sight – being my father's sister, it didn't run in her family.

I brought the conversation on to my parents' house – some work to the roof was needed – it was an old house – it's been in our family for generations . . . I saw my chance.

Was there ever a Mary living there?

"Mary? Let me think. Well, it's an old house, and Mary used to be a very common name . . . Why do you ask?"

I dished out the excuse I had prepared. *Researching a book.*

"Oh, a book, that's nice." She adjusted her glasses on the bridge of her nose and stirred her tea.

I quickly scrawled: *Do you have any stories about a Mary living in Glen Avich from when your gran was young?*

"Well, I don't know how much help I can be, dear. My granny passed away when I was wee, and your grandfather never talked about his childhood much. Why don't you go and have a look in the Heritage Collection in Kinnear? Sheila Ramsay swears by it, you know she's big into family trees and all that." I nodded – it was a good idea. "Inary, now listen, love. Don't take this the wrong way, but about your voice, dearie . . ."

I sighed. Another remedy? Because nearly everyone seemed to have one, and I'd tried them all. Milk and honey, peppermint tea, mint tea, ice-cold water or near-scalding water, warm compresses on my chest, an ice pack on my throat, anchovies. Yes, anchovies. Apparently they work wonders at keeping singers' voices strong and clear. So maybe my voice would return and I would start a singing career . . . but all that those anchovies had done was stink out our fridge and make me drink a gallon of water.

I plastered a smile on my face, waiting for Aunt Mhairi's suggestion. Dried ground newt to be taken on the night of a full moon, maybe?

"Well, you see, Maggie and Liz, you know my friends . . ."

Oh yes, the funeral experts.

"They were wondering if maybe the well . . . St Colman's well. It's supposed to perform miracles . . ."

I laughed. *It's supposed to help women have babies!*

"Yes, well, I know, but these are exceptional circumstances. St Colman will know what you need. I would ask Father McCroury to see what he thinks, but you know he's not fond of all that, the well, the people who come drinking . . ."

With my luck, if I drank the water I'd *still* be mute, and pregnant.

Thank you. Tell Maggie and Liz I'll think about it, I wrote and stood to go.

"You going already? Wait till I wrap up some of this tablet for Logan . . ."

I took the tinfoil-wrapped tablet obediently and I held Aunt Mhairi tight. She was the closest thing to a parent I had left. In her own clumsy way, she tried to look out for us, and I was grateful. She reciprocated the hug, murmuring *dear, dear Inary* – and I knew she was thinking of what we'd lost. *Thank you*, I mouthed.

"No worries, dearie . . . And think about the water from the well. You never know . . ."

I stifled a smile and nodded. It would be better than anchovies anyway.

I stepped out of the cottage in the lilac light of dusk, the soft scent of water enveloping me. A fine mist was gathering on the loch and I wanted to be home quickly. I didn't like being too close to it at the best of times, let alone when the fog crept in.

I headed away from the cottage, leaving the hazy loch behind me with relief. I kept thinking about Mary as I walked on, a chill breeze in my hair and night closing fast around me. I hoped with all my heart that she'd come back to me soon, that she would keep telling me her story.

I couldn't see Emily, even if I kept calling to her; for some reason, it'd been Mary who had come instead. I could only accept the way things were, try to live with the constant yearning for my sister and unravel Mary's secrets. She'd come to me for a reason, I realised as I stepped onto the small stony bridge across the River Avich. She wasn't just a momentary apparition, shimmering through time like a reflection on running water. I leaned against the parapet and watched the water flow below. So many precious things have been taken away from me – my parents, my sister, my own voice – Mary was something to hold on to.

★

As I was approaching my house, I saw that there was someone standing in front of our door – a man. Tall, slightly built, a mop of caramel-coloured hair . . . He turned around all of a sudden, and I could see his face. Taylor.

I stopped in my tracks and considered turning away, but he saw me.

"Inary!" he called with an open smile. I couldn't help but smile back. He looked so . . . untroubled. His face was as cheerful and open as a blue sky.

"Hello, just passing by . . ."

Hello, I mouthed, and let him in.

"Hi . . . oh, hi Taylor," Logan greeted us. "Cup of coffee? I've got to warn you, though, Inary made a cake earlier. Have some . . . What doesn't kill you makes you stronger," said Logan, taking my tiramisu out of the fridge.

Very funny. Okay, it came out a bit liquidy, but still tasty. You just needed a spoon, that was all. I'd bought a Nigella book online and I was going through it, one recipe at a time. Or to say it like Logan, I was *butchering* it one recipe at a time.

"Yes to the cake, please. No to the coffee. I don't drink caffeine."

How do you stay awake? I scribbled quickly. I was addicted to

141

coffee. Less than three cups a morning and I'd get the shakes.

"My energy levels are a lot higher, actually, than when I used to drink coffee," he said vehemently, like he was announcing something miraculous. I smiled to myself.

"I'll pour you a drink, then," said Logan, taking out two spirit glasses from the cupboard. My heart sank.

"No, not for me. Not on a Monday night," laughed Taylor, putting his hands up. Logan hesitated, but then he poured himself one.

"I guess I'm going to have to drink alone, then." He shrugged.

Taylor dug into my cake. "Mmmm. Inary. This is . . ."

"Ghastly," Logan interrupted him.

"Of course not! It's good. Just the consistency . . . maybe . . . a bit . . ." He didn't finish the sentence. I simply went to the cupboard and passed him a packet of Hobnobs.

We chatted for a while, mainly about outdoors stuff, but soon I lost the thread of the conversation. My head was somewhere else. I kept thinking about last night. About Mary. About Emily.

". . . so, what do you say?"

I realised that Taylor had just told me something, and I had no idea what it was.

I frowned and shook my head, mouthing *sorry*. I felt myself blushing.

"I was wondering if you wanted to come and see the site tomorrow. The crannog excavation. My office, in other words!" he laughed.

Really, was there any other choice than to say yes? Unless I tried to explain that I was scared of the loch . . . obviously I couldn't tell him the real reason for my fear. I'd have to make up some excuse, like not being able to swim, or some phobia of water, when actually I was a good swimmer and had no phobias whatsoever (except for alligators, after I saw a documentary as a wee girl, but you don't see many of those in Scotland). It would be so humiliating to say I couldn't swim, for someone born and bred a few hundred yards from the loch shore.

Maybe it was time to get over my fear. After all, it had happened thirteen years ago.

I nodded.

"Great!" He ran a hand through his thick, wavy hair and I read something in his gesture. A tiny, near-invisible touch of shyness that I hadn't thought could exist side by side with his larger-than-life personality.

"You sure you're not up for a drink, guys?" Logan asked.

I shook my head and brought my hand to my forehead, mimicking a headache – forget about the writing, all this miming was going to land me an acting job sooner or later.

"Are you okay?" asked Logan.

Bit of a sore head, that's all, I wrote. I waved goodbye to Taylor briefly, and ran upstairs to my room.

So, it looked like I was going onto the loch with Taylor. I already regretted saying yes, but it was too late. Anyway – no more agonising over American lads or ghosts from long ago; I slipped my glasses on and sat in front of the computer. I had psyched myself up for it all day: I was going to start writing again. I had no idea *what*, Cassandra having been given the boot (to both my relief and dismay). But I had to try. It had only been a short while without writing, but I missed it already.

I had been writing since before I could remember, on school jotters and notebooks, on my dad's computer and then my

143

own. When I wasn't writing, I was reading anything I could get my hands on. I *ate* words. I still found time to go out and have fun – Logan was the solitary one in the family – but I always returned to my books. Books were home.

I'd written heaps of stories and poems that nobody read but Emily. As an editor, I knew how many people wrote in, sent manuscripts for consideration and were rejected. Very, very few succeeded; most had to deal with disappointment, and still they kept trying and trying. I admired them because, unlike me, they had *guts*. I never showed my work to anyone in the industry; not even Rowan and the rest of the editorial team at Rosewood had ever read anything of mine. *Because it's not good enough*, a voice in my head kept saying, and I always believed that voice, though it hurt me. I never believed that what I was writing was quite ready. The next story would be. But not this one. I could never satisfy myself.

Now that Emily was gone, who would read my stories? Funny, how multifaceted grief is: like a prism, casting its tear-born rainbows all over your life. I choked back tears again.

Not being able to stand it any longer, I switched the laptop on and opened a Word document.

I stared at it for a few minutes.

And then I got up and brushed my hair, then I sat down again, and stared some more.

I got up and sorted my underwear drawer. I wrote a few words – a possible title, a possible plot – then deleted them.

I looked around. I had to put a washing on. And my bookcase needed tidied. And I had to shave my legs, and look at those cobwebs! Suddenly, I had developed an unhealthy and entirely out of character interest in housework . . .

I sighed. I was getting a headache for real. The screen was

very white and very empty, and my mind was blank. I looked at my watch. Forty minutes I'd been at the computer, and two words had been written: *Chapter One*. That was it. Next it'd be *it was a dark and stormy night*.

I switched the laptop off, exhausted from doing nothing. I just hoped Mary wouldn't come. I couldn't cope with otherworldly encounters, that night; the world of the living was complicated enough.

21

Take me home

Inary

The next day there I was, back at the laptop, but this time editing yet another book written by someone else, someone brave enough to let her work see the light of day. Someone who had written a literary novel so intensely boring I was losing the will to live: the nearly autobiographical story of a woman who really, *really* loved crows. I was wrestling with a sentence with a lot of birds dotted through it – birds flying, birds pecking, birds perched on branches – when there was a knock at the door, immediately followed by Logan walking in, waving his phone.

"Taylor texted, he asks if it's okay to come and get you at two."

What? I mouthed.

"To show you the dig."

Oh yes. The crannog site. Had I agreed? Oh God, I had. I looked at Logan with pleading eyes.

"It's up to you. You don't have to," he shrugged. "Just say no." He always captured the shades and subtleties of human relationships.

Told him I would, I wrote on the back of some A4 paper from the printer's tray.

"Yeah well, you can change your mind."

You coming? I chanced.

"No time. No one is around to watch the shop this afternoon, I've got to be there."

I thought about it for a second.

Tell him yes.

"You sure?"

I nodded.

"Right. Here's his number, just sending it to you . . . there. I'll make lunch before you go. Something stodgy, to keep you going."

I smiled. He was such a mother hen. A scruffy, grumpy one, but still a mother hen.

I switched the bird woman off without regret.

★

We drove to the loch in Taylor's Land Rover. It was only ten minutes away and there was no need to drive at all, but I suspected Taylor wanted to show off. It was sweet, though.

Shame I had these niggling thoughts about Alex in the back of my mind. As much as I tried, I couldn't quite manage to stop thinking about him . . .

No. I was lucky Alex was talking to me again in the first place. I couldn't let myself go back there, not after it had caused so many problems. I'd made a promise to myself.

With a huge effort, I brought my mind back to the present, back to Loch Avich. It was a cold, clear day, and I was relieved there was no mist on the water. Taylor's boat was a tiny, pretty wooden thing. It was painted blue and shaped like a peapod, and looked a bit like the boat my dad used to have. I couldn't help smiling – I was expecting something high-tech – and Taylor read my mind.

"This is the advanced technology we can afford at the excavation, Inary," he laughed. "Seriously, we concentrate our funding on diving equipment, and this is the best way to travel on the loch, I find. It's quiet, it doesn't disturb the wildlife, and it's fast enough. Also, I got to name her . . ." He pointed at the name painted in navy letters on the side of the boat: *Rover*. Weird name for a boat.

Your girlfriend? I wrote on the notebook I'd brought with me. I hoped he'd get the joke.

Taylor laughed again. "Silly, Rover was our dog when I was a kid," he explained. He was charming, an All-American kind of charming. I had to give him that.

I climbed into the boat. It swayed quite wildly, but it wasn't the rocking motion, or the fact that it was tiny, that worried me. It was a different concern entirely. It was that a thin mantle of mist was beginning to rise on the loch, and the water was so black . . . I sat rigidly, holding on to the boat's sides. Taylor must have noticed my anxious expression, because he studied my face, frowning.

"Are you okay? We don't need to go if you don't want to . . ."

I shook my head with a smile brighter than I felt. I was sure it was time to win over my old fear. Thirteen years avoiding something that frightened you was a long time. Also, I didn't want to disappoint him – he seemed so keen to show me the dig, so enthusiastic about the whole thing.

There was my pride as well. I couldn't chicken out of it now and let him believe I was scared to go on a boat! Too humiliating.

He pushed *Rover* into the water, took hold of the paddles and slowly, hardly making a ripple, we left the shore. The silence was unbroken, the water a black mirror, and the sky bright and cloudy at the same time, the way a winter sky can be sometimes – pure white shining from within. We passed Ailsa, the little rocky island in the middle of the loch. It wasn't much wider than a hundred yards in diameter, and was covered with dark, wind-bent trees and hardy bushes. It reminded me of that painting by Arnold Böcklin, *The Isle of the Dead*.

Okay, maybe it wasn't the right moment to make that comparison. I tried to un-think that thought.

"Don't worry, this is perfectly safe," Taylor tried to reassure me in between paddle-strokes. "And once we get to the platform you'll be on dry land, in a way."

I took my notebook from my jacket pocket and wrote *I'm not afraid of the water* (lie) *I'm a good swimmer* (truth).

"So that's not what's making you nervous? Is it me?"

I laughed and shook my head. It'd be impossible to be nervous around Taylor.

I relaxed ever so slightly and sat back a little, taking in the beauty of the landscape and enjoying the gentle rocking of the boat. Maybe I could allow myself not to think about anything, if only for an hour. Just for a short time, just as long as I needed to start breathing deeply again, without the anxiety of grief, or the fear of lost chances. To just *be*.

The water was perfectly black, but I could see silvery fish darting by on the surface every once in a while. It was the first time I had gone out on the loch in many years, and it didn't feel too bad at all, I conceded. Maybe I had just been silly to avoid the water for so long – what happened that day, thirteen years ago, seemed like a distant dream. Or a distant nightmare, more like.

"Look! You can see the dig from here," Taylor said, jerking his head to the right without letting go of the paddles.

A wooden platform stood above the water, about a hundred yards from the shore. A white and blue caravan sat in a clearing opposite it, just past the tiny pebbled beach, and I could see the remains of a bonfire. A marshmallow-roasting session after work, I imagined.

"The weather is okay today, we should be able to see underwater," said Taylor, panting slightly with the effort of rowing. "I can't wait to show you what's under there. It's just amazing . . . On a clear day, when the water is transparent, you can see the poles that used to hold the crannog up. Some of them are still standing. It's quite incredible, to think this stuff was laid there so many years ago, by people like you and me. It gives me a thrill every time," he continued, and suddenly my heart started beating faster. His face had the kind of glow you only see when someone is truly passionate, truly inspired. I'd been feeling so empty of passion recently – I wanted to breathe in his enthusiasm, to drink from it, to feel that zest for life again.

I didn't want to be the girl sitting in front of a blank screen, all her stories gone.

I sat up as we approached the platform. Taylor tied the boat to one of the poles and climbed up. Then he crouched and extended his hand to me. "Come on," he said, and he helped me step on to the wooden planks. I had seldom been on this part of the loch, so much wilder than the side that faced the village. It was beautiful, full of the peace you can only find in truly ancient places, made heavy by the weight of eras.

I closed my eyes for a second, letting my other senses take over – the sound of the water lapping around the platform, the tap-tap-tap of the boat against the pole she was tied to, the scent of water, fresh, moist, misty. I could understand

150

why Logan spent so much time in the wild. I understood the peace it gave him and how it helped him cope with all the complications of his life, the weight he'd felt on his shoulders for many years.

I opened my eyes and the beauty took my breath away, as if I was seeing it for the first time: the glens cradling the loch; the smooth expanse of the water, wavy with tiny ripples, reflecting the white sky; the soft mantle of clouds, endless, ever-changing.

Suddenly I realised Taylor was looking at me, his head leaning slightly to one side, thoughtful, as if he were looking at an artefact in a museum. I blushed.

"Come and see ..." He took my hand, and he kneeled at the edge of the platform, peering into the loch. I stood, holding his hand, hesitating. I wanted to reach him and kneel beside him, but I wavered. Even if I couldn't feel any of the physical signs that announced an apparition, my last memory of having my face so close to the water was ...

I didn't want to remember. My heart had begun to flutter again, and it wasn't because of Taylor's flirting. I checked myself again: no tingling, no buzz in my ears. It was going to be okay. It *was* okay.

"Don't worry, Inary," smiled Taylor. "I'm a very good swimmer, I promise I won't let you drown."

I was a bit piqued: so when I'd said I could swim he hadn't believed me. Well, I was going to let him think that. I couldn't explain what really happened anyway. I took a deep breath. It was time to let go of old fears.

I made myself kneel beside Taylor and gazed down into the black, still waters.

"Can you see the outline of the house, Inary?" Taylor

began. "People lived here, people like us, men and women and children, hunting and working the land and sleeping together in their home on the lake. They lived here for generations. You'll think I'm crazy, but I often daydream about them . . . What they must have looked like, their names, their lives. I suppose archaeologists are obsessed with the past . . . We must be . . ."

His voice was hypnotic as he kept chatting about the excavation and what had brought him here and what they had found. Nobody could understand the way he felt about people from the past better than me.

The ripples in the black water, the perfect silence broken only by the soft sound of his voice and the lapping of the waves, it all melted into me – or I melted into them. Suddenly I couldn't quite decipher his words any more, because my ears were full of the soft drone I knew so well – and still, I tried to deny it. Shapes were beginning to appear in the water – it's the reflection of the clouds, I reassured myself. It's the poles the crannog stood on. I had counted three of them standing up, a broken one, its rugged stump like a cracked tooth, and a few more lying scattered among the stones.

I heard myself whimpering as the tingling started in every limb, joining the drone in my ears – the usually harmless sensations were subtly hurting me, like a knife working its way over my skin in a shallow, slow, impossibly painful cut. I tried to move, but I was paralysed by fear. And more than that: something was keeping me still, and tied to the water. Something was keeping me prisoner. From the whirlwind of my thoughts came a prayer – *please, let it be the people of the crannog, let it be their ghosts showing themselves to me . . . and not* that other thing *in the loch.*

But I knew that it wasn't. Never before had I felt like this, except that once. No other vision could cause me such terror.

My face and my chest felt like I'd been plunged in ice all of a sudden, and I knew that whatever it was, it was near. A silvery, blurred shape appeared in front of me, whirling in a crazy pattern. An overwhelming feeling of loneliness, of abandonment, filled my soul, bringing a tide of tears with it.

They left me.

They left me here alone.

Take me home.

I knew those weren't my thoughts, my memories – I knew it was something else, some*one* else, invading my mind. I made another helpless effort to tug myself away, but I couldn't, as if the thoughts overriding mine were hands, cruel hands keeping me where I was – kneeling on the wooden planks, my head facing the water and my hair cascading on either side of my face, my hands clutching the edges so hard they hurt. I must have let out a gasp, because Taylor wrapped his arm around me. I could hear him talking, but I had no idea what he was saying; his voice came to me like from the other end of a tunnel.

My eyes were following the swimming shape, as fast as a salmon, but too big to be one; as white as the reflection of a cloud, but too solid.

They left me here alone.

I'm cold.

I want to go home.

Take me home . . .

The alien thoughts were screaming in my mind, clawing at me. Over the words in my head, over the pain that had spread through my body, I became suddenly aware that my chest was

153

rising and falling so fast I could end up passing out – I could already see stars sparkling in the corners of my eyes.

I seized the edge of the platform harder, praying that I wouldn't fall into the water, where that *thing* was. That it wouldn't pull me in.

The white shape kept swimming frenziedly around the platform, coiling and uncoiling like seaweed carried by the current. I knew it had come for me.

I heard Taylor call my name, and I tried to beg for help, to implore him to tear me away from the spirit, away from the loch, but I couldn't. My mouth was open in a silent scream. It wouldn't let me go. *She* wouldn't let me go.

The shape stopped and floated right in front of me, just beyond the water level. I thought I would die of fright. But instead, mercifully, every feeling left me and I was empty, hollow, beyond fear and terror.

I watched as the spirit rose up without making a sound, without making a ripple, as if she'd been made of water herself.

22

Black waters

Inary

She looked just like I remembered – her skin white and her flesh swollen with water, her eyes black and empty, her long, tangled hair woven with seaweed. She was a child. A little girl lost.

The first time I saw her, the day I lost the Sight, I was a child myself.

Take me home, she whispered once more, and the sound of her voice came from inside my head and echoed all around me, in my heart and my bones. She hovered in front of me, her face so close it was nearly pressed against mine, and her small, blue-nailed hands touched my cheeks. They were wet and very cold. I looked into her eyes and I fell into them, fell into nothing.

Listen to me, she pleaded, and all of a sudden, she somersaulted backwards and melted back into the loch, her hair dissolving in the black water, her face losing shape, her body liquid once more. She was a white shadow floating in the water, and then she disappeared.

I fell backwards too, like a puppet whose strings had been cut. Everything went dark for a second, but I came to almost immediately. Taylor's arms were around me, but I was dizzy and disorientated, and in my confusion I must have believed that the spirit girl had taken hold of me, like she had when she pulled me off my dad's boat and into the loch. I panicked, and jerked away from Taylor with such force that what I feared the most happened – I fell over the edge of the platform with a splash.

The water closed above me and I couldn't breathe – I was too frightened to open my eyes, in case I saw the little girl again. My body went into panic mode – all I could think about was air, oxygen, the need to breathe. My arms and legs were flailing in blind terror, and my skin burnt with the cold. Instinctively, I opened my mouth and a draught of water rushed down my throat, into my lungs. As the fight or flight instinct kicked into overdrive, I opened my eyes and there she was, floating in the murky waters, her arms extended to me. Our eyes locked, and at that moment I thought I was dead already.

It was just a few seconds, but it seemed like an eternity of fear, before I felt Taylor's arms holding me again.

Next thing I knew I was on the shore, spitting out water and coughing so hard I thought my lungs would tear. A memory flashed into my mind: *drowning hurts so much*. I knew where that thought had come from, and it wasn't my own consciousness. It was the girl, still echoing her thoughts feebly into mine. I took my face in my hands and let Taylor hold me, hoping the link between me and the spirit girl would be severed completely – she was so frightened, so lost. I couldn't bear it.

I should've known. I hadn't been silly at all, in avoiding the loch for so long. She'd come looking for me, a poor soul without peace, just like she had thirteen years ago. I realised that now, after all this time. She was trying to get my attention; she was trying to speak to me. And just like back then, she'd begged me to take her home – but I had no way of helping her, no way to answer her plea.

★

I sat shivering in front of the gas fire, my teeth still chattering, wearing nothing but an oversized Fair Isle jumper someone from Taylor's team had left in the caravan and a pair of long woollen socks. I was still freezing, but the gas fire was incredibly hot and I could feel myself warming slowly, and my hair was beginning to dry. Taylor, having changed into a black T-shirt and chinos, handed me some coffee in a mug with a cartoon picture of Nessie on it. I recognised the mugs that Peggy sold in her shop; we had a set of them too. Funny, the little things you notice when your thoughts are all jumbled up.

I drew a deep sigh. It felt good to wrap my fingers around the steaming mug, to be away from the water.

"Better?" he asked. I nodded, looking into his face. He seemed younger than he was, and . . . earnest. Yes, he looked earnest. Uncomplicated. I was so thankful he'd been with me. Had I been on my own, who knows what might have happened . . . I shivered again, and he noticed.

"You'll get warmed up in a minute. This fire is so strong you could roast a boar on it!" he laughed. I took a sip of my coffee. It was revolting.

"It's chicory. A great coffee alternative, no caffeine whatsoever!"

I mustered a smile, willing myself to take another sip – I didn't want to seem ungrateful.

Taylor's eyes turned serious. "What happened out there, Inary? You looked . . . terrified. I tried to move you, but you

157

were rigid. And then when you fell I wanted to hold you, to help you . . . but you pushed me away." His fingers went to his face, absentmindedly. Only then did I notice that there was a purple bruise just under his left eye. It looked nasty. It must have happened when . . .

Oh my God.

I did that!

I clasped my hands over my mouth, gazing at the bruise in horror.

"Oh, this? Don't worry, its fine. It's not sore. If I keep it closed."

Sorry, sorry, sorry! I mouthed over and over, and followed the contours of the bruise with my fingers, gently. *Sorry*, I mouthed again.

"I swear on . . . on Rover's life that it does not hurt at all."

I raised my eyebrows. The dog he'd had when he was a boy? It was obviously dead. Not much point swearing on his life.

"Honestly. It's not your fault. You were upset. That was pretty scary, man. When you fell in, for a moment I just couldn't see you. Like there was something above you . . . Like something covered you."

I looked down into my cup.

"Tell me what happened, Inary," he said gently.

I shrugged and showed the palms of my hands, as if to say *I can't*. My notebook was in my jacket pocket – either in shreds or soaking like everything else. There was no point in even looking for it. It was a good excuse, anyway.

"Sorry, I forgot about . . ." He touched his throat, embarrassed. I smiled and shook my head – I didn't mind. He'd been great. I was pretty sure he'd saved my life. And got a black eye as a thank you.

I looked into Taylor's frank, clear blue eyes and I wondered if I could explain what really happened. About the way I see things . . . About the girl in the loch.

Could I? No. That wasn't an option.

Many people in Glen Avich knew that the Sight ran through the McCrimmons and a few related families. But only six people in the world knew about the true extent of my gift, and four of them were dead: my parents, my grandmother, Emily, Logan and Lewis. Nobody else. Nobody else could have imagined that the gift, for the women of my mother's family, was a lot more than the occasional dream that hinted of the future, or feeling a presence once in a while. It was so much more than that – so much stronger, more vivid. Real. And, my grandmother had said, nobody in the last few generations had had a gift as potent as mine. Which was why when it ended so suddenly, she was astonished. I never told her – or anybody else – about the girl in the loch.

I'd regretted telling Lewis. I'd regretted it at once, as soon as I saw his face when he realised I wasn't joking. I'd told him in a moment of weakness, an intimate moment when I felt I wanted him to know everything about me. At the beginning, he thought I was messing with him. When he grasped that I was serious, he was spooked. And he told me never to mention this to his parents – as if I would – because they would not want me in the house again. As if my gift were somehow demonic, akin to witchcraft – something intrinsically evil, when it was really just like a sixth sense. Neither evil nor good in its substance, just the way I was, the way many women in our family were.

"Inary?" Taylor said softly and pulled me gently out of my thoughts. "Wait. I'm sure we've got . . ." He hunted around and landed on a pile of printed sheets that looked like spread charts,

159

and a capless blue biro. "There you are," he said, handing me one of the sheets and the pen. "You can write here."

Oh.

What excuse could I find for what happened today?

"More chicory?"

God no, no more of that brown broth. I shook my head so hard I was dizzy for a second.

I paused and rested the tip of the pen on the paper, biting my lip. What about *I see dead people*? I chuckled to myself, somewhat hysterically.

"What's funny?" whispered Taylor, amusement replacing the concern in his eyes. He was sitting very close to me, and his arm was brushing against my bare leg. Dusk was falling outside, and the light in the caravan was grey and opaque, a prelude to darkness. The fire shone warm and orange on Taylor's face, like a window in a darkened house.

"I'm sorry I asked you out on the water. I could tell you were worried and I should've listened. I'm sorry you felt obliged to come and see the excavation . . ."

I shook my head again, more firmly this time, and lay a hand on his arm. I couldn't stand the idea of him feeling guilty for something he had no responsibility for. I should have said no.

So much had happened, and I was cold and shaken and I had so much on my mind. I sprang to my feet. I just wanted to go home.

★

I stepped into the house in a daze. Thoughts of the ghostly child filled my head in a messy tangle, and I couldn't pick up the threads.

The girl's empty black eyes.

Her pleading words.

Drowning in the black waters.

Take me home.

And then I was shaken out of my reverie, as I noticed something on the kitchen table – a little parcel, tied with string, and beside it a note in Logan's handwriting: *This came for you.* I didn't need to open it to know who it was from.

Inside the parcel was something nestled in layer after layer of bubble wrap, and a small, flat present encased in lilac tissue paper and held together by a raffia thread. I ripped the bubble wrap – within was an exquisite porcelain owl, white and blue, and Blu-tacked to it was a tiny Danish flag. I then untied the raffia thread and gently opened the lilac tissue. Inside, a purple leather notebook, its cover soft and buttery.

Owl number two, and something to use until your voice comes back.

A.

PS. You might guess I'm in Copenhagen.

Now I had two owls, sitting side by side on my desk. I was glad that the Polish one had another little owl to keep it company.

The day had been so long, so eventful. It was definitely time for a Lesley chat. She didn't even know about what had happened between Alex and me yet . . . and I needed to find out if he'd said anything to her. Maybe that could give me an insight into his thinking, because right now our relationship was so jumbled up I couldn't make sense of anything.

From Inary@gmail.com
To LesleyGayle@aldebaran.co.uk

Hi Lesley,

I wish I could phone you and actually talk. Everything is okay here. Relatively speaking. Things between Logan and me are a wee bit better, it seems. He's stopped having a go at me on a regular basis, so that helps. What worries me is that he's not doing that great. I try to keep an eye on him and hide bottles away, but it's not really working. He sits there and drinks. I just wish I could ask Emily what to do, what to say to him. She always knew how to take him, you know? How to make him snap out of his black moods. It doesn't bear thinking what would happen if I weren't here, Lesley.

Will you come up? I mean, if you can? I know you came for the funeral, and it's a long way, but with my voice gone, I'm still scared to leave Glen Avich. I haven't been anywhere yet. Also, I don't want to leave Logan. But if you can't, I understand . . . I know it's a lot to ask.

Alex sent me a purple notebook. I'm writing instead of talking. It helps. At least it's a way to communicate.

So . . . Something happened between Alex and me before I left. It shouldn't have happened and I'm not sure how to deal with it now. It's too much. I told him it was a mistake and I hurt him a lot. Has he mentioned anything to you?
I thought it was better if we didn't speak for a while, but everything was so painful and horrible here, I texted him, so we're back in touch.

Well, please visit if you can. I just can't wait to hear your voice and see your face.
Inary xxxx

From LesleyGayle@aldebaran.co.uk
To Inary@gmail.com

Oh, Inary. The two of you, honestly. He didn't mention anything, no, but I did feel he was a bit weird. I thought it was just because you were away.

I'd love to come up. Let me just sort out a few work things and I'll get back to you . . . I'll let you know the earliest I can make it.
Take care,
Lesley

23

She isn't you

Alex

I was in one of my favourite places in the world, Copenhagen, having a coffee in Café Kys and logging a few new colours into Chromatica, when I got an email from Inary.

> Hi Alex,
> I got your Danish owl, thank you

– wow, the courier had been faster than light; I'd only sent it the day before –

> And how's Chromatica going? Any more purples found?
> I don't think I'll be back for a while. Months, probably.
> Apart from the fact that I can't speak, which is bad enough, the worst thing is Logan. Yesterday he spent three hours chopping wood – without stopping. Afterwards, his hands were all blistered. He acts normally, but I can see that inside it's a different story.
> So I won't see you for a while. I'm really sorry.

Dismay filled me like a tidal wave. Suddenly, the coffee tasted like dirty water.

I think I owe you an explanation, about what happened between us, and the way I was afterwards. You know, the way I said it had been a mistake. I never planned to be in a relationship again, after Lewis. But with you . . . I don't know, things just seemed to happen. The problem is, my life is a bit of a mess right now. I can't think of anything but Emily and I can't speak and my brother is in a bad way. Yes, it's all a big mess. I just couldn't cope with more complications. It's so much better if we are just friends. I hope you understand, and please don't be hurt. It's just me being all wrong, right now.

Inary x

I closed the email without replying.

As soon as I got home I phoned Kamau, and we went out places. Various places, not sure exactly where. I don't remember much of the night – just a few hazy scenes, blurred words, the sense of nothing being quite right. I recall having a long, loud conversation in a club, shouting over the noise and downing brightly coloured, unidentified cocktails.

"So that's what happened. And now she's gone . . ."

"That's tough."

"It is tough indeed, my friend." Words were quite difficult to form at that stage, but I soldiered on.

"She won't be back for months. If ever . . ."

"Can you not go see her?"

"I don't know. Can I? Does she want me to?"

He shrugged. "Worth trying."

"Nah. Not after what she said to me . . ."

"What did she say?"

165

"That she couldn't cope with any more complications and it's better if we are just friends. And I quote. Because I know that email by heart."

"You're in a bad way, mate," Kamau concluded.

I downed another bright-blue concoction, and after that it all went black.

Kamau must have dragged me home sometime in the early hours. He'd taken my shoes off and put me to bed. I woke up in my clothes, hating myself and the whole world.

As I got up and as everything spun and unidentified sludge sploshed in my stomach, the thought hit me again: Inary and I were to be just friends – in case I didn't get the message before. Then why did she keep talking to me, turning to me every time she needed someone, like some kind of torture she'd planned for me? Why?

I dragged myself to the kitchen. Kamau was still there, and he was awake, smartly dressed and sitting with a smirk on his face.

"Rise and shine! How you feeling?"

"Rise and shite, more like." I moaned. "How come you had a change of clothes?"

"I sort of knew what kind of night it was going to be." He smiled. He was sober, not hungover in the slightest. And he was smug. Had I not been so grateful, I would have hated him too, like the rest of this planet.

"Drink this. And take ... these." He handed me a cup of black coffee and pushed two Nurofen out of their packets.

"This coffee is practically *solid* . . ."

"It's what you need. And by the way, it's half past eight, so you have to finish that and get dressed in the next ten minutes. I'll drive you to work."

166

I nodded, and it was so painful I just wished somebody would chop my head off. "Ouch . . ."

"Well, you only have yourself to blame, like my mum always used to say!" laughed Kamau. "'Mon, get going."

A few agonising minutes later, we were out. The fresh air did take the edge off a bit, but by the time we were in front of my office I just wanted to lie down and die.

"Thank you, mate," I said as I opened the car door.

"Any time. Oh, and Alex?"

"Mmmm?"

"You know something else my mum used to say?"

"What?"

"What's for you won't go past you."

"Ah."

"I mean, if she's meant for you, she'll come back. Or you'll go to her. It'll work out."

I wasn't so sure.

★

I walked into my office, every step a stab between my eyes. It was just Sharon and me.

"Hi, Sharon," I called. My voice sounded very *loud*. I winced.

"Hi. Good night?"

"Not exactly," I replied, hanging my jacket up. The office was oddly quiet for this time of morning. "Where is everyone?"

"Gary is on holiday, Molly and Clark are in Manchester, and Alena is sick with the flu. She phoned this morning. Looks like it's just you and me. You look terrible. Coffee?"

"God, no."

I sat at my desk, and for a second I thought I was having some alcohol-induced hallucination. There was a toy owl sitting in front of my computer. It was a plush one, baby blue, with huge round eyes and a patchwork of textures. How did that thing get there?

For a wild moment, I thought – I hoped . . . of course, it must have been Inary! I looked around frantically, as if she were about to jump out of a filing cabinet. I lifted the owl up, and a small envelope – the same blue as the owl, appeared from under it.

I opened the note.

For your collection, it said.

What?

I met Sharon's eyes over my computer. She was smiling. Her lips were very red and her hair styled in smooth, silky waves. Sharon wasn't just pretty – she was beautiful, cinnamon-skinned and dark-eyed beautiful.

It dawned on me.

"I got it for you," she said.

"Oh. Oh, thanks." I didn't know what to say. Why an owl? How did she know . . . ?

"Gary told me you were hunting for owls. Not literally!" she laughed. "He said you were looking for a nice one in Copenhagen. That you collect them. So I thought . . ." Colour was rising in her cheeks.

This couldn't be happening. And my head was killing me. Oh God please make the drilling in my head stop, I prayed.

"Well, they were for a friend . . . But thank you."

A cloud passed over her face. "Oh."

Oh indeed. I suppose if a man is buying statuettes and says they're for a friend, it's likely they're for a woman.

"Well, you can give it to your friend." She laughed a brittle laugh. I felt terrible for her. What a mess.

But we were adults. Professionals. We could handle it.

We were professionals who left plush toys on people's desks. I pressed my fingers to my temples. Please Lord, make me die. I'll never touch a drop of vodka again, ever, as long as I live.

"You okay?" she asked. "Look, I'm sorry. It was a bad idea. What was I thinking? Honestly, just give it to your friend and let's forget about it. I'm going for a coffee across the road . . ."

"No, I'll keep it for myself."

"You don't have to . . ."

God, I felt for her. She'd really put herself on the line. Like she really cared about me, and she was willing to take a risk to get closer to me.

Like I mattered.

"Listen, Sharon . . ." I took a breath.

"I'll be back in ten, okay?"

"Sharon. Please stay."

She stopped in her tracks.

I had to move on.

"Yes?"

I had to try again to free myself from Inary.

"Alex?"

I owed it to myself. It'd been three years, for fuck's sake. And she still felt *confused*.

I'd had enough.

"I've been in the mood for Thai food for ages. I don't suppose you . . . ?" I blurted out.

169

"Oh . . . I love Thai food," she replied, a tentative smile on her lips.

"Great. I'll book somewhere. Should I come and get you at eight?"

"Sure." She was smiling now. "Sure."

★

It was a good night. We never ran out of things to talk about, we made each other laugh, and whenever she brushed my fingers with hers – not on purpose, of course, by complete *accident* – her skin felt soft as silk. There was a candle on the table, and its light made her eyes liquid, like dark honey.

Later, I invited her home and into my living room. On the very spot I'd held Inary, I let Sharon wrap her arms around me. She smelled deep and dark and womanly, like some night-blooming flower. I stood still for a few seconds, and then I took her face in my hands and kissed her.

★

I woke up sated and starving all the same time. She was in a peaceful, undisturbed sleep, her dark hair scattered across my pillow, her arms cradling her head. She looked very young, though I knew she was my age, thirty-one. She looked vulnerable. Spending the night with her had been . . . good. And it hadn't been enough, somehow.

I stroked her hair and wished with all my heart I could fall in love with her. And I would – once Inary was out of my system.

24

In our blood

Inary

Taylor was around a lot. He was a live wire, full of life, full of energy. He told me stories of his work and how it had taken him around the world before he'd landed a job with the Scottish Underwater Archaeology Association. He'd dived off the coasts of Turkey and Japan, swum among the ruins of long-lost cities in Greece and recovered Viking jewellery from frozen lakes.

Everything he said took me a million miles away from all that weighed on me those days. He didn't seem to mind my inability to speak – he simply kept talking. The purple notebook lay mainly untouched.

One afternoon he'd come up to the house for coffee (me) and herbal tea (him). I'd been at the kitchen table, jotting down a few notes about what I knew about Mary, everything I'd uncovered from my visions. She was different from any other spirit I'd seen. She moved me in a way that no other had done – like I was meant to get closer to her. Like I *needed* to get closer to her.

"Working on a project?" asked Taylor, looking at a little pile of scribbled sheets.

Oh, yes, it's just about this ghost I see, I considered replying. But of course I couldn't. I thought quickly. *It's for a book. About a girl who used to live here*, I wrote on my purple notebook.

"Cool! Logan said you write. Can I read it?"

I smiled. *Nobody reads my books.*

"Right. So what do you write them for?"

He had a point. I shrugged. *I'm waiting for the right time.*

"Oh, okay. Well, while you wait, let me know if there's anything I can do to help."

Oh. Suddenly, I had an idea. I wanted to find out more about Mary, and Aunt Mhairi's suggestion to visit the Heritage Collection in Kinnear sounded promising. I'd been there for a project when I was at high school, and I remembered them having parish archives from Glen Avich and the surrounding villages. Maybe I could find out something there. The problem was . . . I couldn't leave Glen Avich, not without being able to speak. I just didn't feel ready. In Glen Avich everybody knew me, but in Kinnear it would be so much harder. I just found the idea of going alone very hard. Impossible, really. But, with Taylor maybe . . .

I sat up and scribbled quickly.

There is something . . .

"Fire away," he said, taking a sip of his tea.

Would you come with me to the library in Kinnear? Research for my book. I just don't feel like going by myself, without being able to speak . . .

I looked down. I suppose I was embarrassed. I never thought I'd have to ask someone to come with me to the bloody library. But just the idea of standing in front of strangers, and having to write down everything, and miming, and nodding . . . I wasn't ready.

"Sure. Now a good time?"

I smiled. *You sure you're not busy?*

"Not today, otherwise I wouldn't be here, but I will be all next week, so perfect timing. Let's go."

I grabbed my notebooks and pens, threw on my jacket and followed him outside. I hadn't left Glen Avich in weeks. It was strange. I felt a bit dizzy – as if I'd been somewhere shady and sheltered, and I was now blinking in bright sunlight.

As I got into his car, a flower of anxiety bloomed in my chest. Would I be able to keep the pretence up, that I was researching a book? Would he think that there was something strange going on? I hardly knew Taylor, after all. And suddenly, he was helping me with something so important, so precious.

The Aberdeenshire countryside flew past us as we drove on the rural lanes between Glen Avich and Kilronan, and then on the road to Kinnear. Glen Avich and Kinnear were only half an hour away from each other, but they were like two different worlds. I often thought that Glen Avich seemed frozen in time, in spite of the Chinese takeaway and the new fancy coffee shop – it still felt a bit remote, just like it had when I was growing up. Kinnear, with its grey sandstone buildings and even its little suburbs, was very much part of modern Scotland.

We'd arrived in no time. "So, do you want me to do the talking?" Taylor said. "Oh, of course. Sorry." He gave a light laugh.

I couldn't help laughing too. I gestured for him to wait, took out my notebook and pen, and scribbled a summary of what I was trying to find out.

Mary
Probably lived in St Colman's Way, Glen Avich
Probably turn of the century?

"Mary . . . probably lived . . . okay. How did you find all that out?"

Good old Google, I lied.

"Okay . . . So, in this library . . . do they have archives or something?"

They should have old parish archives from the area. They all go under the name Heritage Collection.

"Cool. Let's see what they say. Ready?"

I nodded. We stepped out of the car and walked up a small hill, towards the community library. I was a bit nervous, and frustrated that I couldn't do all this myself, that my confidence had taken such a blow, I needed someone to speak for me.

Behind the counter there was a girl with her hair piled on top of her head and bright-red lipstick, looking at a computer screen. She was about Emily's age, I thought.

"Hello," said Taylor, smiling brightly. The librarian looked up and brightened visibly as she saw him. "Maybe you can help us. We're doing some research for a novel . . ."

"Oh, that's exciting! Are you a writer?" she squealed.

"No, *she* is . . ."

I smiled a tentative smile. I could feel my cheeks burning.

"Oh, wow! So what is this book about? How can I help?" She seemed really sweet. I allowed myself to relax a little.

"We're looking for information from the Heritage Collection. About someone called Mary . . ."

"Half the women in the Heritage Collection are called Mary," she said cheerily. "But don't worry, I'm sure we'll find her. Follow me . . ."

We trailed after her, behind the counter and through a back door. It was a high-ceilinged room, covered wall to wall in bookshelves, with filing cabinets filling every free corner. It would take us days to go through all that – no, weeks . . .

"We're a bit short of space, but the stuff is all in order. So, this Mary. Where did she live?"

174

"Glen . . ." Taylor began, but I put a hand on his arm. *I* wanted to speak. This was *my* thing.

I looked at Taylor and gestured to my throat, and then at the librarian. Taylor got my hint.

"She can't speak. She writes instead," he explained.

The librarian looked bewildered for a moment, then she recovered herself.

"Oh, okay. No problem. Handy that you're a writer, then?" she said kindly.

I smiled. I could do this. Voice or not, I could do this. I took a deep breath. Out of the corner of my eye, I could see Taylor looking at me with something very similar to pride. I opened my notebook at the page where I'd written what I knew about Mary, and I showed it to the girl.

"I see. Glen Avich . . . this section. Right. The address is no use for now because the parish archives go by dates of birth and death. Do you have an idea about the time . . . Oh I see. Turn of the century . . ."

I did a quick calculation. In my visions, Mary looked about twenty. I took the notebook from the librarian, gently, and scribbled: *Probably from around 1880 to 1890 or so.*

"Smashing. Well. It's all in here." She gestured at a small row of computers, sitting on desks against the opposite wall. "Everything has been scanned and catalogued. It's on microfilm, and on PDF as well. The PDFs are handier."

My vision of us sifting through fragile yellowed papers dissolved. It was all shaping up to be a bit easier than I thought.

"Thank you . . ." Taylor began.

"Lucy," said the librarian. Had I imagined it, or was she blushing?

"Thank you, Lucy."

She cast her eyes quickly around the room, and finally her gaze rested on us. "So, I'll leave you to it. No coffee or tea allowed in this room, but if you want a break just come through. My mum made cupcakes yesterday," she added, looking straight at Taylor, and she was gone.

"Okay. Let's do this thing, then," said Taylor cheerily, and he sat at the desk, folding his long legs under it.

Thank you, I mouthed, taking my place beside him.

"Well, when I have something ultra-boring to do at the excavation, I know who to call for help. Once I logged and classified seven hundred and twenty-two pebbles. It took me six weeks."

I laughed. I felt a weight had gone from my chest. I'd left Glen Avich and negotiated my way with the librarian. Yes, I'd had Taylor's help, but I'd done my bit.

I was still me. Still Inary. Without my voice, but still me.

I started studying the records, one by one. The librarian wasn't joking when she said that half the women in there were called Mary. There were also a lot of Annes, Catherines, Elizabeths, Margarets and a few Floras. Their lives, otherwise forgotten, were on the screen in front of me. And still, even if they weren't individually remembered, their blood flowed in the veins of Glen Avich. There were so many names I recognised – Monteith, my own surname, and then Watson, Buchanan, Walker, Duff. I'd gone to school with these women's descendants – these women were us, all of us. And so many McCrimmons . . .

Anne McCrimmon, dead at twenty-three of tuberculosis . . . Emily's age.

Morag McCrimmon, dead at eighty-nine. After nine children, five of whom had died before three years of age.

Elizabeth McCrimmon, born in Glen Avich and, said a wee note beside her name, dead at thirty-eight in Nova Scotia . . .

Had any of them had the Sight, I wondered? I felt them around me. I could hear them whispering . . .

I was beginning to feel quite strange – light-headed, and the hairs on the back of my head were rising. My hands were tingling too. I kept looking around, but I couldn't see any spirits. It was probably their stories, having that strange effect on me. I was beginning to lose my concentration and felt drained by the weight of those weird feelings.

"You look a bit pale. Are you cold?" Taylor rested a hand on mine. "You're freezing! Maybe we should continue another time . . ."

Do you want to go? I wrote.

"I'm happy to stay. Just you don't seem to be feeling well . . ."

A little bit more. There weren't many birth certificates left to go. I was sure that I would find her.

And I did. At last. The low drone in my ears announced it – and there she was.

Mary Gibson, Born in Glen Avich, St Colman's Way, the 1st October 1895.

As I saw her name, my heart started beating faster and for a second I felt like I was floating. It was like a shift in the atmosphere, an echo of voices and sounds taking physical form and sweeping my body from head to toe . . .

"Inary?" Taylor turned towards me. I just pointed at my screen. "Mary Gibson . . . Do you think that's her?"

I'm sure, I scribbled quickly, my hand shaking.

"How can you be sure?"

Because I feel it in my bones, I could have said, but I didn't – *Everything fits*, I wrote instead.

And then I heard them, the whispered words – a warm breath on my cheek, as if somebody's face was right against mine, a woman's mouth against my ear.

Find her.

I gasped and stood up so quickly that my chair fell backwards. Taylor wrapped an arm around my waist, steadying me, his face full of alarm.

"Inary? What's wrong?"

I shook my head. I couldn't say.

"Sorry guys, it's closing time . . . Everything okay, yes?" The librarian came in, holding her jacket and handbag.

"Sure, all fine," said Taylor, and I nodded feebly.

I took hold of my notebook and pen and leaned on the desk. *I found what I was looking for. Thank you.* I tried to smile.

"You sure you're okay? Would you like a glass of water?"

I shook my head.

"We'll just go. Thank you . . ." Taylor intervened.

"I'm in every day. Come back whenever you want," she said, giving Taylor a red-lipped smile.

"Yeah. Will do . . ."

Once in the car, I rubbed my face with my hands to try to dispel the light-headedness. *Find her.* It had been Mary's voice, I was sure – but who was she talking about?

"So you found your Mary. Mary Gibson. Will she end up in your book?" said Taylor, starting the car.

I nodded. We drove in companionable silence, until he stopped in front of my house.

"When should we go back? I'm not free until next week . . ."

I can come here by myself. I feel fine about it now.

"Oh." He seemed deflated.

I don't want to inconvenience you . . . I wrote quickly. It was true. I was happy to have company, but I was sure he had better things to do than accompany me to the library to find out about a ghost. I mean, wouldn't you?

"I enjoyed today, Inary. I'd love to come back. I guess I can be kind of your writing partner – intern-assistant," he laughed. "Seriously, it's cool. How about next Thursday?"

I had to give in. I nodded, smiling.

"In the meantime . . . maybe we could go for a drink, just you and me?"

Uh-oh. Just what I needed. More complications.

I poised the pen to write – something like *I'm so busy this week* . . . and then I sighed and put the pen down. I gazed at him.

His handsome face broke into a smile. "Right. Right. I think that's a no . . ."

I have a lot on, Taylor, I started writing as he was watching over my shoulder, *I just can't get into this kind of thing now . . . I'm sorry if I gave you ideas, I didn't mean . . .*

He put a hand flat on my notebook, interrupting my writing. I looked up, alarmed – but he was smiling.

"Hey, it's okay. Honestly. Look, I like you. I can't lie. But I can see it's not the right time . . . Maybe there's someone else?" he asked kindly.

I went to deny it, but I couldn't. I nodded.

"In London?"

I took a deep breath and nodded again.

"An awful long way away . . ."

I looked down.

"Well, lucky dude," he said with a sigh.

I studied his face. He looked a bit deflated, but not entirely crushed.

You sure you want to come back to the library with me? You don't have to. I mean, I would understand ...

"Of course I want to." He smiled again and looked me straight in the eye. He meant it. Thank goodness. I breathed deeply. I couldn't have coped with more tricky situations. And I enjoyed his friendship; I didn't want it to end.

★

"So ... you and Taylor seeing each other then?" my brother said during dinner, pretending to study the label on the back of a bottle of HP sauce.

I shook my head, eyes wide.

"Right. Good."

I grabbed my notebook. *What do you mean by 'Good'?*

"Nothing," he shrugged. "He told me he liked you, but he doesn't seem your type much."

How do you know my type? My brother, the relationship expert.

"Keep your hair on. Just saying."

I rolled my eyes.

"Sorry, forget I ever spoke."

Logan didn't look good at all. He was pushing his food around the plate. I was sure he'd lost weight. I had tried to suggest he go and see Dr Nicholson many times, but he kept putting it off.

I had to find another way. Sort of make him go without him realising he was actually going.

I'm very worried about my voice, I wrote. It was true, of course.

"So am I, Inary," he said, gazing at me. His face was full of concern. Bingo, I thought. Push the 'looking after' button, and with Logan you'll get results.

I'd like to go and ask Dr Nicholson again, see what she says ...

"You should."

Actually no, better not.

"Why? You really should."

Don't know, too stressful.

"She could have some advice ..."

I'll ask Aunt Mhairi to ask for me.

"Aunt Mhairi? You crazy? Bless her, you know the way she is!"

Yes. Let's just forget about it, I wrote.

Logan didn't reply, but I saw from his face that my plan had a good chance of working.

25

Tomorrow

Logan

I'd only closed the shop for a few days, when Emily was dying and then over the funeral and the immediate aftermath. It was better for me to be busy. I knew Inary would be working from up here, but I thought she might need some extra money and something to do, so I asked her to help.

I didn't mind having her around, I must admit.

I'd left Inary and the usual shop assistant in the Welly, and walked down to see Dr Nicholson. I didn't tell my sister where I was going; I didn't want her to know that I was looking for advice about her.

I sat, leafing through the pages of a medical magazine. The photographs were horrifically graphic. I started browsing the leaflets: diabetes, high blood pressure, flu and all its complications. Alopecia, depression, asthma, arthritis. Suddenly I was sore everywhere. I left the leaflets alone.

It was strange to be in the surgery without Emily. I couldn't remember the last time it had happened – doctors are not really my thing. They always seem to give bad news, or so it worked with Emily. But I had to go – I was worried about Inary. Her voice was showing no sign of coming back, and it broke my heart to see her writing in that notebook. I knew she was just trying to work her way out of what had happened, but it had been a long time now. She hadn't said a word for *weeks*. Not one. I tried not to show her how anxious I was, just be with her the way I'd always been, but she could probably guess.

"Logan? Hello, come on in." Dr Nicholson waved me into her office and gestured to the chair. "Have a seat. How can I help you?"

I took a breath. "It's Inary. She's still not speaking at all. Not even a whisper."

Dr Nicholson looked at me thoughtfully. "And how is she feeling?"

"She seems okay. She's upset, no wonder, with all that happened . . . But she's bearing up. She's working, she's helping me in the shop . . . I make sure she eats, of course."

"And who makes sure *you* eat?" Dr Nicholson said quietly.

I was taken aback; I was there to talk about Inary, not myself. I never went to the doctor for myself. For a moment I felt completely exposed, and I just wanted out.

"I'm fine."

"You know, when someone you love is ill you dedicate all your energy to them. It happens quite often that carers need nearly as much attention from me than the people they care for do . . ."

"So how can I help Inary?" I said sharply. I refused to be dragged into a conversation about me. It annoyed me to see the concern in Dr Nicholson's eyes as she looked at me. One of my sisters was dead, the other couldn't speak – and there we were, talking about me. It made no sense.

"You can't do anything more than what you've been doing already. Grief takes its natural course. But if it doesn't get better, we might need to support her further . . ."

Support her further? How? "What do you mean?"

"I mean give her some psychological help. Maybe look into medication, certainly refer her on. What she has is called dysphonia. It's caused by stressful or traumatic events. It usually corrects itself over time, with help, but sometimes it might need professional guidance. I explained all this to her when she came to see me. But there's nothing I can do if Inary doesn't come to me again. Herself."

"She won't."

"Why, do you think?"

"I've had this conversation with her. She doesn't think you can help."

"Maybe she's right. Maybe it's something she needs to find her own way out of. But if you feel things are getting too much for her . . . if her voice doesn't come back in a reasonable time . . . she might need some extra help."

"It's not that straightforward. I could never tell Inary what to do."

"Quite a lot of people are like that, around here," Dr Nicholson said with a smile. I looked away.

"Thank you, then," I said quickly, and I dived out of the door.

"Logan . . ." Her voice reached me through reception.

"Yes?"

"Take care."

I'd take care of Inary, yes. Like I used to take care of Emily.

"I will." I just wanted out of that place. I'd spent too much time in there. And there was nothing to report to Inary, anyway, apart from 'you need help'. What was I hoping for, anyway? That Dr Nicholson would suggest some miracle cure? Maybe she knew a way to stop drinking until it made you sick.

I rushed back to the shop and busied myself, trying not to think of anything.

184

26

You couldn't have come at a better time

Inary

I'd spent all morning in Logan's shop – he'd asked me to help out once in a while, and I thought it was a good way to keep an eye on him. My brother had been AWOL for over an hour on some mysterious errand in the village, and as soon as he'd got back he'd disappeared into the stock cupboard without a word.

My worry about him hadn't subsided. Just the opposite. I worried about him pretty much constantly. But what could I do to take his sadness away?

Just be there for him. It was all I could do.

I sighed and looked outside. It was a sunny, cold, pure winter day; from the window I could see a tantalising square of blue sky, and the hills were beckoning. I wanted to be out in the frigid sunshine . . .

The door opened, with the soft chime of the bells above it filling the place.

"Do you have wellies?" a woman's voice said all of a sudden.

I turned around to see who thought it was okay to walk into a shop and not even say hello. A woman was standing in front of me, frowning and holding a bright-red welly in her hand. Instinctively, I looked down at her feet; she was bare-footed, her toenails painted a bright turquoise. I must have gaped, because she said, her face hard and unsmiling: "Taking pictures in the loch, got a great shot, fell in. My camera is now swimming."

Only then I noticed that her long hair, the colour of dark chocolate, was dripping wet, and she was shivering. Oh, so that was the reason for the bad mood.

"Sorry. Cameras aren't cheap," called Logan from the cupboard.

"No they aren't. Anyway, I lost a welly. Need a new pair . . ." She looked around. She had a west coast accent. Probably Glasgow.

"No prob—" Logan started, then turned around "—lem." He'd seen her. I couldn't help grinning as Logan stared. He stared because she was barefooted and dripping wet, and because she was so pretty, standing there like a selkie who'd just come out of the loch.

He coughed. Then coughed again. Then recovered himself. "Do you need somewhere to get dry? My house is just up the road. My sister—" he pointed to me "—can go with you . . ." he mumbled, so she wouldn't think he was a perv luring her to his house. I nodded emphatically – said sister was willing to take the mysterious girl home to get dry.

She smiled, and her face brightened up a bit, the frown between her eyebrows smoothing. "That's kind of you, thanks . . . But I'm okay. I'm just staying at the Green Hat round the corner. Only the shop was on the way and I thought I'd stop to put something on my feet. They're sore. And cold."

Logan gaped. He'd just seen her toes. "Did you walk all the way from the loch to here on bare feet?"

"Well, with one welly," she said, lifting up the surviving red boot. "So humiliating." She rolled her eyes.

"I'm sure nobody noticed," my brother replied in his earnest way. *He* wouldn't notice, no. Anybody else would.

"Oh yes, I'm sure nobody spotted the tourist hopping through the streets on one welly. Dripping wet," she said, her mouth curling up in the beginning of a smile. My thoughts exactly.

"Anyway, what size?" Logan disappeared into the stock cupboard again.

"Five!" She called.

"Let's see ... Oh, look. Red, like yours. Here, take these ones," he said. The girl extended her hand to take the wellies from him, but Logan placed them on the counter – no doubt to avoid the risk of their fingers touching. I knew my brother.

"They're perfect, thank you. How much do I owe you?"

"Don't worry about it. You've had a bad day. Just take them."

She shook her wet head and started rummaging in the bag she carried across the shoulder. "I can't accept . . ."

"Well, I'm not taking your money, so you have to accept," he said simply.

"Oh ... thank you. I don't know what to say. Look, I still have the right one, I only need a left . . ." she stopped for a moment, then burst out laughing. "No, that wouldn't work!"

"Unless a pirate came in. You know, one wooden leg . . ." He attempted a joke, examining an invisible dent in the counter. He likes her, I thought.

"Oh well, you never know!" she laughed again. "No seriously, thank you."

"You just lost your equipment. If I lost my camera, I'd be in pieces."

I offered her the stool I was sitting on, and she sat in my place with a whispered *cheers*.

187

"Wait! There," Logan said, fishing a pair of new, dry socks from a basket and throwing them to her. Honestly, throwing stuff! She's not radioactive . . .

"Oh, thank you! Mine are also soaking," she replied, slipping her hand in her pocket and taking out what had once been a pair of stripy socks, and was now a muddy, waterlogged ball of wool. She started putting her socks and wellies on. I really loved her nail polish. I made a mental note to buy the same, as soon as I could muster the courage to go shopping in Kinnear.

"Oh, did you take these?" the girl asked Logan, looking at the rows of framed photographs on the shop walls.

"Yep."

"You're a photographer!" she exclaimed, like she'd found another member of some secret society.

"Well, not a professional photographer . . ."

"Wow, I love this one." She had noticed my favourite picture: Glen Avich on a day that had somehow managed to be snowy and sunny at the same time, land and sky glittering like the inside of a snowball. "It's just beautiful."

"That's kind of you," my brother said bashfully. His cheeks were scarlet. "You probably see much better every day . . ."

"Don't," she smiled.

"Don't what?"

"Underestimate yourself."

Logan smiled back, embarrassed. This girl had a strange knack for reading him instantly, I thought.

"I'm Aisling, by the way."

"Aisling," he repeated, like tasting the word. "I'm Logan. And this is my sister Inary. She can't speak."

Cheers, Logan. That was pretty blunt. I smiled and held out my hand. Aisling shook it; she had a strong, warm grip.

188

I liked her.

"Nice meeting you. And thanks for these," she said, wiggling a foot and then looking straight into Logan's eyes, a smile brightening her face.

"No worries. So . . . you here for work?"

"Yes. I'm a photojournalist, taking shots of a digging site. I live in Aberdeen, but I'm originally from Dublin." My infallible instinct for accents again. "Oh, by the way, I'd love a copy of that picture . . . Are they for sale?"

"Yes . . . I use that one for display, but I should have a couple of copies done soon."

"I'll give you my number; call me when they're ready. I'll be around for a while anyway," she said with a smile to melt ice, and she walked over to the counter. I handed her my pen and a piece of paper to write her number on.

"So let me know," she said, sliding the paper towards him.

"Sure," he replied, turning around to pin the number on the corkboard over the counter.

He won't call, I thought sadly as I watched her walking out of the shop and down the street, her red wellies a splash of colour against the steel-grey pavement.

27

Love remains

Inary

I was sitting at my laptop, in a haze of sleepiness, editing another unbelievably boring book – about birds. Again. And this was worse than the first. *Wings Like Souls* was about a man who lived alone on an island for a year, to study a colony of Arctic terns. It was the chronicle of eleven months watching birds under the pouring rain (most of the time), pondering the human condition (all the time), his mental state deteriorating slowly (no wonder). In the end, he threw himself off a cliff. Quite understandable. Rowan's choices of books to publish had been so gloomy, recently – I prayed for a bit of romance, a bit of action. A bit of anything that wasn't birds.

Mary. Mary and Robert, I doodled idly in my notebook.

I hadn't seen or felt any sign of Mary since she'd whispered those words to me in the library. I missed her. It was strange how fond I'd grown of her, how much I was looking forward to her presence, even if she'd come instead of my sister. And I had no idea what could have happened. I longed to see her, and to know more of her story.

But it still felt strange, and cruel, that it should be Mary coming to me, and not my sister, given my shattering desire to see Emily again. I called to Emily every night, hoping that sooner or later she'd hear me, that sooner or later she'd return from wherever she was, even if just once, just for a moment. I had resolved not to go out and look for Emily again . . . not for a while, anyway. It was too heartbreaking, and my heart was in pieces already. Any more mangling and I'd have to do without a heart at all.

Maybe Emily was somewhere else already. I often asked myself why some spirits remained and some didn't, or only stayed for a while. Maybe because they had something left to do, something left to say. Sometimes, though, I had the overwhelming feeling that what I was seeing wasn't a ghost as such, but a memory – the memory of something that had happened. Spirits and memories were somehow subtly different in the way they presented themselves to me.

With Emily, I had neither. Her spirit was gone, and the memories were only in my heart. But still, I'd look for her until I knew for sure.

I sat at my desk and gazed out the window. The sky was clear and dotted with stars, and the view of the pine-covered hills was so lovely that I leaned my chin on my hand, letting the splendour envelop me and sink into me. I had missed this wide, endless sky so much – how had I never realised it? Alex would love the colours streaking through those clouds, purple and blue and a shade between grey and pink that has no name . . . I thought about emailing him. He hadn't written back to me, and I had so much to tell him. But maybe he'd read my email and he preferred silence . . .

I was about to switch the computer off when I registered that something was moving in the street below, and my eyes were drawn to it. It was a lonely figure, right in front of my door. It seemed to have appeared out of nowhere, out of the darkness. Logan? He'd gone to the pub; maybe he was back.

No, it was a woman. Someone visiting at – I looked at my watch – half past eleven at night?

I narrowed my eyes. A slender-framed woman hovered in front of our door for a few seconds, and then . . . she walked in.

She'd got into the house.

I jumped up and ran downstairs, wishing I could call out *Who's there?* And wondering who'd walk in without making herself known, or at least knocking; doors were nearly always unlocked in Glen Avich, but you still didn't walk into people's houses like that. My hands were shaking a little on the banister as I reached the last step, and all of a sudden, the tingling in my limbs and the low buzz in my ears began. Of course. I recognised her now – Mary.

She was taking her coat and gloves off, and her face was twisted with anguish. I stood still as she ran towards me, *through* me, and up the stairs – a sudden feeling of nausea hit me, making me heave slightly. It's difficult to explain what having somebody walk through you feels like. I turned quickly to see her running up the stairs, and then it happened again – something walked through me, and the feeling of nausea returned, though not as strong. There was somebody else. Emily?

I leaned heavily on the banister for a second, trying to get my bearings. I'd been *walked through*. Twice. Ugh. I shivered, and all of a sudden I realised I was chilled to the bone. I shook myself and followed Mary and the second spirit upstairs, taking each step slowly, as my head was still spinning. I allowed myself to hope: please, please, please, let the second spirit be Emily . . .

As I staggered onto the landing, I saw Mary disappearing into my room. I stepped in. The room was in darkness, apart from the computer screen on my desk. Mary was sitting on my bed, and the second spirit – still blurred, its features impossible to make out – was beside her.

"We'll never see her again," she whispered between her tears, as the second shape began solidifying, becoming more visible. I focused on her, looking for her mind, and finally I touched the edges of her consciousness. I felt despair, endless, icy sorrow, strong enough to make me hold my breath. At that moment I saw her, but only for a second – it was Mary's mother, the woman who looked so much like my own mum – and then they both started waning away as they cried together. Already their shapes had lost consistency, and I could see my pillows and duvet through them.

They'd nearly completely vanished, now. The prickling was gone, and so was the faint drone in my ears. My head had stopped spinning and I was steady on my feet again.

They were so full of sadness, crying like their hearts had broken – and those words, *We'll never see her again.* What were they talking about? Who were they talking about?

That night I couldn't sleep. Everything felt wrong, like my organs had swapped places with each other, like my skin once again was too tight. Emily's absence tore me apart.

I waited and hoped in vain that Mary would come back to me and keep me company, but she didn't. Where are ghosts when you need them?

I opened the curtains and lay awake, looking out of the window. There was a world of difference between Mary and me. She was so much in love with Robert, while I had closed the door to vulnerability . . .

And the message, *Find her.* Who was she talking about? And why were they crying? Who would they never see again?

I tossed and turned half the night, my mind working, working. If only I could tell Alex everything. If only I could tell him about the Sight, about Mary . . .

I kept wondering what Alex was doing. Of all the thoughts I had, there was one that I tried to silence repeatedly, but that kept coming back: I'd never felt a peace so great as when I'd been in Alex's arms. Snippets of our night together flashed before my closed eyes, each one tender, each one digging the knife further into my wounded conscience.

He'd stroked the hair off my face and placed a kiss on my eyes, my forehead, my nose, and then, finally my lips. He'd looked into my eyes and said *you're so precious to me* . . . and other memories that I can never share, memories so sweet they shattered me. I tried to convince myself they would fade, but I knew they wouldn't.

Finally, at first light, I couldn't take it any more and I got up. Five in the morning. It was going to be a long day.

To Alex.McIlvenny@hotmail.co.uk
From Inary@gmail.com

Dear Alex,
How are things with you? I haven't heard from you in a while. I'm okay. Sort of. You know, before she fell ill, Emily was making a shirt. She was so good at designing and sewing clothes . . . Remember my white dress, the one I wore to your birthday party a few months ago? She made it for me. God, was it only a few months ago? It seems a lifetime. So much has happened.

So there's this shirt, and it's unfinished. I can't bring myself to take it out of the sewing machine; it's still there, with the needle in.

The house is so empty without her. Every time I walk in front of her room, I think I can hear her voice. Her perfume is still in the air, everywhere.

I'm doing some work for Rosewood and helping Logan in the shop, but nothing really seems to hold my attention much. I don't seem to be able to write. I tried, but nothing comes out. I think I'm empty . . .

But Mary had come to me. And I needed to find out more about her, and I went to the library in Kinnear and . . .

I wished I could tell him.

But I was afraid.

. . . Anyway, better go. Speak soon?
Inary x

28

A flying thought

Alex

"So, a cold spell, you say?"

Brenda, my eldest sister, laughed. "Yes. Why are you so interested in the weather in Scotland, all of a sudden?"

"No reason. Just making conversation," I replied.

"Right. You're okay, yes?"

"Yes, of course."

"You seem worried about something." She knew me too well.

"No. I'm fine. A friend of mine is up in Aberdeen now, I was just wondering . . ."

"A friend? As in, a girl?"

"Brenda. Enough. I've got to go."

She laughed. "Fine. I'll find out anyway, you know that, don't you?"

Of course she would. And then she'd probably want to knock some sense into Inary.

I got off the phone and rested my chin on my hand, gazing at the laptop screen, email open. Inary sounded so low, and there was nothing I could do.

And then there was Sharon. My *girlfriend*. I couldn't justify speaking to Inary as much as I had done before all this. I couldn't justify it to myself. And still I did it.

To Inary@gmail.com
From Alex.McIlvenny@hotmail.co.uk

Dear Inary,
I remember that dress. It looked like it was made out of foam,
and you'd just walked out of the sea . . .

Lame. I deleted all that, and started again.

Dear Inary,
I remember that dress. Emily was so talented, and so are
you. You'll start writing again, of course. You have to be kind
to yourself and take your time. I can only imagine how you're
feeling right now . . . I wish I could take away your pain, I
really do. I wish I could help more than I do. Sorry for being
AWOL. Busy!
Alex

I agonised over adding an 'x' or not. I didn't. I pressed 'send'.

A few moments later my phone rang again – Sharon's name
flashed on the screen. I was picking it up and pressing the
phone to my ear when an email appeared in my inbox: Inary's.

"Hey . . ."

"Hey . . . How are you?"

"Good, yes. You?"

Dear Alex,
No worries. Busy is good sometimes. You help me a lot. Sure
you must know that. Your emails always make me smile; I
love hearing about Chromatica and your trips . . .

Sharon sighed. "Alex?"

"Yes. Sorry. What were you saying?"

... so where are you going next? Your life is so glamorous. All
the places you get to see ... and still, right now, I only want
to be here in Glen Avich, where I can feel closer to Emily ... I
have so much to tell you, but I need to get on with some work.
More birds, Alex! Remember what I told you about Rowan's
literary novels? Honestly, this one is torture.
Speak soon,
Inary x.

"Alex? Is it a bad time?"

"No, of course not. Sorry. You were saying about tonight ..."

"Not if you have too much on." She sounded piqued.

"Of course not. Mine or yours?"

"Come to mine. I'll cook dinner. Speak later then. I love
you ..."

"Yes. Speak later."

There was a small silence, and I realised what I had just
said. What I hadn't said. "I love you," I added quickly, feeling
sick to my stomach.

29

Separation

Inary

I sighed and forced my eyes back to the screen, trying to summon the energy to work, when my phone beeped.

I'm just outside.

It was Taylor – we were due to go for a walk in the woods. I stood up and waved at him from the window. He was leaning against his Land Rover, waiting for me. He waved back, breaking into a smile. To my surprise, I spotted Logan walking across the street towards Taylor, his camera around his neck.

I ran downstairs and stepped out under a pink sky, as soft as a hug. It had just stopped raining, and a few rays of sunshine had broken through the clouds, making everything – the trees, the street, the stony bridge – glimmer with raindrops. The air smelled of after-rain, one of my favourite scents in the world.

"Coming to take some pics of trees," Logan said as we settled into the car. "I have something on, a project with textiles for the art gallery," he explained. "Do you mind me tagging along?"

I shook my head with a smile.

Taylor switched the engine on. "So, guys. I was thinking along the shore, past the crannog?"

I felt the colour drain from my face. We'd be going very close to the loch. But then, I could just avoid the shore.

We stopped the car in a small opening, safely back from the water. I could see the still, dark loch in the distance, and the silhouette of Ailsa, the isle in the middle of it, but I was far enough not to be afraid. Taylor and I began walking slowly, breathing in the fresh air, while Logan kept stopping to take shots of leaves and roots. We were just walking past a small pebble beach when I gazed briefly to the loch shore. There was a figure on the stones. Terror gripped me for a second, but only for a second – I saw at once that it couldn't be the girl in the loch. It was a grown woman, a slender shape crowned with wavy hair. Was she a live person or a spirit? I gazed at Taylor quickly – he showed no sign of having seen her, but that didn't necessarily mean she was a ghost. Maybe he simply hadn't spotted her. I checked myself – no pins and needles, no soft hum in my ears. But it could just be because I was too far away.

I stopped and stood still. Taylor stopped too and turned around, looking at me. It was as if he could sense that something uncanny was happening.

Right at that moment, I had my answer: wet pebbles shimmered through the woman's feet, and the quiet surface of the loch blurred through her body.

I left Taylor – I couldn't have him keeping me on our side of reality, I had to stand alone – and walked a little closer. Her blue dress – her black hair in a long braid down her back – her slight shape – *Mary*, I called silently.

I stopped myself from running in case I disturbed her, and instead walked as slowly and quietly as I could, leaving Logan and Taylor behind and advancing alone. My limbs began to prickle gently and my ears started humming, as reality shifted nearly imperceptibly around me. The closer I got to her, the stronger the sensations became.

And then, all of a sudden, a wall of sadness hit me and made me swoon slightly. It was almost physical. I brought my hands to my chest and held my heart as I stood a few yards from Mary. Mary's thoughts were grey, dripping with sorrow, and my eyes filled with tears.

I could hear my brother and Taylor calling me, but I couldn't force myself to step out of my semi-trance and turn on my heels. I had to know what was happening to her. I stood immobile, my hands still clasped on my heart, staring. Mary had stepped on a flat stone at the edge of the waters. There was something in her hand.

The loch was now frighteningly near and the idea of stepping closer terrified me. But Mary was so sad . . . I wanted to touch her, I wanted to hold her. I wanted to tell her I was there. I made myself take a step, and then another, and another. The pull towards Mary was stronger than my fear of the water.

I trod softly on the grass towards the small pebble beach, my eyes fixed on her, until I stood just behind her. I extended my hand . . .

"What is she doing?" I heard Taylor calling behind me.

"She saw something. A heron, maybe," Logan replied quickly. Thanks, Logan, I hazily thought.

Slowly, as if it pained her, Mary raised a hand and let go of something – a piece of paper – a letter. Then another one, and another. One by one she let the letters go, anger betrayed by the arc of her arm, by the arch of her back, and then she threw a whole bundle in. I followed its flight with my eyes, and then it vanished at the highest point, never touching the water. When my eyes left the pile of letters and returned to Mary I saw that she was vanishing too. Her silky hair, her slender arms, her graceful frame were dissolving into the air, becoming one with the stones and the loch.

The tingling in my limbs disappeared and there was silence in my mind again, apart from the gentle lapping of the water on the pebbles. But the deep, deep sadness remained. Mary's gesture had been laden with loss. Something had happened. She had thrown the letters away, into the water – were they Robert's letters? Something told me that they were.

Suddenly, Logan was at my shoulder. He said nothing, but stood very close to me, arm to arm, and touched my hand briefly. He would not put an arm around my shoulder when someone else was there. Very Logan.

"Is it gone?" Taylor had reached us. I nodded, unable to look away from where Mary had stood. "That's too bad. It would have made a great shot for you, Logan," he said, and he sounded like he was reciting a script.

Taylor suspected something, I realised. I looked at him, eyes wide, and he held my gaze, without giving anything away.

All of a sudden I remembered how close I was to the loch. I turned around and hurried back inland, followed by my brother and Taylor.

"So, back for a beer?" called Taylor as we climbed back into the car. He kept looking at me, badly concealed concern in his eyes. I wanted to go home – I wanted to be alone and ponder what had just happened, but I didn't know what excuse I could find that wouldn't have them both worried about me.

It turned out that sitting in the pub with a dram in my hand was the best I could have done, because some of the sorrow I'd felt through Mary drained away with the warmth of the liquor.

When Logan stepped out to make a call, Taylor took his chance. "Inary . . . What happened there . . . ?" he began once Logan was out of earshot. He glanced to one side, looking for the right words.

I gazed at him, a host of lies spinning slowly in my mind – which one would I choose? I was used to lying about the Sight, I'd done it whenever I had to.

"Is it the same kind of thing that happened at the dig?"

And then my mind went blank. All excuses were gone. I just couldn't think of anything. I looked away and took another sip of my dram.

"I hope one day soon you'll tell me, Inary. Because believe me, it's *freaky*."

You're telling *me*.

★

I managed to convince Taylor and Logan that I was tired, that I needed an early night. I wanted Mary to come to me again so that I could find out what had happened. I felt in my bones that she would visit me that night.

I was right. I was reading under the duvet, my face to the wall, when I felt a weight beside me, like someone had sat on my bed. For a split second I let myself hope it was Emily, but deep down I *knew*. I turned around and there she was: Mary, sitting so close to me that my legs, bent under the blankets, nearly touched her hip. Her back was hunched as if under an enormous weight, her chin lowered into her neck. Her hands were folded on her lap, something scrunched between her fingers. Like the tide, her mind swept mine, making me gasp softly. Over the low drone in my ears, I could hear her thoughts. It was as if all her vitality and passion for life had gone, sucked away by whatever had happened. She smoothed the piece of paper and looked at it – a gentle sob escaping her lips.

Dearest Mary,

I'm sorry. I can't leave her. Anna is going to have our child – it happened before I met you, and I had no idea, but I still have to stand by them. I'm so sorry, with all that your family has gone through.

I hate myself, but I'm not strong enough to walk away.

Please forgive me,

Robert

Every word was a stone hitting her, and I could feel every blow. So that's why she'd thrown his letters away.

How sad, how cruel it was that Mary and Robert should meet just as the die was rolled, and rolled forever. Like life was mocking them, all three of them.

Poor Mary, how I wished she hadn't had to go through what I went through. And in a way, poor Robert too, what a wrench of a choice.

Still, at least he'd had a choice. Unlike Mary, who could only accept his.

Miracles

Inary

Eilidh and I had taken to meeting at La Piazza every Wednesday morning for coffee and cake. I always looked forward to my Wednesdays; Eilidh and I were the core of our meetings, but there was a constellation of women, with or without children in tow, coming and going around us. I have to confess I had the best time when I could have Eilidh all for myself.

The appearance of La Piazza had caused much excitement and, at first, a touch of diffidence. The old ladies went first – they checked and reported to friends and families. The place offered some fancy stuff, especially in its lunch menu – couscous and goat's cheese and pesto and chicken tagine – and it had all sort of coffee-based drinks like caramel espresso, mochaccino and – lo and behold – chai latte. In Glen Avich, yes. But it also served the basics, like tea, scones and toasted teacakes, and the Old Ladies test was passed with flying colours. The rest of the Glen Avich citizens followed suit and were immediately charmed by the lovely Debora, a Scots-Italian woman with black eyes and endless energy.

"Wonder what potpourri they have today," Eilidh whispered, leaning towards me.

Potpourri? I raised my eyebrows.

"Yep. Have you not noticed? Debora changes the potpourri

in the bathroom every week. On rotation. Lavender, peach, berries, rose, lemon . . . Let's bet on what it is this week. What shall we bet . . . a cream cake, Sorley? Deal?" She shook Sorley's wee hand playfully, and he squealed in delight from his high chair.

Lavender, I wrote.

"Okay. I say peach. Sorley?" Sorley said something between *don* and *won*, which we took as lemon.

"Right. Lavender, peach or lemon. If it's none of these . . ."

"Da!" yelped Sorley.

"He means we'll have a cream cake anyway. Good man. I'm going in . . ." And she disappeared into the bathroom, under Sorley's watchful eye.

"*Mna?*" he asked. I smiled and stroked his arm, which was my wordless attempt to say *Mummy will be back in a second, but in the meantime, you're safe with me.* He smiled back – he'd believed me, and for a moment my heart was made of melted chocolate.

"Inary, dear . . ." It was Maggie and Liz, Aunt Mhairi's friends.

"How are you?" said Liz.

Fine, I mouthed and smiled.

"Still no voice. Poor dear. And who's this lovely baby?" she replied.

"It couldn't have been the water already!" laughed Maggie, with Liz joining in mirthfully. I was dumbfounded, then I remembered. The water from St Colman's well. They thought I should try drinking it to sort out my voice. I felt cold, thinking that Sorley could be mistaken for mine, even in jest. Don't get me wrong, he was the loveliest baby, but I was miles and miles away from being ready to be a mother.

Eilidh McCrimmon's son, I wrote.

"What's that?" said Liz, squinting. "I don't have my glasses."

"Wait a minute . . ." Maggie rummaged in her handbag and took out a small zipped case. She slipped her glasses on. "Eilidh Mc . . . oh yes. It's Eilidh McCrimmon's son," she explained to her friend. "Of course you are! I didn't recognise you there, without your mummy. Hello, cheeky toes! Cheeky *cheeky* toes!"

"Aaaaw, he's gorgeous! You *really* should try the water, Inary . . ." whispered Liz.

"Absolutely. You might have some nice side effect!" laughed Maggie. "If you have a young man, of course. How old are you, dear?"

Nearly 26, I wrote and prayed silently they'd let it be.

"Twenty six! At your age I had all my three daughters!"

"And I'd been married for years!"

I shuddered inside.

But then, maybe, it was a good plan. The miraculous water of St Colman's well would cure me *and* give me a baby, then we could put my story on Facebook and market Glen Avich as a place of miracles.

"Or go see Father McCroury. He'll bless your throat," said Maggie solemnly. I felt my lips curling up before I could stop myself. "You can laugh if you want, young lady, but that's how my husband was cured when he had gallstones. A blessing."

"And Isobel, remember?" Liz reiterated. "Oh, Isobel was terrible with her joint problems. *Joint problems*," she repeated and nodded to emphasise her point. "She got a blessing from Father Sartori up in Kinnear, and it was all gone."

"Gone. Like they'd never been there," Maggie echoed.

I smiled in a manner that I hoped looked grateful more

than amused. They meant well. My grandmother believed in the miraculous powers of blessings and holy water, after all. Maybe it was all in the mind.

"Anyway, my dear. Hopefully they won't have run out of scones. They always do, on a Wednesday," said Liz eyeing the counter.

"It's the old folk from the sheltered flats. They take them down early on a Wednesday now. They're like locusts with their scones," Maggie whispered.

"*Locusts!*" echoed Liz.

"Lemon! Sorley wins!" Eilidh was back. "Oh hello," she said to Maggie and Liz.

"Hello my dear. What a lovely boy you have! And how's Jamie's daughter . . . ?"

"Maisie. She's great, thank you."

"You have two great children there, Eilidh," said Maggie with real, heartfelt kindness.

"I do. Thank you."

There was a flurry of "take care my dear", and "look after yourself, love", and they went to sit at the table by the window, with one last whisper from Liz: *try the water!*

"What are they on about?" murmured Eilidh.

They think the water from the well can cure me.

"Right. I thought it was only supposed to make you pregnant? I always suspected Peggy slipped some in my tea, because Sorley truly was a miracle. Anyway! The boy gets the cream cake. Oh yes you do!" She tickled Sorley's little feet and he giggled.

"Ready to order, girls?" it was Debora, chirpy as always. We managed to secure two muffins and a cream cake – the sheltered houses' locusts had left that much.

"Mum!" A little girl's voice resounded from behind us. I turned around to see that Peggy had come in with Maisie. Eilidh's face lit up and opened into a smile in seeing them. Eilidh had mentioned to me how much it pleased her that Maisie had taken to doing that. When I was in London I'd seen Janet Heath, Maisie's birth mother, in the papers and on posters all over the place. Alex was a fan of her work, but not so much of her as a person, after I told him how she'd left Maisie and severed all contact with her. I was so glad to see Maisie and Eilidh so close, so happy – they both deserved it. I watched her slipping an arm around Maisie's waist, Sorley on her knee, so contented in her little family, and I wondered what the future held for me.

31

Rivers of time

Inary

"You ready?"

I nodded. Taylor opened the car door for me. It was a cold Thursday, a throwback to winter, and I was all wrapped up in a scarf and a red beret.

"What are we looking for today?"

I grabbed my notebook. *Marriage records.*

"Right. We need to find out who Mary Gibson was married to?"

Yes. Thanks for doing this, Taylor.

"No problem. I can't think of a better way to spend my free time than sitting in a library."

I laughed, and he looked at me, surprised. "I'm not joking. I'm an archaeologist, remember? We love this kind of thing."

As we drove, I stole a glimpse of his profile. He was squinting in the winter sunlight, his hair golden, a hint of freckles on his nose . . . and beyond him, the infinite shades of browns and purples of the landscape darting to each side of us. My heart tightened all of a sudden, and I wasn't sure why – what thought, what memory had just hurt me, like a jab in my side? Oh, yes, of course. The colours. Alex. I wondered what he was doing, if his life had kept going, while mine seemed to have halted. On replay, like a groundhog day. Suspended.

Lucy was very happy to see us. Okay, she was very happy to see Taylor. She showed us into the archives room again and wished us luck. We needed it, because three hours later we were still scouring documents. The marriage records for Glen Avich, for some reason, were grouped together with ones from Kilronan and Kinnear – that made *a lot* of documents.

"Tea and a scone?" Lucy peeked in.

"Let me guess. Your mum made them?" said Taylor.

Lucy blushed and giggled. "She did, yes! Good day for you to come."

On you go, I'm good, I wrote.

"Won't be a minute," said Taylor, following Lucy next door.

Left alone, I sat back into my chair and sighed. I knew I was becoming obsessed with Mary and her story, but it was something to distract me from the constant ache in my heart. And I couldn't help thinking that I was meant to find out more about her.

After a few minutes, Taylor walked back in with a cup of tea and a scone. I made an inquisitive face, remembering the librarian's words on our first day: food and drink were not permitted in the Heritage room.

"She likes me," he whispered. "So she let me bring this in for you."

I smiled and dug in.

"Wait, Inary. Is that not . . ." Taylor pointed at the screen. "Look, Mary Gibson . . ."

I sat up, alert. There had been a few false alarms – apparently Mary Gibson was a common name–surname combination at the time . . .

"Mary Gibson, born 1 October 1895 . . . that's her!"

I nodded frantically and scrolled down. Married to Alan Monteith . . . Monteith, my own name! But . . . Alan? Not Robert?

211

"High five!" He offered me his open palm. I slapped it with mine, laughing. He was so . . . American, at times, in an expansive, funny way. He always dragged a smile out of me. "Looks like you're related. Of course," he said, "you're related to everyone! I'm surprised that you don't have three legs and one eye in the middle of your forehead . . ." I couldn't help laughing. He had a point – everybody was related around here. Thank goodness for newcomers . . .

I nodded, taking note of the document. The excitement of the find was beginning to wear down as it was sinking in: Mary and Robert hadn't married, in the end. Robert broke up with Mary for good. He must have married Anna, the beautiful woman from my vision, and Mary married Alan Monteith.

"Are we finished here?"

I nodded, feeling a bit deflated.

"Thanks for this, Lucy," he said to the young librarian and actually winked. He *winked*. I rolled my eyes, but I thought it was funny.

"Oh, you're going already? When will I see you again? I mean, is there anything else I can do . . . ?"

"I'm sure we'll be back," said Taylor.

"I'll see you again, then," Lucy replied. Subtle.

There had been no happy ending for Mary and Robert, then. She'd given him her soul, like I'd given mine to Lewis. And when they went, there was nothing left of us, nothing but a little spark, threatening to be extinguished any second. Gone was the strength and the joy and the hope of happiness.

You shouldn't have loved him as much as you did, Mary. This is what happens when you love too much, when you love at all, I thought sadly.

212

32

In search of a heart

Alex

Everything was going great. And then she mentioned Scotland.

Sharon and I had spent the day in Hyde Park, and then we'd gone back to mine; she'd cooked some mezze for me, and we put music on, and it was all good . . . until she asked me when I planned to go home next.

The vision of a city with a volcano in the middle and a stony castle on top of it appeared in front of my eyes. And more: windy hills and moors and heavy skies and endless beaches – home.

And in a weird way, home was Inary.

The spell was broken. I was distracted for the rest of the night – I could see the worry in Sharon's face, and I hated myself for causing her pain. Was I stringing her along, had Inary been stringing *me* along, both of us unwittingly? Was this some sort of misery dance, where each one of us was bound to one another in a set choreography, and each one of us was destined to get hurt?

It was just typical that after having spent the whole evening with Sharon, it had to be Inary who came to me in my dreams. I dreamt of an afternoon we'd spent in Regent's Park, at the open-air theatre. I was still at the stage where I thought there could be something between us, before I realised how determined she was to keep our bond within the realms of friendship. Or within the realms of torture, depending on the point of view.

In my dream, every detail came back to me like it had happened yesterday. She was sitting beside me, reading the programme, an aqua-coloured cardigan folded on her lap and auburn tendrils wrapped around her ears like seaweed around a shell. She was wearing a short flowery dress in the tones of green, teal and blue, to bring out the startling, pure blue of her eyes. The setting sun shone on her hair, making it shimmer copper and gold. In my dream I could even smell her scent, sun cream and something flowery, like her dress. Her presence beside me – tenderness and excitement and the promise of soft skin – and the dreamy scenes of *A Midsummer Night's Dream* melted together, and by the time it was finished I was in a dream too.

And then the dream turned strange. Inary touched my face and leaned in to kiss me – but in the fraction of a second before our lips met she began to vanish, like a vision. Like the fantasy she'd always been.

Beside me there was an empty plastic chair, the programme bent and muddy at my feet, and no sign of Inary.

She was gone.

This was our reality now, whether I liked it or not. Inary was away on the other side of the country, miles and miles away from me. We'd been blown apart – no, wait. We were never together.

33

Colliding

Inary

I opened my eyes in full light – strange for me, I usually woke up a lot earlier than that. The dream had been so real, so powerful.

I hadn't thought of that night in a long time: the night Alex and I went to see *A Midsummer Night's Dream*. That night at the theatre I was unaware of just about everything but the fact that it had been my birthday the day before and Lewis hadn't called. I didn't *want* him to call, but it was surreal. It seemed impossible that I would not speak to him on my birthday. Or ever again.

Like I had woken up in a nightmare.

In the days leading up to that birthday I'd been frantically active, unable to stop – work, shopping, exercise classes I hated, clubbing – anything but being alone and thinking about what a mess my life was. I was exhausted, and my activity overload hadn't had the effect I'd hoped anyway – my mind was still working constantly, taking me to lonely, wintry places. So I welcomed Alex's invitation to spend yet another night out of the house, trying to distract myself. Alex's presence calmed me. Even just hearing his voice relaxed me, gave me respite from the chaos of my emotions. Apparently, he had the same effect on a lot of people.

It was a peaceful evening. I nearly felt happy again for a few moments – not quite, but nearly. After the play we went for an evening walk, eating chips from a newspaper cone – we laughed about being able to read the paper on our fish. When he took me home and left me on the doorstep I remember feeling truly bereft. I wanted him to come in with me and help me forget, but I stopped myself. And I should have stopped myself that *other* time, too.

In my dream I relived the whole night, still frame after still frame of calm companionship and easy joy.

When I woke up I expected to see the lilac walls of my London room, and to hear the low noise of traffic through the window. It took me a few seconds to realise I wasn't in London, but in my Glen Avich home, and Alex was so, so far away.

34

Headland

Inary

I made a little calendar with the days left to Lesley's arrival –
and every morning I crossed one day off. I just couldn't wait.
Finally, the day was here, and she had sent me a text to say she
was only an hour away.

When I saw Lesley's car appear at the bottom of the street
– I'd been checking at the window every ten minutes since
she'd texted me – I ran downstairs and started waving like a
windmill. She didn't even have time to get completely out of
the car before I was holding her tight, breathing in the sweet
vanilla scent that was her signature.

"I missed you!" she said, as we did a little hug-dance in the
street. "Let me look at you." She held me at arm's length, her
hands on my shoulders. "You've lost weight . . ."

I need a curry of yours, I wanted to say, but I couldn't. *I'm
fine*, I mouthed instead. Her eyes grew sad all of a sudden. Yes,
still not talking, I'm afraid. She knew about that, of course, but
I could imagine how it was still a shock for her to see it with
her own eyes.

Don't worry, I mouthed. But I knew she wouldn't be
reassured.

"Oh, Inary . . ." she said and hugged me again. I smiled and shrugged, trying to pretend that it was fine, that I'd got used to it.

We carried her luggage inside – two suitcases for a weekend! That was the Lesley I knew and loved. I gave her the present I'd prepared for her – a necklace made by Jamie McAnena – and she ooohed and aaahed over it just like I'd hoped. Then she took out something from her bag. "For you," she said, and handed me a gift wrapped in red polka dot tissue paper and tied with white ribbon. I opened it carefully, minding not to rip the lovely paper. It was a teddy bear dressed like a Queen's Guard, tall hat, red uniform and all.

"To remind you of your home in London," she said, and we both had tears in our eyes. And there were more tears to come, because I had to give her something too.

I took Lesley's hand and led her into Emily's room. I opened the little drawer at the side of her bed and I took out her bright-green iPod. I handed it to Lesley.

"Is this . . . was this Emily's?" she asked, taking it gently from my hand.

I leaned on Emily's desk to write. *It's all her music. She said that you should have it.*

Lesley brought her hand to her mouth, choked.

"Thank you," she said finally. "I'll treasure it."

★

Half an hour later we were at the Green Hat in front of two vodka oranges.

"So what's the story with your voice?" Her forehead creased in a frown.

I shrugged and looked down. I hated to see her so worried

for me. And I was afraid she'd try and convince me to go to the doctor again. I wasn't ready to do that. Not yet.

"God, what do you do for trauma? Therapy? Anti-depressants?"

I shook my head. *Time*, I wrote.

"Honey, it's been three months . . ." A pause, then a sharp intake of breath. "You're not coming back to London, are you?"

Oh. I wasn't expecting that question. *I don't know. Logan is on his own. Haven't resigned from my job yet. If I do stay, I'll give you notice, for the flat I mean.*

"Don't worry about that. I understand." There was another moment of silence, and then: "Is that the one Alex sent you?" she asked, pointing at my notebook.

I smiled. *Yes.*

"I spoke to him yesterday."

I just didn't know what to say to that. *Did he know you were coming to see me?*

"Yes. But he didn't say anything."

Oh.

"By the way . . . I think he's seeing someone. I'm not sure, though . . ."

I blinked once, twice. A firework of confusion exploded in my head, so that I couldn't make out what Lesley said next.

Sorry, what did you say?

"I said I think Alex is seeing someone. This girl at work, Sharon. I'm not a hundred per cent sure they're together as such, but I saw them together recently and there was definitely something there. Probably just as well, Inary. You couldn't keep toing and froing, the two of you."

The fireworks kept going off, and I desperately tried to

219

silence them before Lesley noticed. I was furious at myself for feeling that way. I'd refused a relationship with Alex. He was free to see whoever he wanted. Actually, it was supposed to be a relief for me. I was trying to put distance between us, wasn't I? Alex had to be celibate forever and keep pining, otherwise I'd get upset. Selfish and completely absurd.

So good to have you here, I wrote, trying to smile back. Like everything was good. Like I *really* didn't have feelings about Alex at all, secret or otherwise.

★

We all went out to Kinnear together, Lesley, Logan, Taylor and I. My head was somewhere else. I couldn't help it. I kept thinking of Alex seeing . . . *that girl*. I couldn't bring myself to say her name.

"I got a call from Lucy earlier," said Taylor as we were left alone for a minute.

Who? I mouthed.

"Lucy, the librarian, remember?"

I smiled. *So you gave her your phone number! Smooth*, I wrote on my notebook. Clearly my rejection had left him heartbroken . . .

"Not like that! I mean, not as such. She said in case she found out something else that might interest us . . ."

And what did she find out? I wrote, suddenly alert.

"She told me there's somewhere else we can look for information."

I nodded, encouraging him to continue.

"Do you know the Ramsays, from Glen Avich?"

Oh yes. They're cousins of mine. On my mother's side.

Taylor laughed. "Of course! I should have guessed! Well, apparently Lord Ramsay is a patron of the library. Lucy did some work for them in her own time, cataloguing stuff. She said they're big into local history . . ."

Lord Ramsay . . . Torcuil, I mean . . . was at Emily's funeral. I have his number, I wrote, taking out my phone.

"Do you want me to phone him?"

Would you mind?

"No problem. Give me your phone . . ."

Ten minutes later, he stepped back into the club. "Torcuil is in London right now, but he will get in touch when he's back," he smiled. "By the way, Lucy said, for your voice . . . have you tried anchovies?"

★

Later, Lesley and I sneaked out to get chips from the Golden Palace. We ate them sitting in the St Colman gardens, just the two of us. It would have been perfect, had my mind not insisted on going back to Alex every two minutes. I had a horrible suspicion I'd met that girl once. Horrible, because if she was the girl I remembered, tall and dark with silky hair that fell in waves across her shoulders, she was beautiful.

I'd messed up, hadn't I?

"You know, the flat is just empty without you, Inary . . ." Lesley said.

Empty without my mess, you mean! I wrote, laughing, leaving a tiny mark of chip grease on the page. I realised that that notebook held the whole story of the last three months – each word, each stain, each mark, held a memory. My whole life in a notebook, its pages battered, its leather cover scratched, stains of tea and grass and make-up, telling the story of my days.

Lesley sighed. "I'd take the mess any day, to have you back."

35

It will be soon

Inary

"I'd love to come up this summer, maybe with Kamau . . . You won't be able to get rid of me!" Lesley's smile had a touch of sadness to it. Again there would be nearly the whole of Britain between us.

You know you'll always be my best friend anyway. Distance doesn't matter, I wrote, then took her hands in mine, negotiating our muffins and cappuccinos.

"When I'm rich and famous I'm going to buy a holiday home here. No, seriously! Scotland is amazing. Alex always said he wasn't planning on coming back to Scotland to live, ever again . . ." I looked down. ". . . but weirdly enough, a while ago he told me just the opposite. That he missed Scotland. He missed being near his family."

My heart skipped a beat.

"He said he'd looked up the exact distance between Glen Avich and London: five hundred and twenty-three miles."

Oh, I mouthed. *What else did he say?*

"That it was an awful long way."

I'm sure Sharon will fill the void, I wrote, a bitter taste in my mouth.

"Maybe. Hey, Inary, give the guy a break. You said you only wanted to be friends. He's trying to move on. Sorry, don't

223

mean to stir things up. Just, Alex is trying to deal with things too."

I nodded. She was right.

Lesley gave me a hug. "Anyway, enough about *boys*. I never asked you about your writing! How is Cassandra?"

Cassandra is no more. Deleted.

"Seriously? That's a shame!"

No it isn't.

"So . . . you taking a break from writing? I mean, with all you've been through . . ."

Yes. A sort of break. Maybe indefinitely.

"Oh, no . . . Honey, that's a waste! You've got to write. Promise me you will . . ."

I don't know.

"Promise you won't give up," she repeated. "You have to make your dream come true."

At that moment, the softest hint of a tingle filled my limbs, and I felt like I'd just put my ear to a shell, because I could hear a low whisper, like waves breaking on a shore far away.

Emily.

Lesley's words had echoed Emily's: you have to make your dream come true.

"So, she's away," Logan said to me as I stepped into the shop.

I nodded.

"I'm sorry."

I glanced at him. He was busy over a pile of invoices, so I thought the conversation was over. I began tidying up the cycling accessories, half-heartedly. For three years Lesley had been the first person I said hello to in the morning and the last person I saw at night. We'd shared toothpaste, three break-ups (one mine, two Lesley's) takeaways and hours of TV dramas on our living-room sofa with a tub of Häagen-Dazs between us. She cooked for me, I proofread her press releases; she kept me awake telling me all about her latest crush, I inflicted on her my out-of-tune singing in the shower; she let me lean my head on her shoulder whenever bad news about Emily had broken me, I went with her to the hospital when her dad needed an urgent operation. And now, once more, a whole nation stretched between us.

"Do you miss your life in London?" Logan said, mock casually.

Oh, I see. We were having The Talk. The one I'd seen coming for a while. Whether or not I was going to stay in Glen Avich for good. This required some more than nodding or shrugging. God, this not-talking thing was taking its toll.

Yes, I suppose I do.

"So when are you going back?" His tone was harsh, but there was a note of vulnerability in his voice.

I don't know if I am. Alex seeing Sharon wouldn't be a strong enough reason to uproot myself again – but it did sway me . . .

"Right. Inary, listen." Logan looked straight into my eyes. "You must do what's best for you. If you want to go . . ."

Was it really Logan speaking? How things have changed.

For a moment I hesitated – but from over Logan's shoulder I could see the Glen Avich hills framed in the window, a shroud of soft mist veiling them. Holding their breath, just before fully falling into spring . . .

I don't want to go, I wrote, and then looked at the page in amazement. It was true. I didn't want to go. I didn't want to go away from Glen Avich, and I didn't want to leave my brother.

"Oh. Okay then. I suppose I'll have to put up with you,"

225

he said abruptly, and walked off to sort out something in the stock cupboard. But before he turned away, I noticed the look of relief on his face.

I smiled, a smile of genuine joy.

Decision made.

It's my turn to look after you, Logan, like you always looked after us, I thought. But I didn't write it down. Some things would never be put in words.

Dear Alex,

Lesley was here. She told me about Sharon.
Just to say, I wish you happiness.

Inary x

I switched my laptop off, and my phone too. They would stay that way for a while, until I was ready to face this new world, the world where Alex had a girlfriend and I'd messed it all up.

36

523 miles

Alex

Sharon's skin looked even darker against the white sheets, and her sleeping form was as inviting as warm water. She loved sleeping late at the weekend, while I was always up early. Inary was a lark too. Sometimes we'd get together with Lesley to have a Chinese and watch a DVD, and Inary was asleep on the couch by ten.

There. She'd come into my thoughts twice already, and it was barely nine o' clock. No doubt there would be more thoughts of Inary when I'd make breakfast in bed for Sharon – granola and yoghurt. Inary hated granola, she loved a bacon sandwich on a Saturday morning. Then it would be time to go to feed the ducks in Hyde Park, and Sharon would take an hour to get ready – Inary brushed her hair and she was ready; she never wore make-up, except for a night out. And so on, and so forth, and so totally and completely wrong.

"Hello . . ." Sharon was resting her head on her hand, and was looking at me. "Been awake long?"

"No . . . just an hour or so," I said, and I sat on the bed to give her a kiss. Thank God thoughts are silent and they don't hang over our heads in big speech balloons.

Hyde Park was beautiful, sun rays dancing in the trees and happy people everywhere, on bikes, lying on blankets, playing with frisbees and feet. Spring had come to London, at last. Scotland was over its cold snap, but still a bit chilly, my sister told me – there was no way that Inary would wear her summer dresses, yet ... But I had to concentrate on there and then. Sharon had slipped her hand into mine, and her deep, musky perfume was in the breeze around me.

We strolled on the grass and then sat to eat the picnic we'd prepared. Sharon had made some tiny apple tarts, fragrant with cinnamon. The last time Inary had made a cake, it could have bounced off the floor – I grinned at the recollection. Weird thing was, she never gave up: she kept cooking, disaster after disaster. I remembered eating plastic roast beef and burnt potatoes just to make her happy. I loved her spag bol. Or spag bog, like Lesley called it. It was terrible, but it tasted of home, somehow.

Sharon was breaking bits of a slice of bread and throwing them to the ducks. I shook myself from my thoughts and imitated her. Except I'd been so distracted, I kept the slice of bread and threw the loaf instead, plastic wrapping and all. It hit a duck on the bum and there was a flurry of feathered panic.

"Oh God! I'm sorry!"

"Oh no, Alex ... poor duck!" said Sharon, but she laughed, and her whole face lit up. She really was beautiful. My stomach knotted up, because in the middle of all this, right in the middle of mine and Inary's mess, was a woman who had showed me nothing but kindness. A generous, sweet, funny woman who did not deserve to be my rebound girlfriend.

"Sharon ..."

"Yes?" she replied. Her face fell when she saw mine. "Is everything okay?"

"It's just that . . ."

Her eyes clouded over, mirroring my solemn expression. I couldn't bear it.

I couldn't bear to spread more hurt, like there hadn't been enough of that already.

"It's just that I was hoping you'd stay tonight as well. At mine, I mean."

"Sure," she smiled, all the worry melting away from her face.

I hated myself. Inary had hurt me, but she'd done so unwittingly; she'd never asked for me to be in love with her. Instead, I was hurting Sharon while knowing very well what I was doing.

★

On the way home, in passing, I checked my email. There was something from Inary. My breath caught as I read her words . . .

She knew about Sharon.

Of course, she was bound to find out sooner or later. I should have told her.

I should have told her because I had nothing to hide, did I?

Rage bit me suddenly, unexpectedly – because of her tone, *betrayed*, as if I'd done something wrong, as if I'd broken a bond between us. When she'd been the one keeping me at arm's length, sleeping with me and then saying it was a mistake, telling me we could only be friends.

But I still wasn't allowed to see anyone.

"Don't tell me you're working . . ." Sharon's voice interrupted my thoughts.

"Sorry. I'll switch off, now." And I did. I switched the phone off and resolved, in my red-hot anger, not to deign to reply.

But later that night, of course, I gave in.

From Alex.McIlvenny@hotmail.co.uk
To Inary@gmail.com

Inary,

It was three in the morning and I couldn't sleep. All the things I wanted to say to Inary whirled in my head, and I couldn't silence them. They had to come out of me.

You and I are not together, are we? You don't want us to be together properly. You've had three years to think about it.
Yes, I'm seeing Sharon. I couldn't keep playing your game.
I'm so sorry for all that happened and I swear to God if I could make it better for you, if I could help you . . . if you'd allow me to be there for you . . .
You push me away. And then you look for me and I always answer. I'm sorry, but this can't keep happening. But don't act all offended if I'm seeing someone who's not you.
Of course we can be friends. It's up to you. But I won't stop seeing Sharon to keep having this weird thing with you where we both end up alone.
Alex

37

Rapture

Inary

I'd been in Glen Avich for nearly four months. Spring was there at last, and with it came change. I could feel my life moving forward, every part of my heart and soul wrapping themselves around new possibilities. Everything was shifting, as inevitably as the drift of continents over the ocean. But two things stayed the same: Emily's absence burnt as sore as the day she died, and my voice showed no sign of returning. Writing what I needed to say, or miming it, had become second nature.

Maybe silence didn't feel that bad after all. I was strangely comfortable in my bubble, even if it made the simplest things more complicated.

And there was something that made me fearful of my voice returning. My voice had gone just when my Sight had come back, like one sense had been swapped for the other. What if when I regained my voice, the Sight went away again? Before I could see Emily?

I couldn't risk it. Even with everybody insisting I should go back to Dr Nicholson, I would bide my time and keep my silence. I had become a secret person, whose thoughts and feelings couldn't just be blurted out – they had to be translated, taken out of my throat with pen and paper, carried into the

231

world with time and effort. If you have to write everything you need to say, you'll end up omitting most of what you would have just spoken without thinking. What used to be on the surface had burrowed deeper, and as I sunk into my world of silence, so many things started getting clearer and clearer. Lies and illusions began to melt as I got slowly closer to my core, closer to the essence of me.

A secret and silent person. Not someone I'd ever thought I would be, but it suited me. After all the pain of Emily's loss, it was impossible to still be frightened. I might have filled a river with my tears, but sooner or later rivers flow into the sea, and what hurt, what cut you to the bone, becomes a memory.

I was editing when Mary came to me next. It was early afternoon, and the noise and movement of life were all around me – Mary's presence melted with the present seamlessly. There were children playing football outside; the occasional car driving up St Colman's Way; the soft noise of the radio seeping from downstairs; and Mary, sitting at my dressing table. She was at the centre of my perception, stronger and more real than anything else. Calm, silent tears were rolling down her cheeks – there was no more anger in her devastation, like there had been when she'd thrown Robert's letters into the loch. She was resigned.

The words she wrote resounded in my mind as clear as if she'd spoken them.

Dear Robert,
I thought you might want to know that I'm getting married. He's a kind man and he loves me, and nothing else matters. I suppose we'll never know what could have been, we'll never know if you

and I would have been happy. But after all, does anyone know?

I was on the loch the other day – the sky was perfect blue and the sun was shining, and then, all of a sudden, black clouds came over me and the heavens opened. It was so sudden, so harsh a contrast between before and after, it made me think of us. We were together; you were my life. Then all of a sudden you were gone.

Like the sky goes from sunny to stormy in the space of half an hour, joy turns to sadness so quickly – but the opposite happens too. There was no written path for us, Robert, life would have been what we made of it.

I often wonder about the life we would've had. After what happened to my family, after what happened with you, I often feel like I'm broken and I'll never be whole again. It looked as if I had nothing to lose, while your whole life was at stake. But that's not true. I could drown – and I did. And I think I should stop now, in case I say too much.

I wish you all happiness and joy and a long, peaceful life with Anna. Please give her my love, whether she accepts it or not. She must be due soon. I hope it won't be long before Alan and I have good news soon too – I am sure it's the only way to bring some joy back into my life. And I do hope that life has some happiness in store for me, even if it seems impossible now, that today's tears will be just a memory. I hope the years will take my pain away. But I can promise you something: I'll keep you in my heart forever, whether you like it or not. Whatever happens, you will not fade from me.

I see no reason to write more: it's just words and more words, isn't it? And we've had so many. Just one thing. Robert, if you turn you and me into a poem, make it a happy one. Make it about you and me that day on the loch shore, in May, remember? No more sadness.

Listen to the words unspoken and you'll know how I would sign
myself, if I could. But all I'm allowed to say right now, is
I wish you much happiness,
Mary

When she went, every ounce of strength left me and I fell to my knees on the wooden floor, drained. Her state of mind had left me grey, listless. There was no hope left for Mary and Robert.

Or for Alex and me.

Except Mary hadn't deserved it; she hadn't done anything to bring all this sorrow onto herself. But I had, by lying about my feelings for so long, to Alex, to everyone and, most of all, to myself.

For the first time in days, I switched on my laptop and my phone . . . Among the dozens of emails I'd accumulated, there was the one I wasn't expecting. From Alex.

. . . You push me away. And then you look for me and I always answer. I'm sorry, but this can't keep happening. But don't act all offended if I'm seeing someone who's not you.

Even though his words stung, he was right.

I wondered if it was serious between him and Sharon, or if he was simply in *lust* (the thought killed me) or if he was doing it out of spite after what I'd done to him.

Or if he was in love. *That* was the most painful scenario: that he was in love with her. That he'd look at her like he'd looked at me, the night we slept together.

It hurt. Suddenly, I was angry.

Alex,
I know I messed up. I'm sorry. But it didn't take you long to find someone!

I pressed 'send', my chest heaving with rage. Why was I furious with him? He didn't deserve it. Maybe I was furious with myself.

I sat staring at the screen, hoping he'd be there – and he was.

I can't speak like this. Switch on your Skype.

As soon as I logged on to Skype, an instant message came through.

It didn't take me long? Three years, Inary. Three years!

To my dismay, I felt a tear trickling down my cheek, and I hated myself for it. It was exactly the kind of situation I'd fought so hard to avoid – to be involved again, to be hurt again.

I can't explain why I am this way. I have no words to tell you why every time I get close to you, I run away.

I typed. I felt the truth welling up in my heart, threatening to overspill into my fingers. I wanted to tell him. I wanted to tell him everything . . .

Alex: Find the bloody words, for God's sake! You're a writer!

Me: Right. Fine. You want to know what really happened? Lewis left me because he thought I was a freak. And maybe I am.

Alex: ?

Me: What if I told you that I see ghosts?

Alex: What?

Me: Alex, I see ghosts.

Alex: ~What?~

I took a deep breath. I would have given anything to be able to speak.

Me: Have you seen *The Sixth Sense*? Well, my life is a bit like that. Only less scary (mostly). I actually see dead people, excuse the cliché. My granny was the same. It runs in my family. It really is like a sixth sense . . . it feels normal when you're born this way. It started when I was six, but then stopped when I was twelve years old because I got a huge fright, and the trauma took the Sight away. A bit like losing Emily took my voice away. Anyway, I told Lewis and he thought I was crazy. I think that scared him enough to break up with me. I don't know for sure, but I think that's what really pushed him, in the end. No one else knows except my family. And now my voice has gone but the Sight is back. I was hoping to see Emily. I looked for her everywhere, but I couldn't find her. So this is it. Now you'll think I'm crazy.

Long, long minutes I waited for his reply. He was probably in shock.

Alex: You're pulling my leg.

My heart sank. He thought it was a bloody joke.

Me: No, I'm not.

Alex: Is this for real?

Me: Afraid so.

Alex: So this is the gift you told me about, the gift Lewis couldn't accept?

Me: It was, yes.

A pause. I could see he was typing, but nothing was coming through, as if he were writing then deleting message after message.

I'd done it. I'd told him about the Sight. The enormity of it was making my heart pound in my chest, in a mixture of terror and relief . . .

Finally, I saw that he was calling me on Skype. But why? He knew I couldn't speak. I took the call, and seeing his face on the screen made my heart skip a beat. There he was: Alex. My Alex. His black hair was standing up in tufts, in a sweet end-of-the-working-day kind of way. He was wearing a shirt, opened at the collar. In the background, I could see the familiar scene of his living room – the fireplace, the photographs of his nieces and nephews on the mantelpiece . . . My gaze went back to him, and as our eyes met, he smiled. Alex had this thing, that when he smiled his eyes wrinkled up and he looked so young, like a happy child. I wanted to smile back, but I was too anxious.

"Hello," he said, and I waved. Suddenly I remembered that he could see me too, and my hands went to my hair, self-consciously. I probably looked like something a cat had dragged through a bush.

"You look lovely," he said, and the hint of a smile finally curled my lips. "I have something to tell you."

I nodded. I couldn't do much else.

He lifted up a piece of paper, with a few words scribbled on it in red Pantone: *You're even more amazing than I thought.*

Hope soared out of me like a balloon floating to the sky.

I clasped my hands over my mouth. He believed me. He understood. He didn't think I was Satan's daughter or mentally ill and hallucinating.

A pang of longing swept through me.

I missed him so much.

I loved him.

Oh, God.

That was the first time ever that I'd admitted, even to myself, that my feelings for Alex weren't as clear-cut as I always pretended them to be. Which was probably something everyone knew, but me. I'd pushed him away because of my fear of getting hurt, but I was stronger now. Maybe I would be given another chance. Was it too late?

I hastily looked for my notebook and wrote: *I can't wait to tell you everything! About this one ghost, Mary ... and about all that's been happening.* I lifted the notebook up against the webcam.

"I can't wait to hear it. Anyway, I suppose it makes sense, for us to be friends ... with all we've been through."

What? How could we be friends? *I love you*, I wanted to say, but it just seemed impossible to write down something like that. I nodded, waiting with bated breath for what would come next . . .

"I don't want to lose you, Inary. I mean, with me seeing Sharon and all that . . ."

Oh. My stomach sank all the way into my ankles. I felt sick with disappointment.

Yes, I wrote simply, and lifted the notebook up.

"Great," he said, and my heart broke. "Now tell me all about Mary . . ."

Email, I wrote. He nodded and we both switched Skype off.

Instantly, I felt the tears that had been gathering behind my eyes start to spill. I'd tried so hard while we were talking to keep them in because I hadn't wanted him to see me crying.

I told him everything, about what happened that day on the loch, thirteen years before, about Mary, about my research. I was so relieved at his reaction, so touched that he should believe me, and understand me . . . but I sobbed throughout.

We were to be friends.

Maybe he loved her.

I'd had my answer, then. Like I'd feared, it was too late.

38

To see her face

Inary

A few days later, Taylor and I embarked on our journey to Ramsay Hall. It was as magnificent as a castle, albeit small, and its grounds were lush and green and dotted with deer. The long gravelled driveway took us to grand stony steps and a door that was twice the size of the front door of our cottage.

"Come in, come on in," Torcuil said in his quiet way. "Mrs Gordon is off today and I just couldn't quite work the heating . . . I'm usually okay with it, but this time I seemed to have jammed it . . ."

"Maybe I can have a look?" said Taylor.

"Sure, that'd be great. I'm Torcuil, by the way," he said, and shook Taylor's hand. "Come this way . . . So I hear you're writing a book?"

I nodded, but he was walking ahead and didn't see me. He turned around and gazed at me. "So, you're writing a book . . ." he repeated, thinking I hadn't heard. "Oh, gosh, sorry! Taylor told me on the phone you couldn't speak! So sorry. I'm mortified. It must be the cold going to my head," he said, perfectly serious. I had to laugh. With his enormous blue eyes covered by round glasses, he looked a bit like an owl blinking in daylight. He led us through an endless succession of rooms and corridors and down two flights of stairs until we came to some sort of basement. I stood next to Torcuil as he showed Taylor the boiler. It was gigantic and it looked positively ancient.

"It's here. What Mrs Gordon . . . my housekeeper . . . usually does is she bangs it twice here, and once here and it always works. But it doesn't seem to work as consistently with me. It sort of recognises its master. Or its mistress, I should say."

"Right, twice here and once here?" said Taylor, unfazed by it all and, as ever, keen to help. "Okay, here we go!" He slammed the boiler three times, and the thing started emitting a long, sinister wail. The wail dissolved and turned into a buzz, and then a low, reassuring hum.

I smiled and turned towards Torcuil, who'd been standing at my side – except it wasn't Torcuil. It was someone else entirely. A man whose pale, smiling face was just a few inches from mine.

I screamed with all my might and jumped back, but the shadow was gone already.

"What's wrong?"

"You okay?" Taylor and Torcuil were both beside me. Right then I realised that my arms and legs were tingling, and that the humming in my ears had been hidden by the wail of the boiler.

The man began to dissolve in front of my eyes, but my heart showed no sign of slowing down. Sometimes it happened, with the Sight. You saw things you'd rather not see, especially in ancient places like Ramsay Hall.

I smiled a brittle smile and made a gesture with my fingers on Torcuil's arms, to signify a spider.

"Oh, yes, there's a few of them down here. Sorry."

As we walked back upstairs, I saw Taylor gazing at me

sideways. I wondered if some aspects of my behaviour puzzled him.

We sat in the hall, a splendid room with wooden floors and huge windows that opened onto the lawns. I'd always loved Ramsay Hall, since I was a child and I'd come to play here with Torcuil and his sister, Sheila. From the window I could see the tree house we used to play in, and it brought a smile to my face.

"Another life, huh?" said Torcuil, following my gaze. "Happy memories. Except I had a tendency to fall off the tree. I broke my nose there. Twice. You probably remember because the second time I fell on you . . ."

I laughed. I remembered.

"Anyway, this is the stuff I dug up . . . Mary Gibson used to work here. My great-grandmother, Lady Edwina, employed her as a maid. She's in a few pictures . . . look," he said, and handed me a thick, leather-covered photograph album. "She must have been about twenty when this was taken. Not long before she married Alan."

I smiled in recognition. Yes, that was her, my Mary. The dark hair in a bun crowned by a braid – the slender, small frame, her tiny, feminine hands. Finally I could see her face better: the sweetheart shape of her forehead, her eyes, so full of life that they seemed to shine, even if the picture was in black and white. The corners of her mouth were curling up – she was trying to look solemn as the picture was being taken, but not quite managing. She was arm in arm with another girl, slightly taller and plumper than her, with fair hair and a look of calm about her – Leah. I recognised her from my vision, but I couldn't tell Torcuil, of course.

"From what I know, Mary and Alan struggled quite a lot. Alan came back from the war badly wounded and couldn't

242

work for a long time. My great-gran gave her a job here on the estate, and Lady Kilpatrick helped them a lot too."

Lady Kilpatrick?

"Anna Kilpatrick."

Of course! Anna, Robert's fiancée, was Lady Kilpatrick! Did she not know about what had happened between Mary and Robert? She must have. But she'd helped her anyway. I thought of her beautiful face, and how graceful, how dignified she looked. She stood out in a crowd – and still, it was Mary that Robert had loved. But not the one he chose.

Only then did I realise that a photograph had slipped out of the album, somehow, and was lying on the floor.

I picked it up. It was a child – a girl, wearing a white dress and buttoned boots. Her long black hair was in braids, white ribbons tied in bows at each end. Everything twirled around me. All of a sudden I could hear a low noise, like water lapping on a shore in the distance.

I couldn't believe my eyes.

It was the girl I'd seen in my visions.

It was the girl in the loch.

"Are you okay, Inary?" asked Torcuil, but his voice came to me from far away.

I nodded.

"You sure? You look a bit green."

I'm fine, I wrote. *Do you know who this girl is?*

Torcuil took the photograph from my hand, and severing the link with it so suddenly made me slightly nauseous. "I think it's Mary's sister. I don't have pictures of them together, I don't think . . . She vanished, not long before Mary's wedding. Poor wee thing."

Mary's sister and the girl in the loch were the same person.

Mary's sister had drowned – *find her*, she'd implored. The two sisters were pleading to be reunited. So that was why she and her mother were crying, the day they came into my house.

Do you know her name?

"I'm not sure . . . But I can have a look through the papers and pictures and see if I can find out."

The girl in the loch was the person they'd never see again.

Thank you. Can I borrow this album? I'll be careful with it, I promise.

"Of course. And I can't wait to read your book . . ."

I nodded again, looking down.

"Is there a bathroom here?" asked Taylor.

"Yes. Six of them. The closest is the blue door on the landing . . . you know, where we went down to the basement."

"Six bathrooms? Do you use them all?"

Torcuil laughed. "One for me, one for the guests, the others are perfect to keep books in."

Taylor disappeared in the maze to look for the blue door – I was surprised that Torcuil hadn't offered to show him where it was, but as soon as Taylor had gone, I found out why.

"So, Inary. What did you see down there? In the basement?"

I felt the blood drain from my face.

What do you mean?

He smiled. "We used to play together, Inary, remember? I've known for a long time. About you having the Sight. I have McCrimmon blood too . . ."

I looked down. I'd been taken aback, I didn't know how

244

to discuss this with anyone. I liked Torcuil, but apart from at Emily's funeral I hadn't seen him in ages and I wasn't sure I could trust him.

"I'm not going to ask you any more questions, Inary. And don't worry, I won't discuss this with anyone."

I nodded.

"Hey, I'm back," said Taylor cheerfully, striding back into the hall. "I ended up in a room full of severed heads, but it's all good."

"Oh yes, the other blue door. That's the trophy room."

"Cool. This place must be full of ghosts. Have you thought of installing infrared cameras?"

"They'd just catch me roaming the place looking for a bowl of Weetabix," Torcuil laughed, and his eyes met mine.

I wasn't so sure of that.

★

I sat the photograph album on my desk. I was painfully aware of the picture of the girl in it, as if it'd been pulsating quietly between the pages and in my mind. I *felt* it there. I wrote a long email to Alex telling him what happened, how I'd found out who the girl in the loch was.

From Alex.McIlvenny@hotmail.co.uk
To Inary@gmail.com

This is amazing. So do you think that's why she's come to you? And the guy in your cousin's basement . . . Your life is like an episode of *Most Haunted*.

From Inary@gmail.com
To Alex.McIlvenny@hotmail.co.uk

I never knew you watched *Most Haunted* . . .

From Alex.McIlvenny@hotmail.co.uk
To Inary@gmail.com

Oh yeah. It's my guilty pleasure. Love it when they go into
hysterics. And tell me, was the delectable Taylor with you as
you made your discovery?

I smiled in triumph. We were to be just friends, but he was still
jealous.

From Inary@gmail.com
To Alex.McIlvenny@hotmail.co.uk

He was, yes. He's a nice guy, but completely not my type.

From Alex.McIlvenny@hotmail.co.uk
To Inary@gmail.com

Well, I suppose none of my business. Inary, I was thinking,
all this story . . . Mary's story . . . Maybe you should put it all
on paper, don't you think? With Cassandra gone . . . Just a
thought. I have to go.
Speak soon,
Alex x

I sighed. All the stories had gone out of me. I hadn't tried to write in weeks – there was no point. I was touched, though. Alex had always been so supportive of my writing. The thing was, I felt so drained and empty that writing seemed impossible, like climbing Ben Cruachan barefoot.

★

That night I had the first nightmare: black water closing over me, and then floating with no breath in my lungs, my heart still. Long, lonely years at the bottom of the loch. I woke up gasping for air, and when I fell asleep again, it started once more. Drowning, slowly, painfully; water closing over my head; my lungs filling up, my heart stopping – and then silence. And again, and again. Sometimes I could catch a glimpse of my white dress, my childlike hands, my small feet clad in buttoned-up boots, my black braids. I was her. The girl in the loch. Mary's lost sister.

She was so small, and so frightened. Calling for help, but nobody came.

Little did I know that those nightmares would torment me for a long time ... Every night I'd pray it'd be the last night she'd come to me, I'd pray that it would be Emily to come to me instead, but it never was.

39

Little girl lost

Inary

Logan's shop was getting busier and busier as the weather got warmer, and hillwalkers from down south and from the cities started flocking in. Every once in a while, Logan disappeared. Hillwalking, apparently. Often I heard him talking on the phone at night. I was worried, but the thing was, he looked pretty cheerful. I caught him one night in the living room, watching TV with a glass in his hand. Nothing strange about that – he'd always had a glass in his hand since Emily died. But that night it was a glass of orange juice, and I'd noticed quite a few cartons of it in the fridge . . .

So there I was, in the Welly, trying to concentrate, but my head was floating somewhere else. I kept forgetting what I was doing and staring into space instead.

Three nights now. Three nights of drowning nightmares. I was worn out. It was as if seeing the girl's face had unlocked some line of communication between us; the dreams of water had become stronger, and even more distressing. And relentless.

She was talking to me, she was telling me what had happened to her, showing it to me, making me feel every moment of her terrible fate. She was giving me her memories, the memories of her death and of her ghostly existence. The girl in the loch was an elemental force, with all the intensity of a child abandoned. She was draining the life from me. I dreaded falling asleep in case she came – and she always did. She would not let me be.

"Hey! Hello!" Eilidh had just come in with Maisie.

"What can I help you with?" Logan appeared from the stock room.

"This girl needs a new bike helmet. She lost hers."

"Right. Shall we try on a few?" said Logan with a smile. He was just back from one of his expeditions and in a strangely chirpy mood. Maisie went with him happily – she loved my brother, like a lot of children did. There was something warm, something unmistakably kind under his abruptness, and children seemed to pick up on it better than adults. I often thought he'd make a great dad, one day.

"Inary . . ." Eilidh called me to one side. "Listen. I saw Lewis. You know, Lewis McLelland."

I swallowed and nodded. I didn't need the second name. I knew which Lewis she was talking about.

"He asked me for your mobile number . . . I didn't give it to him, of course. But just to let you know, he's looking for you. He says he needs to speak to you."

I felt ill. Just what I needed.

Eilidh and Maisie were sent on their way with a new helmet, and I was left in even more of a daze than before.

"Wake up, Inary . . ." Logan called to me gently.

Sorry, I mouthed.

"Go home, come on," said Logan.

I shook my head and eagerly started refolding some tartan scarves.

"It's not that busy. On you go home. Honestly."

As I walked out of the shop, I briefly turned around to wave

249

goodbye and I saw Logan looking at me. He had a worried expression on his face, and I felt vaguely guilty for giving him even more worry than he already had, with my voice not returning and all that. Still, if I'd told him about the girl in the loch and the real reason why I fell in the water when I'd gone out on Taylor's boat, he would have been even more worried. And if I told him about Lewis looking for me, I knew that it'd be Logan looking for Lewis next. And probably not just for a chat.

I set out to walk home, but it was a beautiful early spring evening, and my feet didn't seem to obey. They took me to the main street, and all the way to the loch. I stood on the shore in the soft light of dusk. The call of a tawny owl broke the silence once, twice.

Take me home, she had begged me. Twice. Once when I was a child barely older than her, and then a few weeks ago. Twice she'd looked for me – she'd waited thirteen years for me to go back on the loch, she'd waited thirteen years to speak to anyone, probably. Hoping I would listen. And her sister had come to me too – I'd always known that there was a reason for Mary's visits. No other spirit had ever come to me so often, or so intensely.

But I didn't know how to get her there. Helpless tears started flowing out of me, and before I realised what I was doing I found myself on the shore, sobbing. I didn't know what I was crying for any more: Mary's sister, or my own, or maybe for the love Mary and I no longer had. All of those things, probably. Two lost girls, and me in the middle, at a loss.

40

And still I found her

Alex

And so, Inary was magical. As simple as that. She had a gift I didn't even know existed, though I'd read about it in books and seen it in films – not the kind of thing you'd ever think existed for real. What were the chances of falling for someone so unique?

And still, I'd found her.

I'd believed her at once. There was no room in my mind to wonder if she was really telling the truth, to suspect that there was something wrong with her. I knew her too well to doubt her.

What she'd told me about the loch girl was disquieting. I didn't really want to think of Inary in the cold waters of the loch, or having nightmares every night. Maybe, if I held her in my arms, she wouldn't have bad dreams any more – I'd scare the girl in the loch away from her.

But it wasn't Inary I had in my arms, at night – it was Sharon. And I wasn't sure how I could keep it going, to have my heart with one woman and be going out with another. Every day I said to myself I'd be stronger, and really try very, very hard to fall in love with the person beside me; every night I realised I'd failed again. How long could I keep Sharon in this limbo? But if I broke up with her, just like I'd broken up with Gaby, would it mean continuing on this awful, lonely road with Inary beside me, and still not there? Damned if I do, damned if I don't. That was me.

41

Broken promises

Inary

The next day, as if I weren't shaken enough, I bumped into him.

Lewis.

The world spun around me, a flood of memories swept me away.

"Inary. I've been looking all over for you . . ."

I folded my arms, looking down. He knew where I lived. Though maybe he didn't dare show his face to Logan. And I couldn't blame him.

"You look lovely," he said, and I fantasised about slapping him in the face, like I should have done three years ago. "To see you again . . . it feels so good."

Good wasn't how I'd describe it. At Emily's funeral I was too stunned, too overcome by everything to have the presence of mind to turn him away. He was lucky Logan hadn't seen him there.

"Look, can we go somewhere? Somewhere a bit more private than the street?"

Is there anywhere private in Glen Avich? Apart from my house. And he wasn't setting foot in there. I shook my head.

"Inary . . . please. Just listen to me. Just this once."

I sighed. Oh, what the hell. Whatever he had to say couldn't hurt me any more. And maybe, finally, I could have an explanation, and know if it'd really been finding out about the Sight that made him leave me.

I started walking towards St Colman's Way, and Lewis followed me in silence. I sat on the bench overlooking the village, sinking into my soft angora cardigan, and braced myself for what he was about to say.

"How have you been?"

Mutinously, I took my notebook out.

Okay. So where's Claire?

"She's fine. At home." They were *living together*. I felt sick. "Good God, Inary . . . you're writing instead of talking! Have you been to the doctor?"

I rolled my eyes. A bit late to start worrying about me. *Trauma, probably,* I wrote. *It'll come back.*

"Oh, Inary . . ." he said, and brushed my arm.

I felt myself folding in two, repulsed – and yet a tiny part of me, the part that was still sitting at the table in our house in Kilronan, reeling in shock, that part of me nearly cried with relief to feel his touch again. I hated that part. I truly, truly hated it.

Were you seeing Claire when we were together? I scribbled, my hands shaking.

"No! Oh God, Inary! Of course not!"

Right, right. Sorry for thinking you were actually more of a bastard than you actually are.

"It wasn't that. It's just that . . . I don't know. It was all so fast . . ."

You wanted to move in together. You wanted to get engaged. My eyes stung with the unfairness of it all. It had been him, the

254

one rushing, the one who couldn't get enough of me, who promised to be with me forever.

"I know. I know. I'm an idiot." He looked into the distance. I couldn't believe his bloody cheek to look for me now.

Was it the Sight?

He looked away.

Got you.

"I'm sorry. I don't know what came over me . . . when you told me that. I panicked."

Why? What did it have to do with you?

"Inary! You told me you see ghosts! How would you have reacted, had I told you that? You told me you were attacked by a drowned girl coming out of the loch!"

I was.

"I just couldn't . . . I couldn't . . ."

You thought I was mad.

"I thought I knew you. And then you sprang that on me."

It was a mistake. I shouldn't have told you.

"No, no. It was the right thing to do. It was me, being an idiot . . . After I left you I was in pieces . . ."

Poor you, I thought.

"Logan came to see me. He said you were in London. To stay away from you. He said he'd break my nose, you know your brother . . ."

Good, I scribbled furiously.

"I know, I deserved it. And then I just didn't have the courage to get in touch. When I saw you at Emily's funeral . . ."

I winced.

Conversation over, I wrote and stood up.

"Inary. Please don't go," he said, and stood in front of me. He took a step closer. "I'm sorry," he whispered, and wrapped a lock of my hair behind my ear. "When you told me about your ... gift ... I should have stood by you. I should have known you were asking for help. And I should have been there to help you."

What? I mouthed.

"There's nothing to be ashamed about, Inary," he continued, a soothing hand clasping mine. "I understand now. We should have faced your issues together ..."

My issues?

I laughed.

I just couldn't help it.

"Inary?"

He thought I was ill. Mentally ill. Well, no point in arguing. I turned on my heels and walked away.

Just like that.

And there was no sense of having to rip myself from him, of a limb missing, like it used to be every time we were apart.

"Inary?" he repeated. I stopped. There was still something left to say. I took out my notebook again and scribbled quickly.

By the way, I see dead people again. All over the place. Tell your mum. She can have me exorcised.

I wish I could say that this gave me some satisfaction, but I would be lying. The truth is, I felt nothing. I walked off and didn't look back, darting down St Colman's Way with the cold wind in my hair and not a tear in my eye.

My gift wasn't an illness. It was a privilege.

And it was about time I used it.

When I got home, I took a long, deep breath. For the first time in three years, I felt free. Free of Lewis, free of regret. He thought I was ill – but the Sight was the best part of me. And now he was gone, and I had my gift back.

256

I was whole again. The heart that Lewis had broken had grown stronger, and there was no reason for me to hide any more, to hide my Sight from the one I loved.

Talking to Lewis had made me see. My gift had come back at the worst time of my life, the time I lost Emily. Just then, Mary arrived to comfort me in my darkest times – now it was my turn to help her. The girl in the loch needed me. Scaring me to death was the only way she thought she could make me listen. She looked like a monster, but her words were those of a frightened child: *Please, Inary. Help me. Take me home.*

There was nobody else. Nobody else to listen, nobody else to take her home.

Nobody but me.

From Inary@gmail.com
To Alex.McIlvenny@hotmail.co.uk

Dear Alex,
I bumped into Lewis. He said he was sorry for what he did, that when I told him about the Sight he should have helped me face my issues.
God, I had a lucky escape.
Inary

From Alex.McIlvenny@hotmail.co.uk
To Inary@gmail.com

I wish it'd been me who bumped into him. Or even bumped him. Tosser . . .

The idea of Alex bumping anyone made me laugh – he was so mellow, it was just impossible to imagine . . .

    Sorry, I have to go now.
    Speak later,
    Alex

Oh. That was hasty. I wondered what he had to do, where he had to go. He was seeing Sharon, so better not ask. I could have kicked myself a million times for having been so blind. But I couldn't turn the clock back.

42

Truth

Alex

She started crying. I couldn't bear it.

But I had to do it. Whether there would be something between Inary and me or not, Sharon deserved to be loved. For real.

"I'm sorry . . ." I rubbed my face with my hands.

"I can't take this any more, Alex. I've been in love with you for years . . ."

My heart skipped a beat in hearing her confession.

"I'm sorry . . ."

"Stop saying you're sorry! It's that Scottish girl, isn't it? That Hillary, Inary, whatever her name is . . ." She forced me to turn around and look at her.

"We're not together."

"No, I know you aren't! Because she doesn't want you, and you keep going after her . . . You're an idiot. And so am I. A complete and total idiot."

"Sharon . . ."

"I'm handing in my resignation, Alex. I can't see you every day any more. I owe this to myself . . ."

"No, that's not fair. I'll go."

"For God's sake, Alex. Let me make a decision for myself," she said, and strode to the front door. She jerked it open for me.

I nodded, my stomach in knots.

"Go."

I made my way towards the door. I was crossing the threshold when she called me back.

"Alex . . ."

"Yes?" I said, turning. Maybe she'd have a word of forgiveness for me. Maybe I was hoping for absolution . . .

"The owls. They were for her, weren't they?"

I nodded again.

"Fuck off, Alex."

I'd earned that one. No forgiveness for me, not from Sharon.

★

The first thing I did as I stepped into the street was text Inary, the craving for her stronger than guilt or shame. Love had turned me into a liar, and it would not happen again. If Inary and I were not to be together, I would not mangle anyone else in the process, ever again.

Sharon and I broke up, I said simply.

The reply came as I was opening my car door. *I'm sorry.* Not what I was hoping for. But then, I was a fool, we'd established that already.

That was it. I went home alone.

43

Drowning

Inary

I hurried towards Logan's shop, a fragrant food parcel of sandwiches and brownies from La Piazza under my jacket, to keep them dry. My mind was reeling with thoughts of Alex. His text. He was free. But he hadn't said anything more. Still, I couldn't wait to tell him all about what I was about to do. Maybe then I'd have the courage to understand my own feelings.

A soft spring rain was falling, the treacherous kind, the one that soaks you fast and subtly. I broke into a run, my hair dripping already. I was hatching a plan. I would answer her call; I would do what the girl in the loch was asking me. I would take her home.

I ran through my options: go to the police and say that there was a body in the loch. How did I know? Never mind how.

No, that wasn't good. And how would we find her? It's a big loch. The only way would be to try and get an idea of where the girl was, and then I needed the means to retrieve her. Diving equipment. Taylor. I couldn't tell him the truth, of course. I would have to find some sort of complicated explanation as to how I knew there was a body somewhere underwater. But first, I had to find out where the girl was. And that meant going back and asking her.

I couldn't go alone. The effect she had on me – pure,

unbridled panic, terror so strong I lost my bearings – that alone was enough to make me want to run away and never set foot on the loch shore again. I didn't believe she wanted to hurt me – but she was desperate, and frightened like only a child could be. If she dragged me in the loch again, and in that state, so panicked that I couldn't even swim – I would drown, whether she actually wanted to harm me or not.

I would explain everything to Logan, and he could come with me to see if the girl could give me any sort of hint as to where her body lay. It was a long shot, but I had to try. Then we'd go to Taylor and . . . invent something.

As I ran through the situation in my head, the constant refrain was, *what am I doing? What am I messing with?* I felt my heart speeding up its rhythm and panic slowly rising again. I ran faster, trying to sweat away my anxiety. The one single scariest thing of my whole existence – and I was going to offer myself to it, again. I knew now that she was just a little girl – but her spirit was so powerful, so full of anger and despair, it terrified me all the same.

I barged into the shop, panting.

"Hello. Here on your day off?" Logan greeted me. "Did you run all the way?"

Very observant, I thought as my lungs were bursting. I handed him the food parcel.

"Oh, cheers! Is this from La Piazza? Brownies as well. Sweet."

I strode to the counter and grabbed some paper and a pen. *Something's up,* I wrote.

"What's wrong?" I could read the apprehension in his eyes.

I took a deep breath. Now or never.

Is anyone around?

"No, why?"

Private stuff to discuss. I need you to come to the loch with me.

"Why?" he repeated.

I took a deep breath and started scribbling as quickly as I could. *Same as thirteen years ago. I saw a drowned girl. Very scary. She asked me to take her home. Please take me to the loch. I need to find her.*

Logan stared at me in silence for a few seconds. Even if his grandmother and sister had the Sight, it was still difficult for him to quite wrap his head round the whole thing. It would be difficult for anyone, I suppose.

She's terrifying. But she's only little. Remember I told you about this girl I've seen a few times, Mary? It's her sister, I wrote, and showed him the photograph I'd slipped in my bag.

"Oh . . . This is her? How did she end up in the loch?"

I don't know. I don't know her first name either. Just her second name: Gibson.

"That's what you saw that day Dad took you out?"

Yes.

"Where did you find this picture?"

Torcuil.

Logan took a deep breath. "Basically, Samara."

? I doodled.

"Samara. The evil spirit child from *The Ring.*"

She's not evil!

"She might not be evil, but you ended up in the loch. Twice. The first time you nearly didn't come out, remember? Mum and Dad were beside themselves. And the second time . . . just as well Taylor was there!"

That's what happened to her. She fell in the loch and didn't come out. There was nobody there to help her. Nobody.

263

"Mmmm."

She's asking me to take her home.

"Yes, you said. As in ... how? Jesus, I can't even believe I'm talking about this ... you're asking me to go looking for a spirit who nearly drowned you twice! Do you even realise that?"

Yes!!! I had thought things over. I wasn't taking this lightly. I was about to get seriously angry, when he said something that softened me.

"I just lost a sister. I'm not going to lose two, Inary." His mouth was set in a thin line, and I knew he wouldn't change his mind.

I had no choice: I'd go on the loch alone.

44

Rose

Inary

My hands were shaking so hard I had to slip them into my jacket pockets. My excuse for Logan had been a visit to Auntie Mhairi for the afternoon. I hadn't told Alex what I was doing – I'd kept the scariest bits of my encounters with Mary's sister from him, because I didn't want to worry him. Telling him I was going to go on the loch on my own, after what had happened there – twice – would have horrified him.

When the loch appeared in the distance, I felt my knees giving way. But I had no choice. She needed me. Mary needed me. And it was that or endless nights of drowning in my dreams.

The little peapod boat swayed as I got in. In spite of my fear, I couldn't help but notice how beautiful the loch was, its black, calm water reflecting the steely sky, and Ailsa in the middle, with its gnarled trees and bushes.

I hadn't been rowing for long when the whispers started, and with them the usual signs that I was about to See. They started low and then grew in intensity quicker than I could bear. It was so painful. My limbs were tight; my ears hurt with the low vibration of a nearby spirit. I fell on my knees on the bottom of the boat, my hands holding my head.

The whispers grew and grew, until the words were intelligible at last.

Rose . . . Rose . . . Rose . . . was all I could hear. So that was her name! Rose Gibson . . .

Rose. Tell me where you are, I begged. *Come and tell me!*

A part of me registered a sudden swaying of the boat, and a splashing of water all around us. In spite of the pain in my ears and in my whole body, I lifted my head to see.

She was there, floating in front of the boat, white and swollen, her eyes two pools of distress, what was left of her lips somewhere between blue and black. Her hair, which in the photograph had been lovingly braided, was lying wet and lank, and was woven with seaweed.

Where are you, Rose? I called in my mind.

I don't know. In the loch. It's dark.

What do you see?

Suddenly, she soared and threw herself on me, her arms outstretched. I closed my eyes tight. I didn't want to see her face, I couldn't bear to see her face . . . but before I could move, I felt her cold, wet hands on my cheeks and her icy breath on me.

Nothing! I can see nothing! I'm in the loch! Take me home!

I lay in a heap at the bottom of the boat, with Rose over me. I could feel her hair dripping on me, her hands searching for me . . . She'd take me down with her. She'd drown me . . .

I had to focus. With a huge effort, I forced my thoughts into shape again.

Where in the loch? Rose, please. It's a big loch . . . where are you?

She tugged me towards the edge of the boat, so suddenly that my breath was knocked out of my lungs. I held onto the edges of the boat as hard as I could.

Take me home! Rose screamed, trying to pull me in. I had to think fast. I had to take control of my terror ... My hands were hurting, and she was pulling, and pulling ... *Let me go. Let me go,* I pleaded with her. She was so strong – the strength of desperation. Her eyes were enormous, black and irisless, her hair falling all the way to her waist, the remains of her dress ripped and rotten. She still frightened me – but I was so full of pity, so full of sadness for her fate. I managed to form a thought. *Where were you when you fell?*

I fell off the boat. I was looking for nests. I want to go home now.

If she was looking for nests maybe she was near Ailsa. Had she been looking on the shore, she wouldn't have mentioned a boat.

I think I know where you are. I'll find you.

All of a sudden, she stopped pulling.

I'll take you home, Rose.

She surged in a burst of longing, and again her thoughts were so powerful that I felt myself losing balance, and I gripped the edge of the boat again. Once more I sensed her little hands on my arms, her cold breath on my face.

Don't leave me here ...

Rose. Listen. If you drag me down with you, I won't be able to take you home.

She froze for a minute, and then, she pulled away slightly, but her spirit was so entangled with mine that my body seemed to follow her, as if we'd been tied together. For a second I hovered over the edge of the boat.

Rose, let me go ...

And she did. She threw herself into the water as swiftly as she had risen out of it, and disappeared.

Take me home. Rose ... Rose ... Rose ... Her thoughts kept

267

echoing in my mind for a few minutes, while I panted hard and tried to calm my heart.

I rowed back ashore, the boat creaking and undulating under me. Finally, I was on dry land. I struggled to stand. All of a sudden, the ground was coming up to meet me, and everything was spinning . . . I saw black, like night had fallen in a heartbeat, and red and yellow stars exploded in front of my eyes.

"Inary!"

I heard calling, and I felt somebody's arms around me and the cold, hard pebbles under my knees and against my face.

★

I came to after some time – I'm not sure how long. I was sitting with my back to a tree. There was someone beside me. Logan.

"How you feeling?"

Okay, I mouthed, and lifted myself upwards, slowly. The world spun around me, but I stayed upright. What was Logan doing there?

"Careful . . ." he whispered, and sat beside me. He curled my fingers around a melamine cup. "Drink this." I did. Hot tea. I felt a bit better. I felt my pockets – the notebook was still there. Thankfully I hadn't ended up in the loch again. I took it out and wrote with trembling hands.

What are you doing here? How did you know?

"You're a terrible liar, Inary. When you told me you were going to see Aunt Mhairi I knew something was up. I phoned her . . ."

You checked on me!

"Earlier you were talking about going to find ghosts in the loch, of course I kept an eye on you! What did you expect! For God's sake, Inary, risking your life like this . . . I can't believe it!"

Sorry . . .

"Yes, you should be! This is the last time, do you hear me? The last time you go on some mad ghost-hunting expedition. Never again, Inary!"

I think I know where she is. Somewhere near Ailsa, I wrote.

Logan took a deep breath. "So you found her?"

I think so.

"This is the end of it, Inary. Okay? Promise me."

I need to sort this . . .

"Fine! Fine, but no more going on the loch alone!"

I nodded and leaned my head against his shoulder. I could have just closed my eyes and fallen asleep there and then.

I need to speak to Taylor. My hands were still shaking so much I struggled to write.

"How are you going to explain . . ." Logan began.

I'll tell him the truth. I don't care if he believes me or not. I just want Rose to go home.

★

I couldn't take any more words, from the living or the dead. I closed my eyes and prayed for no more dreams of drowning . . . But my prayer was not answered, because again Rose tormented me all night with visions of water – waves whirling, immobile, algae-covered shores, falling into the sea, into the loch; water in my mouth, my lungs, blinding me, suffocating me. And the same scene, over and over again: I could see my childlike hands, the hem of my white dress, my little boots

269

as I leaned towards the water, the boat going from under my feet . . . and then cold black water closing over my head and my lungs filling up until I couldn't breathe. And then, silence. Stillness. Complete aloneness.

★

The next day I texted Taylor to meet up at La Piazza. I was going to ask him to retrieve Rose's bones from the loch. Without being able to tell him how I knew she was there.

It would be easy.

I had considered making up some elaborate lie – having found the remains of a little shoe on Ailsa, or maybe a bone, but I decided there was no point in complicating things. I'd just tell him and see what he said.

"Hi there, how's it going?" he said cheerily. "Oh, peppermint tea! Awesome. Thanks."

You're welcome. I need to ask you a favour. For a change, I thought, a bit embarrassed. Taylor was such an amazing friend, but I worried about taking advantage of him. I supposed sooner or later it'd be my turn to help him, I said to myself.

"Sure. Fire away," he said. "More research?"

Sort of. I need you . . . or your team . . . to find Rose Gibson. Mary's sister, remember?

"The girl in the picture, yes. Poor thing. You think she drowned? Well, if she did, it'd be nearly impossible to find her down there. The loch is huge and there are only five of us. It'd take months. I mean, we're supposed to get on with the excavation . . . I'm sorry." He opened his arms.

I know she drowned and I know where she is. Somewhere near Ailsa.

"Oh. Okay . . . Well, if she's anywhere, the island would be a place to start, I suppose . . ."

So do you think you can do it?

"Sure. I'll try. I'll speak to the team . . ."

A pause. I knew what was coming.

"But how do you know she's there?"

I just know. What else could I say?

"Right. Right," he said, and took a sip of his peppermint tea. I sipped from my cappuccino and looked into the fire, hoping he'd drop it. "You just know."

I nodded. *And how's the excavation going?* I wrote hastily, trying to change the subject. He wasn't fooled.

"I know something's up, Inary. When we went out on the loch, something strange happened . . ."

I looked down.

"And remember when we went for a walk with Logan? You saw a heron . . ."

Yes, it was beautiful, I wrote.

"There was no heron, Inary. I'm not blind."

I felt the colour rising to my cheeks and my heart running away.

"In Torcuil's basement, remember? You screamed and jumped. This time it wasn't a heron, obviously . . ."

A spider, I wrote, and my hands were trembling.

"Right. A spider."

There was a moment of silence, and I didn't know what to say, I didn't know what to do. I couldn't tell him about the Sight. In a short space of time, Taylor had become a good friend to me. I cared for him, and he cared for me, and in a way, I trusted him. But I couldn't bring myself to tell him. It wasn't so much because I was scared of the consequences,

271

of him thinking I was mad – though that was a distinct possibility – it was more because it was such a precious, secret part of me . . . I just couldn't.

"Look, Inary. I'm not sure what's going on. But we'll look for Rose. I'll find an excuse . . . Maybe tell them I found some arrowheads on the island a while back and it's time to start working around it, or something."

Thank you.

"I'll let you know, then," he said, standing up.

I nodded. Then, on impulse, I got up and threw my arms around him. "You owe me a pint . . ." he said, laughing.

I owe you an explanation, I suppose, I thought. But you're not going to get it.

45

You only love once

Inary

It was a grey, rainy spring morning, and I was overflowing with thoughts and emotions and fear and hope and worry. I didn't know what to do with my jumbled-up mind. I slipped my glasses off my nose, switched the computer off and I went for a long walk, letting the wind and rain take the edge off my feelings. I was . . . pining. Yes, pining. For I didn't know what.

I had to be honest with myself, I thought as I walked. I *did* know what I was pining for. Alex.

Missing him was as ever present as breathing. I missed him with every minute that went by. Even if we were back in touch, I could still feel his absence, ever present, like white noise in my ears.

Alex and Sharon. Sharon and Alex.

It didn't sound right, did it? And even though they weren't together, he still hadn't said anything about what that meant for us, if anything.

Love didn't do Mary much good either. Her story didn't have a happy ending. Love doesn't conquer all, does it? It doesn't always find a way. Sometimes it loses its way and drags us astray with it.

Thank goodness it was Wednesday, the day of my weekly

catch-up with Eilidh at La Piazza. Sometimes, when you're really stressed out, only a chat among women will do, especially if accompanied by coffee and cake. I couldn't chat the traditional way – actually speaking – but nothing would come between me and a girly blether.

I let myself fall on a squashy sofa beside the fire, my favourite spot. The rain was tapping on the windows and both the land and the sky looked grey, melting in a sea of fog. Eilidh wasn't there yet, so I took the chance to text Taylor.

Any news?

Nothing yet. We're diving again tomorrow.

I sighed. What if they kept finding nothing? What if Rose was nowhere to be found, her bones scattered and hidden and impossible to retrieve? What if she was lost forever?

But I couldn't think like that. I had to keep hoping.

"Hello! Sorry we're late!" said Eilidh with a smile, sitting beside me. Sorley was asleep in his pram. Debora came over to take our orders.

"A scone with cream and jam and a cup of tea," said Eilidh. "Inary?"

Same, I mouthed.

"Sorry, no scones left. It's retirement-flat day. They're like locusts with their scones."

I laughed. I'd heard that before.

"What's the chef's special, then?" asked Eilidh.

"I made an almond and cherry tart to wake the dead."

Please no, I thought.

"Lovely." Eilidh looked at me, and I nodded. "Two please. Cheers." Debora went away and Eilidh and I resumed our conversation. "Anyway . . . Inary, don't take this the wrong way, you know I don't want to meddle but . . . It's been what? Four months now? No sign of your voice coming back. Maybe you need to go back to the doctor . . ."

Last thing I want.

"I know. Listen, I'm not sure I ever told you this, but two years ago I was in a very bad place. Before I came back to Glen Avich. My doctor gave me antidepressants and the likes . . . they made me feel like a zombie. On the day I drove back here, I put it all in the bin. It just wasn't right for me. But it's right for some people. Or even necessary. You might be one of them . . ."

I hope not.

Eilidh sighed. "I suppose. You know what's right for you. I'm sure time will do its job. That's all you need. Time to heal after your loss. And then your voice will return."

I wasn't so sure, but I drank Eilidh's words up like fresh water on a hot day. I needed them. I thought it was a good chance to ask her something I'd been wondering about for a while.

What made you stay in Glen Avich? Jamie?

"No. Most people think that, but I made the decision to stay before things with Jamie got serious. What made me stay was Glen Avich, simple as that. Mmmm, thank you, Debora, this looks amazing!"

"Enjoy! By the way, I meant to tell you for ages, Inary, your hair is gorgeous!" said Debora, running a hand through my hair. "I've always wanted red hair. You look so Scottish."

I blushed. That, I did. My hair had grown again, and it was

now just below my ears, all curled up. *Thank you*, I mouthed, and attacked the cherry and almond tart. Blissful.

"So yes, I belong here. For all that it's tiny and everyone knows everything about everyone . . . It's my home."

I nodded. I understood.

There was someone, in London. I messed up with him. And now it's too late, I wrote, and suddenly Debora's tart tasted like cardboard.

"My gran used to say what's for you won't go past you. Bit of a cliché, but I found it's so true."

I've been an idiot. I was so scared, after what happened with Lewis. I let him go.

"I know exactly what you mean! When I met Jamie, I couldn't . . ." A shadow of sadness passed over her face, and her voice trailed away. "I nearly lost him too. And look at us now!" she said, gesturing to Sorley asleep in his pram. As if on cue, Sorley's big blue eyes opened.

"Da!" he said, which I guess meant I'm hungry, because Eilidh took out a bear-shaped biscuit from her bag and lay it on the plate beside her cake.

"Here you are!" she cooed, lifting him up. "Hello!" She gave him a kiss, then handed him the biscuit. Sorley curled up against her, the biscuit in his hand. He needed a minute to wake up. Something in me melted in seeing the way they looked at each other. I took another sip of my cappuccino, and then I grabbed my pen again.

Do you think we only love once?

"Oooh, big question. Yes. I do."

Then I'm done. I've had my once.

Eilidh looked at me thoughtfully. "It's not as straightforward as that. True love is not that easy to recognise. You might think you had your *once*, but maybe it wasn't the real once. I had no idea what true love was. Only when Jamie and I moved in together . . . It's not fireworks and fanfares, really. It's loving every minute together. Looking forward to him coming home. Listening to him speak in company and feeling proud because it's you at his side . . ."

I had all this with Lewis, I wrote bitterly.

"Pa?" said Sorley.

"Do you still feel that way for him?" she asked, taking a battered plush penguin out of her bag and giving it to Sorley. Oh, so *pa* meant penguin.

No, I wrote, and I meant it.

"There you are. True love is forever. Everything else is a crush, or friendship, or lust, or whatever . . . but true love doesn't end."

"Dada," Sorley concluded, and offered me his penguin. I decided that dada meant *give me a cuddle*. He squealed with delight as I took him on my knee and squeezed him and tickled him and covered him with kisses.

Right at that moment, my phone started ringing. It was Taylor. As Eilidh took Sorley back, I pressed the green button and put the phone to my ear – he knew I couldn't speak, so I waited.

"Inary, I didn't want to just text, in case you didn't see it. I'll come and get you in a moment. We found Rose."

★

I watched from the shore as they lifted her out, a parcel of bones, the diver holding them to her heart. The last embrace Rose would ever get, after all those years alone in the loch.

I wasn't surprised when that night I woke up to whispered words in my ear, a voice that had become familiar to me like that of a sister: Mary's. "Thank you," she said, and I half-smiled in the darkness.

46

Sisters

Inary

Word spread that a girl drowned many years ago had been found in the loch. St Colman was full to the brim, and many more gathered at the graveyard. The local press was taking pictures of Rose's coffin and of her remaining family. It was a beautiful day – fresh and full of light. I was so happy for her that it should be spring when she too was finally put into the ground. Torcuil, Logan and Taylor stood all around her white coffin, covered with lilies.

"Inary . . . there's something I have to ask you," Taylor said to me after it was finished. "How did you know?"

I couldn't answer that one. I just smiled, gave him a peck on the cheek and walked away. Apart from my family, only Alex could ever know about my secret.

"Thank you," I mouthed in Torcuil's direction, touching his arm briefly as I went. I needed to be alone.

I wasn't surprised, as I walked home from the graveyard, when I saw Rose and Mary waiting for me by a birch tree, holding hands. Rose looked herself again, her eyes sparkling blue, her cheeks rosy. I could see the tree through her body now, as if her spirit had got weaker. Maybe she was on her way somewhere else, now. To peace, at last.

They both smiled at me, and I smiled back, my eyes welling up with joy and sadness and relief all mixed up. Mary and Rose were together again; maybe Emily and I would be, one day.

47

Writing on the wall

Inary

When I arrived at the Welly the next day, Logan was grinning to himself.

"Oh, hello! And how are you today?" he chirped. Yes, my brother actually *chirped*. I eyed him suspiciously.

Good, I scribbled on my notebook.

"That's great!"

Something was up. I was about to ask, when my answer came through the door, all black wavy hair and eyes the colour of new leaves.

"Hello . . ."

Aisling was carrying a backpack and a camera bag, and this time, she had shoes on.

"Hey . . ." Logan practically melted there, in front of my eyes. He walked over to Aisling, took her in his arms and – shock horror – kissed her!

It was an Irish-woman-induced sort of miracle.

So that's what all those mysterious calls had been about . . . and the disappearances to the phantom bothies . . . and all the cartons of juice that had materialised in our fridge.

"Hello!" She smiled at me. I was too astonished to even smile back.

"You go up to the house," Logan said to her. "I won't be long."

"Sure," she replied, and gave him another peck on the lips. My brother, the dark horse.

So . . . Aisling! I didn't even know you were in touch!

"Yeah, just didn't want to talk about it. Didn't want to jinx it."

So that explains the change in you . . .

"No. I mean, not completely. I've felt better recently, yes. And Aisling helped. But a lot was about having you here."

I couldn't quite believe what I was hearing. Maddeningly, I felt my eyes welling up . . . I was about to write something when suddenly, unexpectedly, Logan threw his arms around me and held me in a tight embrace. The scribbled piece of paper and the pen fell on the floor. A wave of emotion swept me all of a sudden. All the resentment between us, all the words unsaid – the way he blamed me for having left, the way I blamed him for not accepting that I had to go, for making me pay for my decision every single time we spoke . . . everything seemed to disappear, and all the barriers were destroyed. I hid my face against his chest and we remained entwined for a long time.

"A hug fest!" he mocked, but his eyes betrayed his emotion.

*

That afternoon I was on my way home from the shop, walking slowly in the dusky light, when I saw somebody in front of my house – a woman. Her black hair gave her away: it was Mary. She was leaning down, her arm extended . . . holding onto something. There was another shadow, a little one, hanging onto her hand. For a moment, as if a flash had gone off, I saw them both clearly: a dark-haired toddler, with bright eyes and dimpled hands, his wee face turned up in adoration. And Mary – the look of perfect happiness on her features, the pure, joyful, all-encompassing love in her eyes. I'd seen that look before, between Eilidh and Sorley. The toddler must be Mary's son.

The scene dissolved before my eyes, and I took a long, deep, easy breath. So there was my message, the message Mary was still to give me: that when all seems lost, happiness can still be in store for us. She'd lost Robert, but her life continued. And who knows what her *once* had been? Robert and the intensity of first love, or Alan and the long years of devotion and family and hardship faced and overcome? Love takes many different forms: it's not straightforward, like a river to the sea, it's a winding stream that fights its way on. It was true for Mary. Maybe it could be true for me. But who was to be my once? Who was to be my soulmate, if there was one?

I took my phone out and, all of a sudden, my fingers developed a will of their own and decided to text Alex.

I've got to ask you, I typed.

Oh, hello, he replied. *What's up?*

You still angry with me?

Why would I be?

For saying it was a mistake. What happened between us. It wasn't.

I didn't wait for a reply – my fingers did their own thing. Again.

I think I'm in love with you,

. . . they decided to write. And then they tapped 'send', before I could change my mind.

There was nothing, nothing I could do to un-send the message and take my words back.

I felt sick. I'd just told him I loved him. Now I had to wait for the reply. Thank God for technology . . . had we lived in Mary's times, we would have had to wait weeks for each letter to arrive.

I sat in my kitchen and stared at the phone for five minutes, ten, fifteen. No reply. Twenty minutes passed, then an hour, then two. By then I was pacing up and down, trying to distract myself – but I couldn't stop my gaze from returning to the phone every few seconds. I checked there was a signal. There was. I checked it worked by sending a text to myself – how pathetic can you get? I got my own text. It definitely worked.

I had to get out. I threw a jacket on and took refuge at La Piazza. I sat at my usual table beside the fire, staring at the phone.

Debora approached me. "Hey sweetie. All okay? You look shattered." *Great, thank you.* I nodded, and mouthed *double espresso, please.*

She came back with a little cup and a gorgeous red velvet cupcake with a gossamer-thin butterfly on it.

"To take the worry away, darling," she said with a smile. I looked at the cupcake desolately. It was beautiful, but there was no way I could take a bite, my stomach was so knotted up. I raised the coffee to my lips and went to take a sip, when the sound of message notification filled the air. It really filled it, because I had put it on high to make sure I heard it. Two old ladies gave me a dark look and Debora's cat made a beeline for the back door.

"There he is! He texted you!" called Debora from beyond the counter, smirking.

I was frozen, my cup in mid-air. My hands were trembling as I put the cup down and picked the phone up.

I didn't want to look.

But I had to.

Can you buy bread + bin liners. Ta.

What?

Shit. It was from Logan. I swept back my hair in frustration. Shit, shit, shit.

I needed to wash my face. I strode to the bathroom in the back – the potpourri of the day was a lovely peach, I couldn't help noticing – and splashed cold water over my face.

"Your phone beeped again. I think they heard it in Aberdeen, my love," said Debora as soon as I stepped out.

It did? It beeped again? My heart started racing – maybe it was Logan again, sending me on some other errands – I shouldn't get my hopes up. I opened the message.

I'm pretty sure I'm in love with you too.

48

My story to tell

Inary

There would be no more werewolves, no thoughts of what publishers might like or not like, of market trends or what gave me the best chances to get published. I had a story inside me, ready to be put onto the page. Like Emily and Alex had said, it was a Glen Avich story, and it had come to me – it had been there for me to see all along. How come it had taken me so long to understand?

It was like a switch going. I opened my soul, and I wrote for hours without stopping, in a long, blissful gush.

I wrote until dawn broke in the sky. As light began to seep through the curtains, I threw myself on my bed and fell into a deep, contented sleep like I hadn't had for months.

In the next few weeks I just couldn't be dragged away from my computer. I even skipped a few Wednesday mornings with Eilidh, as much as I wanted to see her. Every moment I wasn't working at the shop or talking to Alex, I spent writing. I was eating at the keyboard, stealing a few hours' sleep at night, and feeling happier than I'd been for a very long time. This incredible sense of release had possessed me, like I'd been thirsty for a lifetime and at last I was allowed to drink. Alex's love for me and my writing: for the first time in years, I felt sated.

49

Scotland

Alex

I'd had to break up with Sharon. There was no way we could keep going. And as if somehow Inary had sensed it, as if she'd felt I was once more open and ready, in spite of all my fears – in spite of all that happened in the past – she opened up too.

When I got her message, I couldn't believe it. After all the hope and waiting and love suspended, there we were, at last. Inary and her ghosts and her writing and her little Inary world, the world I desperately wanted to be part of. And finally, I was.

I wanted to be with her straight away; the letters just weren't enough, nothing was ever enough. I had a few things to sort out first. But it would not be long, now.

50

Spring inside me

Inary

It was the morning of my twenty-sixth birthday. On a breezy, sunny day, one of those late spring days where everything brims with life, I strolled along the loch shore listening to the lapping of the water, wearing Emily's green silk dress. There was no fear around the loch now, only peace. The little lost girl was home, and so was I. I had felt besieged by death, with my parents and Emily being taken away from me. And now I was overflowing with life.

Alex had told me that he was preparing a surprise for me, and I was too excited to sit still. I was expecting something owl-related of course, but Alex had given strange hints and clues that I couldn't quite decipher.

The time had come to make a decision. I felt in my heart I couldn't go back to London, that my place was here – I'd had to go away to realise where my home truly was. But Alex was in London. And I couldn't lose him, not again. I knew that sooner or later we'd have to face the small matter that there was a day of driving between us, or a plane flight and neither of us wanted to be so far away.

But just the idea of leaving Glen Avich again broke my heart.

Also, I was scared of going back somewhere as big as

London without being able to speak. I'd been silent for months now, and there was no sign of my voice coming back. How could I negotiate my old life without talking? Here, everyone knew me. I could go to Peggy's shop and to La Piazza, I could spend time with Eilidh and my old friends, work in Logan's shop, negotiate every aspect of life relatively easily. If I went back to London, I would feel lost.

And my stories to tell. My stories were here.

★

I clutched my phone and sent him the text I had prepared, words that had come straight out of my heart. I had to tell him how I felt about Glen Avich. No more birthdays away from here.

This is my home. I don't want to leave it again. I love you with all my heart x

My heart was in my throat as I waited for the reply. I was dreading an *I'll never want to live in the back of beyond*; I was hoping for a *let's talk about it . . .*

I certainly did not expect what I got.

Ready for your birthday present?

Oh. Talk about changing the subject . . .

Yes, of course! x

You'll have it in twenty minutes.

What? As in, a parcel will arrive in twenty minutes? Should I go home and wait for the courier?

What do you mean? I asked.

I mean I'm at the station.

He's where?

What station?

The sign says Glen Avich.

★

I don't think anyone ever ran the distance between Loch Avich and the train station as fast as I did that late spring day.

A chilly wind blew from the loch, and daffodils and crocuses were blooming all around, splashes of colours here and there, after the grey of winter.

I passed Maggie and Liz, about to step into Peggy's shop. I could just imagine the conversation – *I just saw Inary, she was running down the Way like the Devil was at her heels! I wonder what's up with her now . . .* I passed Eilidh and little Sorley in the play park, sitting on the bench – Eilidh jerked her head sharply to see who was running behind the fence, and she smiled and waved as she saw me. Strange, in my excited thoughts they had become like an ancient carving, or a Renaissance painting – a mother and child tableaux.

Laughter sprang from my chest, exhilarated by the running and by the knowledge he was there, there waiting for me already . . .

I spotted his familiar frame – the blue jacket I'd seen a million times, his old tattered rucksack by his side, his strong shoulders and his hands, one burrowed in his black hair – he was anxious, I could feel it. I wanted to call his name, but I couldn't. I stopped, suddenly shy, panting with the effort. I'd been so sure I'd run straight into his arms, but for some reason, I stopped.

We stood in front of each other, awkward and happy and shy and longing, longing. His face broke into a smile, and the sight of his joy in seeing me brought tears to my eyes.

"Inary . . ."

We were together at last, and it could have happened years ago, it should have happened years ago, had I not lost myself, had I not been too busy wandering in the labyrinths of my mind, instead of living. His arms were around me, his face close to mine – how many times I'd inhaled his scent, his Alex-scent – our lips were meeting for the second time, but this time we belonged. I had expected tenderness, and there was tenderness, but not only – my knees went and I felt a rush of desire. I wanted everything to be inside me, the hills and the sky and the spring blooms and Alex. I was hungry for life and for love and for all the time I'd lost and I wanted back.

I wanted to be held and kissed and I wanted to write, and I wanted to laugh and be Inary. And be here, be home.

"Inary . . ." he whispered – how come I'd never noticed how beautiful, how deep his voice was – his accent had always felt familiar in London, surrounded by unfamiliar voices. "I never want to be away from you again."

From over his shoulder, I caught a glimpse of a woman standing looking at us. The glare was so strong that I couldn't make out her features. Some Glen Avich nosy biddy, I thought

291

at once. Two people kissing in the station, in plain daylight, in front of the whole village – they'd dine out on that (or tea out on that more like) for months. But then I felt the familiar tingling in my limbs, and cold spreading on my shoulders – someone was behind me, someone who wasn't alive. Mary, for sure.

I disentangled myself from Alex's arms and stood, looking at her. It wasn't Mary.

It was Emily, my Emily, standing a few feet away from us, smiling.

She waved, and then she turned away to lose herself in the hills of our home.

I opened my mouth, and for the first time in months, I spoke; I spoke the words that had been choking me all along.

"Goodbye, Emily."

EPILOGUE

The dead have been seen alive

The streets of Glen Avich, its woods and hills and the waters of its loch, are full of stories that will not be forgotten. Simple stories of love and strife and rainy days and weddings and illnesses and children playing and men and women making love, the threads of families and lives past woven before my eyes. The men and women who lived and died before me, some of whom share my blood – the tears they cried, their laughter, the days babies were born and the days loved ones died, the love and hate, the joys and separations are written all over these walls, tangled in the trees, rising from the soil like mist.

I hear the stories as I walk, every step a whisper; I see them carved in stone and swirling in corners like whirlpools, waiting to be untangled. I gather them in my hands, they trail after me and envelop me, waiting, wanting to be told. Everywhere I turn I see them, the people who were here before, and they call to me. I see spirits in the children's eyes – I see into their blood as if I were reading a book. I see every generation gone. My dreams might tell the future, but the dead come to me so that the past is not forgotten. I cherish every day and night when the dead have been seen alive, because these are the stories for me to tell.

Other fiction titles from Black & White Publishing

The Half-Life of Hannah
Nick Alexander
RRP £7.99 – 978 1 84502 719 3
Also available in ebook

If your first love came back to offer you everything you ever dreamed of, what would you do?

Thirty-eight-year-old Hannah seems to have it all: a loving husband, a cherished son and a comfortable home. The first half of her life hasn't been as exciting as she hoped for in her youth, but, she reckons, who gets everything they want?

When she rents a villa in the south of France for a summer holiday with her impulsive sister Jill and gay friend Tristan, she's expecting little more than a relaxing few weeks with her family. But when a ghost from her past arrives, secrets are exposed, a lost love is rekindled and Hannah is forced to question everything she thought she knew.

Hannah has been living a lie. But is she brave enough to take the life-changing decisions her future happiness depends on?

Other Halves
Nick Alexander
RRP £7.99 – 978 1 84502 746 9
Also available in ebook

Hannah's and Cliff's gripping story continues in *Other Halves*, the sequel to *The Half-Life of Hannah*.

"If, like me, you read and enjoyed *The Half Life of Hannah* and wondered what happened next after that fateful summer holiday in France, then this is a must-read."
Kindle Book Review

www.blackandwhitepublishing.com